A MERRY LITTLE MURDER

Books by Shelley Freydont

BACKSTAGE MURDER

HIGH SEAS MURDER

MIDSUMMER MURDER

HALLOWEEN MURDER

A MERRY LITTLE MURDER

Published by Kensington Publishing Corporation

A Lindy Haggerty Mystery

A MERRY LITTLE MURDER

SHELLEY FREYDONT

KENSINGTON BOOKS
http://www.kensingtonbooks.com

KENSINGTON BOOKS are published by

Kensington Publishing Corp.
850 Third Avenue
New York, NY 10022

All Kensington titles, imprints and distributed lines are available at special quantity discounts for bulk purchases for sales promotion, premiums, fund-raising, educational or institutional use.

Special book excerpts or customized printings can also be created to fit specific needs. For details, write or phone the office of the Kensington Special Sales Manager: Kensington Publishing Corp., 850 Third Avenue, New York, NY 10022. Attn: Special Sales Department. Phone: 1-800-221-2647.

Kensington and the K logo Reg. U.S. Pat. & TM Off.

Library of Congress Card Catalogue Number: TK
ISBN: 0-7582-0126-5

First Printing: October 2003
10 9 8 7 6 5 4 3 2 1

Printed in the United States of America

Many thanks

To Nancy and Gary Brown and Yvonne Marceau for sharing their knowledge of ballroom competitions and for vetting the manuscript for errors.

To Emilio, designer extraordinaire, for explaining fabrics, trims, and patterns and for his colorful stories of life behind the scenes.

A special thanks to Irene Webb for her hospitality and knowledge of Atlantic City and for introducing me to Lucy.

Chapter One

"—five, six . . ." Lindy Graham Haggerty counted seven toupees as she looked around the crowded lobby of the Grand Pavilion Hotel and Casino. Her hand went reflexively to her own hair, brown, thick, and shorn to a barber's cut. Beside her, Biddy McFee, with a full head of cinnamon-colored curls, handed out room keys to the members of the Jeremy Ash Dance Company.

"That's the last of them," said Biddy, handing Lindy a plastic key card.

"Did you get a look at all the rugs in this place?" asked Lindy.

"Ten if you count the one on the floor." Lindy and Biddy looked up to see Rose Laughton, the costume mistress, looming over them. At nearly six feet, Rose did an impressive loom. "You missed the curly ones. It takes a practiced eye." She grinned. "I just got off the phone with Dawn Gilpatrick. She's in a meeting or she would have been here to meet us. She said to come up to her room and she'll give us the schedule for the week." She waggled her eyebrows. "And if you're lucky, she'll tell you how to spot toupees at a ballroom competition."

They headed for the elevator, past an immense golden Chinese dragon standing guard over the lobby. A giant green wreath hung around its neck and it was surrounded by a dozen evergreen trees decorated with red bows and gold calligraphic ornaments. The dragon puffed out a cloud of smoke above their heads.

Biddy screeched and backed into Lindy.

"Talk about overkill," said Rose.

"You should be used to it," said Lindy as she set Biddy back on her feet. "Didn't you work in Vegas in your misspent youth? I would think it was even gaudier than Atlantic City."

"Yeah, but that was before it turned into a theme park. Somehow it just doesn't have that old magic."

They stopped behind a crowd waiting at the bank of elevators. The elevator doors opened, and two bellhops in Mandarin uniforms pushed empty luggage carts into the lobby. Everyone squeezed inside. Rose nodded toward the head of a man in front of them. "Eleven," she whispered.

"You're awful," said Biddy, struggling with a grin.

"Who, us?" Two male dancers shoved their way past the closing doors, yanking their suitcases in at the last minute. Everyone pressed tighter as the doors closed. Arms reached to press buttons, and the elevator swooshed upward. Several pings and floors later, the last of the passengers, suitcases and dress bags jostled past them and the five members of the Jeremy Ash Company were left alone in the elevator.

"Whew!" The taller of the two men snatched off a black knit hat with a Yankees logo on the front. A shiny shaved head gleamed in the light and refracted into dozens of brown scalps in the mirrored walls. "Did you get a load of all the rugs in the lobby? Must be a convention. Hair Club does Atlantic City."

"Rebo." Biddy gave him a stern look, then barked out a laugh. She immediately clapped a hand over her mouth.

"Welcome to the glamorous world of ballroom competition," said Rose.

"God, remind me to retire before I go bald." Juan Esquidera fingered his hairline and gazed into the mirror.

"Don't worry. You can always shave your head like Rebo does," said Rose. "When you have no hair to begin with, you'll never know when you have no hair for real."

"Is that the name of a country-western song?" asked Rebo.

The doors opened.

"This is Dawn's floor," said Rose. Lindy and Biddy followed her out and the elevator doors closed on the twanging duet of "When you have no-o-o hair . . ."

Corridors spread out from the foyer in four directions.

"Room 1532," said Rose. "That way."

They walked three abreast down a wide corridor carpeted in geometric patterns of yellow, red and purple. The walls were swirls of metallic white against a glittering gold background.

"I'd hate to navigate this after a couple of drinks," said Biddy.

Halfway down the hall, Rose stopped at the door to room 1532. Before she had a chance to knock, the door jerked open, and a man stepped out. He slammed the door, pushed past them, and marched down the hall.

"I guess the meeting is over," said Rose.

The door opened. "Don't think you can get away with this. I'll finish y—"

"Hi, Dawn," said Rose, her hand still raised in the air. Biddy and Lindy stood mutely beside her like a pair of unmatched bookends.

"Oh," said Dawn Gilpatrick, blinking false eyelashes in surprise. She was petite and thin, with a fringe of hennaed hair. Wiry cords of muscle lined each side of her neck. Her sharp-edged collarbone was only partially concealed by the neckline of a flowered camisole that clashed with the wallpaper. She had the hard look of too much makeup and too little flesh. Heavy makeup helped to conceal the large pores on her nose, but it had collected in the fine lines around her eyes and mouth. Lindy thought she must have been pretty—once.

Dawn leaned out the door and looked down the hall, then pulled the door wider and stepped back.

"Come in. Sorry about that. You look great."

"You look pissed," said Rose as Dawn gestured them into a living room that only hinted at the pervasive oriental theme of the rest of the hotel.

"Pissed doesn't even begin to cover it. Do you know what that little shit just did to me?" Dawn stalked toward the window and whirled around. "He just waltzed in here and announced that he's leaving. After all I've done for him. We were this close to a championship." She jabbed the air with two fingers for emphasis. "This close. He and Katja will win Rising Star tonight. I've got it all squared away. After that, there would be no stopping them. But as soon as everyone finds out that Mr. Shane Corbett, God's gift to the dance world, is dumping his partner, no one will mark them. Damn. Shit and damn. And I have a film company coming on the weekend. Major film. *The Secret Life of Fred Astaire.* They'll need a couple to star in it. It could be Shane and Katja. I bet he didn't consider that, did he?"

No one answered.

"It'll be all over the ballroom by tonight if it isn't already. And won't Junie just love this? Shit. I've got to make sure Shane doesn't tell anyone."

Dawn stalked past the couch, snatched the phone from the end table, and banged out numbers.

"This is Biddy McFee, Jeremy's business manager, and Lindy Graham, rehearsal director," said Rose, unperturbed by Dawn's outburst.

Dawn stretched to the end of the phone cord and quickly shook hands. "Glad to meet you. Your schedules for the weekend are on the table." She pointed to a red glossy folder with the words *International Stars Ballroom Competition (ISBC)* embossed across the front and an ISBC logo in the corner. "There's wine in the cooler. Pour yourselves a drink." She turned her back to them and began wrapping the phone cord around her fingers.

Lindy and Biddy stood in the middle of the room while Rose rummaged through a stack of coolers and boxes of potato chips and pretzels that sat on a luggage trolley in the corner of the room. She pulled out a magnum of white wine and held it up. It had a screw top. Rose shrugged and said sotto voce, "For student and staff after-hours parties." She put the bottle on the table by the window and pulled out a bag of plastic wineglasses from another box.

Dawn gave Rose a thumbs-up, then was back fingering the phone cord, while she paced back and forth the two steps that the length of cord allowed. After a minute, she slammed the receiver down. "No answer." She picked up a glass that Rose had just poured and downed it in one swallow. "Shit and damn." She poured herself another drink and resumed pacing, this time from table to coffee table. "Junie's behind this. I just know it. He's judging this week. Can you believe it? I'm one of the sponsors of this competition, and I don't even know how he weaseled his way in. He's probably out there now, bad-mouthing me to everyone who will listen. And if he finds out that Shane is dumping Katja, he'll grab him up before the night is over." Her eyes widened. "Oh, God, tonight—I forgot all about tonight."

Lindy caught Biddy's eye. They flashed each other a "Get out of Dodge" look. Biddy reached for the folder. "We know you must have things to do, we'll just take this and run along."

"Sorry," said Dawn, glancing in their direction. "Sorry. God, I can't believe this is happening. Just wait here for a minute. I'll be right back." She grabbed a large leather purse off the couch and ran out the door, letting it click shut behind her.

Rose sat down and leaned over the back of her chair to snag a bag of corn chips from the trolley. "Just like I never left. The last time I saw her she was ranting and raving about Junie. That was ten years ago and he had just bought a studio down the road from hers in Cherry Hill. Some things never change." She smacked the chip bag between her hands and the top popped open.

"Who's Junie?" asked Lindy.

"Her ex. Ex-partner-ex-lover-ex-husband. Ex-tremely nasty divorce." Rose sighed and poured wine into three more glasses. "You'd think she would be over him by now."

Biddy had slipped on a pair of reading glasses and was leaning over the table, perusing the schedule. She snapped it shut. "This is pretty self-explanatory. I think I'll go see how Jeremy and Peter are making out at the theatre."

Rose made clucking noises and pushed her into a chair. "And let me have all the fun? Not a chance. A few days in the ballroom world will make you long for the backstabbing of the legit stage."

"I doubt it," said Lindy. She took a glass of wine from the table and went to the window to look at the ocean view.

"Dawn's not so bad, actually neither is Junie, separately. They just seem to bring out the worst in each other," said Rose. "I made Dawn's dresses when I first came to New York. They were as poor as the proverbial church mice, but they were young and gung ho. They were the national champions. Everyone thought they would take World. But before it could happen, Junie broke up with her and Dawn filed for divorce. They've been fighting ever since."

"God, how depressing," said Lindy. She turned from the window and saw Rose and Biddy exchange troubled looks. She knew what they were thinking. She was on the brink of divorce herself. She just hoped they weren't comparing her and Glen to Dawn and her obsession with her ex-husband.

Rose lifted the wine bottle in her direction.

Lindy shook her head. She hadn't even touched her first glass. "Don't you think it's a little early for cocktails?"

"Not in this crowd."

At that moment, the door opened and Dawn came back inside. Whoever she had gone to see hadn't helped her mood. She threw her bag on the floor, flopped down on the couch, and threw her arm across her face. Carefully avoiding her eye makeup, Lindy noticed.

"He didn't answer his door," she moaned. "And just what am I going to do now?"

Lindy put her glass on the table. "We'll let you get back to work. We've got to get over to the theatre."

Dawn sat up. "I'm not usually such a mess. It's just that I wasn't expecting this. I'll just bet Junie orchestrated this breakup. He's already stolen my top teacher, but if he thinks he can capitalize on all the work I put into Shane and Katja, he can think again. I'm going to sue his ass. Can you imagine the gall of the man?"

Lindy shook her head and inched toward the door.

"That son of a bitch wrecked my life."

"Which one?" asked Rose. "Junie Baker or Shane Corbett?"

Lindy took another step toward the door.

"Does it matter? They're all alike."

Lindy felt her throat tighten. She didn't want to hear Dawn's tale of marriage woes. She had her own marriage to worry about. She squinted her eyes at Biddy, who stood up and joined her snail's pace toward escape.

"Why don't you two have a visit?" said Biddy. "Lindy and I really need to get to the theatre."

"What? Oh. There are comp tickets for tonight's events in the folder," said Dawn. "Imperial Ballroom. Eight o'clock."

Neither of them noticed when Lindy and Biddy let themselves out the door. Rose was slouched back in her chair, the bag of chips in her lap, and her feet propped up on the edge of the table. Dawn was tearfully recounting the last ten years of being stabbed in the back by Junie Baker.

"It's a good thing this gig is paying so much," said Biddy as they made their way back to the elevator. "Are you all right?"

Lindy looked surprised. "Of course. Why shouldn't I be?"

"All that angsting over her ex-husband. You and Glen are not like that."

Lindy felt the heat rise to her face. Biddy had always been able to cut right to the heart of what she was thinking—when they had been dancers together years before and in the last two years since she'd returned to work as Jeremy's rehearsal director.

"If I ever started obsessing over Glen like she does over Junie, just shoot me."

Biddy slipped her arm through hers. "It will work out."

"One way or the other," said Lindy. "I haven't heard from him since November. It's like he just disappeared. Every time I call the Paris office, his secretary says he's in the field and can't be reached.

Or he doesn't want to be reached. And he never even said he wanted a divorce—just that he wasn't coming back."

"Well, at least Bill is coming tomorrow. That should keep your mind off your nearly ex-husband."

"Biddy—" she began.

"Hmm."

Lindy sighed. "Nothing." She wanted to confide in Biddy; tell her what had happened between Bill Brandecker and her during the last two months. That he had said he loved her. That he had also said he didn't want to be the consolation prize. She was confused and insecure. She was afraid it was too soon to move on in her life. She was afraid of hurting Bill. Afraid of getting hurt, herself. She longed to ask Biddy's advice, but was afraid of what that advice might be.

Biddy in her inimitable fashion gave it to her without her asking. "Look. You can't put your life on hold, because Glen doesn't have the guts to ask for a divorce. You better believe he isn't holding his own around all those Parisian temptresses. And as soon as he settles on some young chippie, you can believe he'll want a divorce—yesterday."

"What am I going to do?" said Lindy. She shuddered. "Criminy. I sound just like Dawn."

"Never, but if I were you, I'd put both you and Bill out of your misery and go for a hot, torrid affair." Biddy grinned. "Then I'd get to hear all about it."

A man was waiting for the elevator. Lindy recognized him as the same man who had stormed out of Dawn's room earlier, Shane Corbett. He was in his twenties, wearing black pants cinched at the waist and a tight stretchy T-shirt. A burgundy dance bag with the white letters of a shoe company printed across it was slung over one shoulder. His hair was peroxided and gelled back from his forehead. He didn't acknowledge them, just stepped into the elevator before them, then scowled at the door as they descended.

They got off on the same floor. Lindy and Biddy stopped between a pair of six-foot Ming Dynasty guardian figures that flanked the elevator and surveyed the hall. Shane Corbett went right toward the hotel's ballrooms and stopped at a counter of phones, where a wiry old lady, wearing a quilted white coat and clutching a battered coin cup from the casino, yelled into a phone, "Hello, Ritchie? You know that new suit I was going to buy you? Well, hon, I just lost the pants."

Lindy and Biddy turned left and followed the signs past the Pagoda Bar and Grill and up a set of steps to the Cathay Cabaret Theatre.

To the right of the theatre door an easel announced the Saturday night performance of *Ballroom Fantasy*. It was a panache of professional theater companies and ballroom dancers, the culmination of the weeklong competition. Pictures of the various participants were arranged below. The Jeremy Ash Dance Company was represented by a picture of Mieko and Rebo flying through the air in Jeremy's *Gershwin Preludes*. The piece was cast for seven dancers, and most of the company had been given an extra week's vacation. Only Mieko, Andrea, Kate and Juan, Rebo, Eric and Paul had come to Atlantic City.

"Hmm," said Biddy. "Us, *Tangos de Argentina, Formation Fixation, Dance with Me*, the Broadway show, and *Dance Sport*. I thought dance was an art."

"It should be an interesting evening," said Lindy and opened the door.

Jeremy Ash was standing in the middle of the theatre looking down at the stage. He was surrounded by tables and chairs. Behind him, tiers of banquettes and couches, each with its own table, rose to the back wall. The entire room was covered with a red-and-black-figured carpet. The seating arrangements repeated the same red and black motif with accents of gold gilt.

"It looks like a can-can dancer," whispered Lindy.

Biddy started humming the Offenbach music under her breath as they walked toward Jeremy.

"It's a cabaret," he said when Biddy and Lindy stopped beside him.

"That's what the sign says," said Biddy, eyes scanning the red, black, and gold interior.

"Check this out," said a voice through the house speakers. The back of the stage began to rise and a double set of stairs appeared between the two levels.

Applause came from the back of the house where Mieko Jones and Kate Cabot sat at a plush banquette. Mieko looked right at home, dressed in black, her dark oriental features expressionless beneath blue-black hair. Kate, the essential Irish lass, looked like she had gotten off the wrong tour bus.

Jeremy groaned.

"Well, at least the girls are happy," said Lindy. "And Peter is probably having the time of his life."

They watched the platform lower into place and shafts of colored lights shoot out across the audience in rapid succession. There was a whoop over the speakers and the houselights popped on. Peter Dowd loped down the tiers of banquettes, followed by Mieko and Kate.

"So what do you think, boss?" asked Peter. His delivery was strictly deadpan, but his black eyes sparkled with humor.

Jeremy groaned again. They stood facing each other, artistic director and production manager, like a pair of theatrical masks, Comedy and Tragedy. But today their usual roles were reversed. Peter was the epitome of the dark mysterious stranger, but his black eyes and naturally serious expression couldn't conceal his good mood. On the other hand, Jeremy, blond, blue-eyed, and Greek-god handsome, was definitely out of sorts.

Biddy slipped her head under his arm. His hand slid to her shoulder and rested there.

"Remind me why we're doing this," he said.

"The money," said Biddy.

"Right."

Chapter
Two

At eight thirty that evening, Lindy walked down the corridor toward the Imperial Ballroom. Black lacquer benches lined each
side of the hallway and were flanked by two guardian figures. Ash
cans were overflowing with food wrappers. On the wall above them,
handwritten signs pronounced No Smoking. Ahead of her, the door
to the ballroom opened and a blast of music shot into the hall, then
died away as the doors closed again. Up and down the carpet, couples were practicing, robes and sweaters wrapped over their costumes.

She jumped out of the way as one of them headed toward her in a
series of hops and chassés that she recognized as a quick step. A second couple, who had been waltzing, came to a dead stop in front of
her. The man flung the girl's arms away and yelled, "Stop hanging
on me, damn it." The girl stuck her middle finger in his face. Then
with a series of disjointed movements, they reattached themselves.
The man's mouth puckered as if he were sucking lemons; the girl
formed her face into a parody of a smile, and they twirled away.
They made it halfway down the hall before they broke apart again.
At the opposite end of the hall, another couple was arguing. The girl
took a step back from her partner and stalked away. He grabbed her

by the arm and wheeled her around. Seconds later they were back in dance position.

Lindy looked from one couple to the other and shook her head. So this was professional ballroom dancing. Not exactly what she'd expected. More like prizefighting. She waited for a path to open between the dancing couples and she headed for the ballroom, humming "Isn't It Romantic?" under her breath.

At the door, she handed her ticket to a girl dressed in a fluffy yellow sweater and matching spandex slacks. The girl stamped Lindy's hand with Day-Glo ink, and she went inside just as an amplified voice called out, "Who's your favorite couple?" He was answered with shouts of "237, 115, 211."

The center of the room was suffused with a harsh yellow light, and the dance floor was filled with a bizarre assortment of people: young couples, old couples, and a combination of the two. The men wore numbers on their backs and sure enough, there were the numbers 237, 115, and 211 among the others. An image of rodeo contestants popped into Lindy's mind.

The music changed from fox-trot to tango and Lindy found herself mesmerized by couple number 211. The man was over six feet tall, maybe in his forties, and sporting one of the toupees that had been prevalent in the lobby. His face went through a series of contortions as he pushed a fragile-looking, older woman into her positions. The woman smiled with delight as he shoved her from one side to the other. He led her under his arm, then yanked her back into dance position, all the time grimacing at the judges who stood at the edges of the floor.

Lindy was beginning to worry about the woman's safety, when the music faded out. The couples all changed their positions on the floor and a fast waltz began. Lindy held her breath while 211 turned at breakneck speed. His partner hung on for dear life as pink and green chiffon flew out behind her. Finally, the music ended, and with her smile still firmly in place, the lady curtseyed on wobbly legs. Lindy breathed a sigh of relief when the emcee said, "Thank you, dancers. Heat forty-seven to the floor please. Silver Two Pro Am fox-trot."

The couples hurried off the floor and the emcee began calling more numbers, while a new batch of contenders took their places.

Each of the new couples struck a pose and stood frozen, waiting for the music to begin. The music blared to life and Lindy began searching for Dawn and Rose. At last she saw Rose's strawberry-blond hair glinting in the residual light from the dance floor. Lindy navigated past tables filled with people and dance paraphernalia and sat down at the table reserved for Dawn's school, Stepping Out.

There were several other people already seated, not watching the dancing, but talking among themselves, though how they could hear each other over the music was a mystery. Next to Dawn, a man leaned over the table perusing the program of the evening events. He was wearing a black vest and shirt and had a towel draped around his neck.

Dawn introduced him as Rusty Lonigan. Rusty nodded, ran his finger down the page and stood up. "Back in five," he said and made his way through the tables to an exit door on the opposite side of the room.

"Out for a cigarette," Dawn explained. "No one is allowed to smoke in the ballroom or this end of the hallway during the competition. Too many people complain and it's not a good image for a dance instructor."

"He's one of your teachers?" asked Lindy.

"Teacher as well as coach and coowner of Stepping Out. He has 150 entries this week."

Lindy looked impressed. "That sounds like a lot."

"It is, thanks to Junie," said Dawn. "Timothy left us in the lurch and Rusty had to take over Timothy's students as well as teach his own. I'd just like to know what Junie offered Tim to get him to leave. He was making a decent salary, plus commissions. And he took some of our biggest accounts with him. Rusty doesn't want to sue, but Timothy's contract clearly states that he can't teach within a five-mile radius of Stepping Out. Junie's studio is four point eight miles. I drove it myself and I'll be damned . . ."

Lindy stopped paying attention. She hoped she didn't become

this self-absorbed once she was single again. She clamped down on that thought and craned her neck to see the dancing couples. She could only see torsos from where she was sitting.

"You can move closer if you want to," said Dawn, not missing a beat. "We've got five tables reserved. We'll probably take top studio as well as top teacher. We would have for sure if Timothy hadn't screwed us. Well, he'll get his—eventually. Just see if he doesn't. And nobody . . ."

Rose was watching the dancers, nodding her head in response to what Dawn was saying, though Lindy could tell she was barely listening. It didn't matter. Dawn was highly self-motivated.

Rusty reappeared. Without a word, he took one of the women's hands and after adjusting the shoulders of her lycra bodice, he led her away.

A few minutes later, midsentence, Dawn stood up. "I wonder if Katja has come down. I'd better go check on her, and I'll see if I can find Shane and make sure he keeps his mouth shut tonight." She pulled a shawl shot with gold threads from the back of her chair and wrapped it around her shoulders.

The music ended at the same time and Lindy heard agitated whispers coming from near the entrance. The sound rippled across the ballroom. The emcee started to speak, then stopped abruptly. His head turned in the direction of the whispers and his mouth dropped open.

Dawn, Rose, and Lindy turned to look. It seemed to Lindy that the entire ballroom was focused on the entrance door. The girl in the yellow sweater held one of the double doors open and the other was held by a diminutive man dressed entirely in black except for a white bolo tie tipped with silver.

A large man in a flowing gold tunic and pants stood in the opening between them. He neither moved in nor out, but posed in the center, backlit dramatically from the corridor chandeliers. Gold necklaces, bracelets, and rings flashed as he turned to slowly peruse the ballroom.

"Holy moly," said Rose. "Is that Enrico?"

The emcee had recovered himself and was announcing the next heat, but no one paid any attention. Even the judges stared at the man who had just entered.

Then with a flick of his head, Enrico stepped fully into the ballroom. The girl disappeared behind the closing door, and the man in black waited at a respectful distance off to one side.

"I don't believe it," said Rose.

Enrico walked the perimeter of the room, each step precise, his head held so that he appeared to be looking down at the room as he held his audience captive. Heads turned as he passed by. The silk of his outfit rippled each time he stepped into a pool of light, and color danced off silver hair that was pulled into a ponytail that hung halfway to his waist.

He gave the briefest hint of a nod when he passed Dawn, then continued on his tour of the room. At last he stopped at the back of the ballroom, paused and panned the room. Then with one last haughty look, he exited through a door, followed by the man in black.

Excited talking broke out over the music.

Rose pulled Dawn closer. "Did you know about this?"

Dawn assumed an innocent expression and shrugged. Then she broke into a satisfied smile. "I have to find Katja. We'll talk later. Just keep your fingers crossed that nothing goes wrong tonight." She hurried away.

"So who's Enrico?" Lindy asked.

"Until a few years ago, he was the best ballroom gown designer in the business. In fact, he was the *only* designer, if you ask me."

"What happened?"

"He went berserk one night at a big comp. Walked up to the dais in the middle of the American Open and reamed the judges at the top of his lungs. He had to be forcibly removed from the ballroom, which, between his temper and his size, was no easy feat. Then he and Luis moved to Italy and he hasn't made a dress since. People have begged him to make gowns for them, but he refuses. One couple even went to Italy to try and change his mind. He threw them out." Rose shook her head. "He was the best, I mean *the best.*"

"That's awful. What was he so upset about?"

"Nobody ever knew. And that is a near impossibility in the ballroom business where everybody knows everything about everybody else. They thrive on it. Thank God I got a job in the theatre. I'd be a raving lunatic if I'd stayed in this business."

"You seem pretty well informed for someone who's been out of the loop for ten years."

"I still run into some of the dressmakers I knew in those days. They keep me up on the gossip." Rose frowned, then looked in the direction of the door where Enrico had disappeared. "I wonder why he's here."

Lindy turned her attention back to the dance floor, where another group of couples was doing the same four dances that had been going on since she arrived. Rusty Lonigan hadn't returned to their table, though she had noticed him dropping off and picking up different ladies who waited for him along the sidelines. He hadn't left the dance floor once.

"How long does this go on?" she asked Rose. "Rusty has been out there for a least a half hour. What if he has to pee or something?"

"Then he holds it," said Rose. "Holy moly, this should be interesting. See number 307?"

Lindy searched the men's backs. She caught a glimpse of 307 just as the man turned and held up his arms for his partner to fit herself into dance position. Black hair was plastered back from a high forehead. His cheekbones were chiseled, his nose was aquiline, and his tan was from a bottle.

"That's the infamous Timothy Saunders, the teacher who left Stepping Out. And that"—Rose pointed to a man just leaving the dais to take his place on the floor—"is the even more infamous Junie Baker."

Lindy watched a thicker, older version of Timothy Saunders and half the men on the floor take his place at the front of the dance floor. "But doesn't Saunders work for Junie now?"

"That's the whole to-do," said Rose.

"So how can he be judging? Isn't that a conflict of interest?"

Rose laughed. "How do you think couples get to be champions?"

"That hardly seems fair."

"All is fair in love, war and ballroom competitions." Rose stretched. "I'm bored. The good stuff doesn't start for another hour. What do you say to a drink in the Pagoda Bar?"

The hallway was blessedly quiet as they walked toward the Pagoda Bar. It was disturbed only by an occasional blast of music as the ballroom door opened and closed behind them. They entered beneath a peaked lacquered entrance and were shown to a table by the hostess, a thin woman with big hair and a Jersey accent. She was wearing a Suzie Wong minidress and a red Santa hat.

"Okay, I confess," said Rose, sliding into the booth. "I'm having a little trouble reconciling the nouvelle Chinoiserie theme with the Christmas decorations."

"Yeah. It's a bit much. And when you add all those pink, yellow, and chartreuse dresses in the ballroom . . . .yuck."

A waiter approached and stood patiently while Rose studied the drinks list. "Hmm," she said. "I can't decide between the Fu Manchu or the Mandarin Mai Tai."

"I'll have a glass of white wine," said Lindy.

"You're no fun," said Rose. "I think I'll go with the Charlie Chan."

The waiter turned from the table and bumped into a man weaving toward the door. The waiter bowed and apologized profusely. The man waved a cigarette dangerously in the air and staggered away.

"I hope he isn't dancing tonight," said Lindy.

"Not up for Bumper Car Ballroom?"

"I already saw a few near misses tonight. I think they better stick to seltzer."

"I'll drink to that." Rose lifted a goblet of green liquid that the waiter had just placed before her. "Hmm, interesting," she said and took another sip.

A couple of drinks later, Rose announced that it was time to go back to the ballroom. "Rising Star," she said.

"I guess the name is self-explanatory. Isn't that what Dawn's couple is dancing in?"

"Yeah. But don't let the name fool you. Couples compete in Rising Star and the Professional Open at the same time. And every time they break up and get new partners, they start all over again with Rising Star. I've known couples on the ascendant for years." She reached for the bill. "My treat."

They were returning to the ballroom when the door to the ladies' room opened and Dawn barreled into them.

"We've got to stop meeting like this," said Rose.

"Thank God," said Dawn. "Katja's in the lounge. Her zipper is broken and they'll be calling Rising Star any minute. Can you sew her in?" She was already opening the bathroom door. "And don't say anything about Shane. She doesn't know that he's leaving."

Rose and Lindy followed her into the bathroom. They turned left into a large lounge filled with brocade chairs and couches and a full-length mirror. Abruptly, Rose came to a stop and Lindy plowed into her.

Lindy looked past her to see what had happened. Rose stood openmouthed, staring at a girl holding a dress to her front. Even unzipped, it was exquisite. Made from lush turquoise silk charmeuse, form fitting to the hips, then opening into a full, bias-cut skirt. A drape of chiffon in the same color swept across the low-cut neckline and fell from the back of one shoulder. There was very little ornamentation. Tiny stones sprayed out in a fan design down one side. It reminded Lindy of a dress from an old 1930s movie. The other gowns she had seen were clownish when compared to this one.

"My God," said Rose. "It's an Enrico."

"Rose, please hurry," said Dawn.

"That's why he's here. He's making a comeback."

"Rose," Dawn pleaded. She immediately began pacing.

Rose snapped to life and took the needle and thread that Katja was holding. She turned the girl around and scrutinized the gap of fabric down her back. "You'll have to hold it closed while I stitch her in," she said to Lindy.

They started at the bottom, Lindy pulling the fabric together while Rose stitched, looped, and knotted. Lindy could feel Katja trembling. "We'll be finished in a minute," she said, trying to reassure the girl.

"Shane will be angry if I'm not there to warm up."

Lindy looked up in surprise. Katja spoke with a thick Russian accent. Perhaps ballet wasn't the only dance form that had benefited from the influx of Russian immigrants.

Rose tore a piece of thread with her teeth and rethreaded the needle. She worked deftly and quickly, with a steady hand that belied the three Charlie Chans she had downed at the Pagoda Bar.

The door opened behind them and two girls came into the bathroom, giggling and chattering. They turned right and went into the stalls.

"I'm telling you, you don't have a thing to worry about," said a voice from one of the stalls.

"That's because you always make the semifinal," answered a voice from the stall next to her. "We would have made it in Ohio, but Shane and Katja beat us by two points."

"Duh. It helps if you're Junie's new love bug."

Katja, who had been shaking her hands, trying to relieve her nervousness, went completely still. Dawn froze in a look of horror.

"Oops," said Rose and continued to sew.

"Shane? He isn't. Really? I thought he and Katja were doing the deed."

"Are you kidding? You should have heard what he called her the other night."

"What?" The answer was drowned out by the sound of toilets flushing.

Heels clicked across the tile floor. "He really said that? That's awful. Maybe they'll break up."

"No maybe about it," said the first girl over the sound of running water. "I heard that Shane is dumping her fat little Russian ass after this comp. That leaves a slot open. Play it right and it'll be you."

They hurried out the door and into the hallway, oblivious that their entire conversation had been overheard.

"Remind me not to be catty when I'm taking a pee," said Rose. "You don't know who might be listening."

Katja moaned and began shaking her head. "How could they say that? It isn't true. It cannot be true." She looked at Dawn with pleading eyes. "Dawn?"

"Of course, it isn't true," said Dawn. She took both of Katja's arms and gave her a little shake. "You know how these girls are. They're just jealous. Now, don't cry. Your eyelashes will fall off."

"Shane loves me," said Katja. "He told me that. He loves my dancing, but most of all he loves me. That is what he said."

Rose shot Lindy an "uh-oh" look and stood up. "You're done," she said brightly and busied herself with rearranging Katja's gown. "It's a gorgeous dress."

The girl's eyes brimmed with tears that she was trying to blink away. One escaped down her cheek. Rose grabbed a tissue from a box on the vanity table and dabbed at Katja's face.

Katja gave her a tremulous smile, but the first tear was joined by another.

The bathroom door flew open and Enrico strode toward them, hands poised in the air in exasperation. "There you are, you silly moo. I've been looking everywhere for you. Shane is having a Jemima attack." He stopped, took a sweeping view of his handiwork and smiled. "I'm good. I am certainly good." Then he refocused his attention on Katja. "Well? What's wrong? You're not upchucking on my charmeuse, are you? It's only on loan."

"The zipper broke," explained Dawn.

"Nonsense. My zippers don't break. Turn. Turn." He stirred the air with his finger. Katja turned. He stopped her when her back was to him. His eyes narrowed. He ran his finger along the zipper, then turned the girl profile. He gave her an open-handed pop on her belly. "Suck it in, I refuse to have tummy bulges." He glowered at

Dawn. "She thinks this is some schmatta? No wonder the zipper broke. She looks like the Pillsbury dough girl. Put her on a diet."

He began stalking around Katja, and Katja burst into full-blown crying.

"Hilda, Hilda, Hilda," Enrico exclaimed in a deafening boom. "Stop bawling. This dress requires a porcelain complexion. Dry your eyes and pull that puss into a smile. And you've lost one of the earrings I gave you to wear. You think earrings grow in my backyard? Luis searched all over Firenze for those. Where is it?" He threw his hands in the air and looked at the ceiling. "Patience. Give me patience." He dropped to his hands and knees, flesh setting off waves of gold silk, and began searching the carpet for the earring.

The door opened again and a voice called out. "Katja. Katja, are you in there? They've called our heat. Get the lead out."

Katja looked frantically at Dawn.

"Here, wear mine. They'll have to do." Dawn pulled off her own earrings and clipped them to the girl's earlobes. Strands of rhinestones hung two inches beneath a crescent of a blue paste gemstone.

Enrico straightened up and struggled to his feet. "Hilda. It's just Hilda."

Again the door opened. "Get out here, now."

Katja jumped and raced to the door.

"Good luck," called Dawn, waving after her.

Enrico turned and scowled at Rose. "I know this face."

"Rose Laughton," Rose said.

"You used to make Dawn's gowns, back in the dark ages."

"Yes, I did," said Rose.

Lindy stared at her. She sounded like an acolyte, not the brazen take-shit-from-nobody person that Lindy knew.

"You knew how to put a schmatta together. I'll give you that. Still at it?"

"I moved to the legit theatre."

"Clever lily." He turned to the mirror and adjusted his tunic.

"I hope she'll be okay," said Dawn. "I could just kill those two half-wits for saying those things. It's probably all over the ballroom. Shane and Junie. An item. Of course. I should have guessed. I'll have Junie's head on a platter for this."

"Don't you think we should be getting to the ballroom?" asked Lindy.

Dawn wrung her hands. "I've never seen her so upset. I just hope she pulls herself together before they get on the floor. They just have to take first tonight."

"Darling," said Enrico, looking back over his shoulder, "my dresses always take first." He turned in a swish of jewelry and silk and strode out the door.

Chapter Three

They ran down the hall and managed to enter the ballroom right after Shane and Katja. The man that had accompanied Enrico into the ballroom rushed up to meet him. He was small, no taller than Lindy, with light brown, closely cropped hair and a pale complexion that looked sallow in the light.

This must be Luis, the long-suffering assistant, as Rose had described him as they sat in the Pagoda Bar.

"Where are the earrings I bought for the dress?" he asked.

"Last call for couples 216 and 307," announced the emcee.

Katja slipped her hand into the crook of Shane's elbow. They pasted on wide smiles and walked down the short aisle to the floor.

"Ah, here is 216, Shane Corbett and Katja Andreyevsky, from Cherry Hill, New Jersey."

As soon as the couple reached the hardwood floor, Shane bowled Katja away from him. She twirled into the center of the dance floor, smiling confidently as if she didn't have a care in the world. The turquoise skirt wafted around her, catching the air and the light with a breathtaking beauty. There was a hum of admiration from the observers. Even the girls on the floor looked on in surprise and envy.

Calls of "216" arose from the direction of the Stepping Out tables. These were met with cries of other numbers from around the hall.

Katja finished her series of turns and made a deep curtsey, then ruined it by lifting both arms like a winning prizefighter.

"She thinks she's playing the Bolshoi," muttered Enrico.

"Ha," said Luis. "Ten will get you twenty that she never made it past the Siberian Folklorico."

Lindy had to agree. The Katja on the dance floor was not the same pitiful young girl that she had been in the lounge. This Katja was working the crowd with a vengeance, but it wasn't terribly tasteful.

"You owe me, darling," Enrico said to Dawn. "Only for you would I let that lead-footed heifer into one of my creations."

Dawn looked hurt, then she smiled at him. "Just wait and see."

"Last call for number 307. Will 307 report to the floor immediately." The other couples were standing, smiles stiff on their faces, bodies lifted in preparation, frozen uncomfortably while they waited for the last couple to appear.

"Remember 307?" Rose said into Lindy's ear.

Lindy widened her eyes back at Rose. "Timothy Saunders?"

Rose nodded.

Suddenly the missing couple rushed to the floor, not slowing down when they reached the aisle, but running full tilt onto the dance floor.

"And here they are. Number 307, Timothy Saunders and Felicia Falcone"—the emcee paused and continued in an amused voice—"also from Cherry Hill, New Jersey."

Felicia spun onto the floor, while Timothy gestured toward her with an outstretched hand. She curtseyed to one side of the room, shot a smug look at Katja as she turned, and curtseyed to the other side.

There was one call of "307" from somewhere inside the ballroom, then dead silence. Felicia was wearing an exact duplicate of Katja's gown. Lindy's jaw dropped and she looked at Enrico. His eyes bugged and his body began to rumble like a furnace about to erupt. Beside him Luis was wringing his hands.

Lindy turned back to the dance floor and took a closer look at the dress Felicia was wearing. It wasn't an exact copy. Even Lindy could tell that the fabric was polyester, the color duller. The skirt was cut straight to the grain, not on the bias, and it had been enhanced with a splotch of jewels at the cleavage and sprinkled generously with sequins all over the skirt.

The emcee cleared his throat. The sound vibrated throughout the room. "Due to the number of couples, Rising Star American Ballroom will be held in two heats. Will the following couples please remain on the floor." He began calling numbers. 216 and 307 were both in the first heat. Seven couples left the floor. Six of the remaining eight couples reassumed their beginning positions. Felicia and Katja stared daggers across the floor. Shane yanked Katja into dance position. Timothy pulled Felicia to the far side of the dance floor and they struck their opening pose.

"And your first dance, couples, is the waltz." The music began.

Enrico burst forward. Luis grabbed ineffectually at his arm. Enrico started down the aisle, dragging Luis with him. To either side, people turned and stared, the waltz forgotten.

He stopped at the edge of the dance floor, feet spread, arms at his side, a colossus in gold silk.

Rose came to stand by Lindy. They both looked toward Enrico. "You are about to witness a Diva attack to end all diva attacks."

"You think he's going to cause a scene?"

"Just stand back when the fabric starts to fly."

Dawn had been inching her way nearer to the dance floor and came to a stop next to Rose. "God, this is awful. How did Felicia get that dress?" she said around the fingernail she was biting.

Lindy tried to watch the dances: waltz, then tango, fox-trot and Viennese waltz, which was much faster than the first one. But it was hard to do with Enrico towering over the dance floor. She couldn't imagine how the couples could concentrate with that force hovering nearby.

Even without Enrico distracting her, she would have had difficulty watching. It wasn't the kind of dancing she had envisioned. Her idea of ballroom dancing was Fred Astaire and Ginger Rogers, all romance and finesse. If the film company was looking for a couple to play those two famous dancers, they wouldn't find them here. This dancing was all hard sell and lots of back bends. And their faces. Ugh.

"They all look like they're suffering from a gas attack," she told Rose.

"It's choreographed that way," was Rose's reply.

A man got up from the table next to them and promptly bumped into Lindy. "Sorry, sorry," he slurred. "Just want to get a better view when the catfight starts." He stumbled into the crowd and disappeared.

"Isn't that the same guy at the Pagoda Bar? Who is he?" asked Lindy.

Rose shrugged. "After my time."

"Vincent Padrewsky," said Dawn. "Once an up-and-comer—he used to be Felicia's partner—now a pitiful hanger-on."

The Viennese waltz ended and the emcee introduced the competing couples a final time. "Aren't they fabulous, folks?" he asked and was answered by applause, yells and whistling.

Couples filed off the dance floor and squeezed past Enrico, who refused to move aside. The two Cherry Hill couples were the last to leave.

After a brief standoff, Shane escorted Katja from the floor. She looked up when she passed Enrico, but he didn't notice her. He was intent on Felicia and the copied dress.

Felicia lifted her chin and marched down the aisle, looking straight ahead. She swept past Enrico as if he weren't there. Enrico turned after her, knocking the hapless Luis into a clump of spectators. With unexpected agility, he reached out and grabbed a handful of Felicia's skirt. The action snapped Felicia to a standstill. She looked back in surprise. With a violent yank, Enrico tore the skirt free from the bodice. Felicia screeched and made a grab for it. Luis tried to wrest it from Enrico's hands. Enrico flicked him away.

He lifted the fabric in both hands as if making an offering, then he tore it in two and dropped it to the floor. Everyone watched, aghast, unable to move, as Enrico grabbed the neckline of the dress, drawing Felicia toward him. She tried to twist away, but to no avail. She screeched and scratched at his hands. Jewels bounced onto the carpet and flew onto the dance floor.

The Rising Star couples who were waiting for the second heat were crowded at the back of the aisle, hands raised to their mouths in astonishment—or to stifle laughter—Lindy couldn't be sure.

Shane and Timothy stared openedmouthed, then simultaneously grabbed for Felicia and pulled her away. Several other male dancers attempted to hold Enrico. He threw them off, but the delay gave Shane and Timothy a chance to scuttle Felicia away. They plowed through the onlookers that had crowded around them and dragged her toward the exit door. Across the dance floor, judges were standing on their chairs to get a better view.

Junie Baker, clipboard in hand, ran across the floor and pushed his way to where Enrico was standing. He took him by the elbow. "Let's deal with this outside. You don't want a repeat of what happened before."

Enrico looked at Junie's hand, then at Junie. Junie dropped his hand to his side.

Then Enrico clipped a slight bow. "Darling. You are so right." And without another word, he let Junie escort him up the aisle. The crowd parted as he went. The emcee's voice cracked over the microphone as he called the second heat to the floor.

Lindy turned to Rose. "Well, you said fabric would fly."

"I didn't mean it quite so literally. Let's go outside and catch the next round."

They wove through the oncoming dancers and stepped into the hall. Dawn and Junie stood nose to nose, even though Dawn had to stand on tiptoe to manage it. Another man, whom Lindy didn't recognize, was trying to separate them.

"You put Felicia up to this," Dawn cried. "You've ruined everything, just like you always do."

"Oh, shut up," returned Junie. "You're totally nuts. I didn't know anything about this."

"You are such a liar," said Dawn between clenched teeth.

Junie threw up his hands. The other man attempted to pull Dawn away.

No one was paying attention to Felicia, standing a few feet away, sobbing convulsively and holding up one side of what was left of her dress. She had lost an eyelash and her eyeliner ran in rivulets down her face. Standing next to her, Timothy Saunders alternated between patting her back and looking daggers at Dawn.

Enrico stood with his arms crossed over his considerable chest, his eyes slowly scanning the group, passing over Dawn, Junie, Timothy, Felicia, Shane, and at last coming to rest on Katja.

"You," he growled and lifted his arm toward her like the Ghost of Christmas Yet to Come. "You stole my design and sold it to that tasteless little bruja."

Katja backed up, her face strained with astonishment. "Me? I didn't," she protested. "I deedn't, I de-e-edn't," she whispered hoarsely, her accent growing thicker with each repetition.

Enrico took a threatening step forward.

Katja cowered back. "Eet was you. You made two. You cheater. One for me and one for Felicia."

Enrico stopped. He took a deep breath and looked further down his nose at her. "You think," he began slowly, "that I would lower myself to make that trash? Honey—I haven't touched polyester since before you were born."

"Eet wasn't me," Katja wailed. She ran to Dawn, who put a protective arm around her.

"Of course it wasn't," said Dawn. "Someone else must have stolen the pattern." She turned and glowered at Shane. "Was it you? Thought you could get two dresses for the price of one, which cost you nothing. Nothing." She turned on Junie, thrusting Katja out of the way. "You put him up to this, didn't you." She lurched at him, but Junie grabbed her by both arms and lifted her off her feet.

"Stop it. Leave her alone, you big brute," cried Katja. "Eet's true. What those girls were saying. You're stealing Shane from me."

Junie rolled his eyes. "You're both a couple of fruitcakes." He put

Dawn back on her feet. "You. You should stop trying to live your life through these girls. Go get one of your own. And you." He jutted his chin at Katja. "You should go get a real job and stop sponging off Dawn."

This time Katja lunged at him. Junie stepped to the side and Katja stumbled forward.

"Maybe not as a waitress," said Junie.

Next to Lindy, Rose whispered, "Better than the soaps."

"Rot in hell, Junie," Katja cried as soon as she recovered her balance. "And you, too, Shane Corbett." She stalked toward him. "You're leaving *me* to dance with that—that whore? You even gave her my dress. After everything. Oh, I could kill you." She burst into a sob and began clawing at the back of her dress. "Take it, take it. You can have it. How I hate you. I hate you."

"Careful!" cried Luis, he tried to pull her hands from the zipper. Katja pushed him away and fled down the hall, groping at the back of the dress.

"You'll get yours, Junie," cried Dawn. "And so will you, Shane Corbett. Just see if you don't." Then she took off after Katja.

"She won't be getting out of that dress without help," said Rose. "Think I should go after her? Nah, this is much more interesting."

Junie watched the two women for a moment, then shook his head. "Sad," he said. Then he pointed his clipboard at Felicia. "You'd better do something about that dress if you're going to do the semi-final."

"What should I do?" wailed Felicia. "I can't go out in this." She looked down at the tattered remains of her skirt.

"Go to Gowns by Marie and tell Marie I said to loan you something. She should be setting up in the vendors' room. Timothy, go with her, and tell the guard I said it was okay to let you in."

"First tell me if it's true," said Timothy. "Are you planning to put Shane and Felicia together as a couple?"

"I don't know anything about this," said Junie. "I have a competition to judge." He jiggled his clipboard at them and went back into the ballroom.

"You owe me. Don't forget that," said Timothy as the door closed behind Junie. He took Felicia, none too gently, by the arm and pushed her past Shane, toward the ballroom.

"You shouldn't have worn that damn dress tonight," said Shane as he stepped back to let them pass.

"Hmm, the plot thickens," said Rose.

Vincent Padrewsky pushed himself away from the wall, where he had been watching the scene with smug satisfaction. He staggered over to Shane and draped his arm around his shoulders.

"So you're Junie's new tickle," he slurred.

Shane threw off his arm. "Shut up, Vincent."

Vincent smiled. "Take it from someone who's been there. Junie has a short attention span. You'll be lucky if you make it to the semifinal before he dumps you for the next sweet thing. Then try and find a decent partner. Nobody will touch you, especially not Felicia."

"You're drunk, Vincent. You don't know what you're talking about." Shane attempted to walk away.

Vincent gabbed him by the shoulder. "Don't I? Don't trust him, Shane, love. He'll wreck your career just like he did mine."

"You wrecked your own career. Now leave me alone."

Vincent shrugged. "Can't say I didn't warn you." He wandered away in the direction of the Pagoda Bar.

"I've got to find Katja before they call the semifinals," said Shane and stalked off toward the elevators. The crowd that had gathered began to disperse.

"Well, the semifinal should be interesting," said Rose. "Not to mention the final."

"You mean there's more?" asked Lindy.

"Girl, these things can go on until two or three in the morning. Come on."

Lindy followed Rose back into the ballroom. A few minutes later Biddy and Jeremy appeared at their table, followed by Juan and Rebo.

"We just got back from dinner," said Biddy. "Did we miss anything?"

Rose and Lindy gave her a look.

The emcee announced the Rising Star semifinal. Anxious couples from the first round waited at the side of the room. The returning couples hugged and kissed and walked briskly to the floor. Those whose numbers had been passed over wandered into the shadows.

"It's like a cattle call," said Jeremy.

Ten couples were called back. Felicia and Timothy were among them. Felicia was wearing a black dress with a wide chartreuse lightning bolt down the front and matching gores in the skirt. Couple 216 was called but did not appear. After the third request for them to come to the floor, Shane Corbett and Katja Andreyevsky were scratched from the semifinal.

"Poor Dawn," sighed Rose.

Once again a slow waltz poured out over the loudspeakers.

"How did Junie know that Felicia and Timothy would be in the semifinal?" asked Lindy.

Rose rolled her eyes.

"Does this mean they'll be in the final, too?"

"Now you're catching on."

"Rigged, like World Federation Wrestling," said Rebo. "What a camp."

The couples once again went through the four dances that made up the American Smooth. Lindy stifled a yawn. "They just keep doing the same thing over and over again?"

Rose nodded.

"It's too bad about Shane and Katja. I wonder what's happening."

"God only knows," said Rose. "And *her* ears are probably burning."

The semifinal finished and the emcee announced fifteen minutes of general dancing while the judges tabulated the scores to determine the six finalists.

"Hey, does anybody want to salsa?" asked Juan. Five faces gave him expressions of "you've got to be kidding."

"Maybe tomorrow," said Rebo. "After I've dry-cleaned my lycra jumpsuit." He looked at Jeremy. "Oops. Let me say it for you, Boss." He lowered his voice. "Over my dead body." He sounded just like Jeremy.

Jeremy broke into a wide smile.

At last the six couples in the final were called onto the floor. Felicia and Timothy took first place. The rest of the spots were taken by couples with names like Dudodovich, Kalensky, Radinikov. Neither Dawn, nor Katja, nor Shane had reappeared in the ballroom.

When the emcee announced one last general dance before the end of the evening, the Ash Company contingent headed for the door.

"Go figure," said Rebo as they waited for the elevator. "There was only one American couple dancing in the American style. And the girl half of that one is Italian. At least they won."

They went their separate ways at the eleventh floor. Lindy was surprised to find Biddy walking alongside her to her room.

"Where are you going?" she asked.

"To our room."

"I thought you would be staying with . . ." Lindy flicked her head in the direction Jeremy had gone.

"Not while we're working. We're professionals after all. Don't you want me?"

"Boy, do I ever." Lindy slid the key card into the door slot, relieved that at least one thing in her life wasn't in the act of changing.

As they got ready for bed, she caught Biddy up on all she had missed at the competition. "And Enrico snatched her dress right off her and tore it to shreds with the entire ballroom looking on."

"Gee," said Biddy. "It makes our company look like Mr. Rogers's Neighborhood."

"Not quite, but it sure puts things in perspective."

Biddy gave her a pointed look. "Just remember you said that. You're going to need it."

Lindy jumped into bed. She knew her life was going to get more complicated before it got better. But somehow, being on tour, with

Biddy in her usual place in the next bed, made it seem very far away and manageable.

"Good night, old pal."

"Good night. Don't forget we're meeting Rose and Jeremy for breakfast at eight. Sweet dreams." And Biddy turned off the light.

Chapter Four

But her dreams weren't sweet, and Lindy was depressed when she and Biddy entered the Rickshaw Café the next morning.

Rose and Jeremy were waiting for them at a table by the panoramic window. Lindy sat down and peered out at the deserted beach. Beyond it, a gray sea swelled beneath an even grayer sky. Whitecaps erupted from the waves, then turned to foam as the waves broke on the shore. It had been cold, but sunny, when they arrived at the hotel the day before. Now, it looked like a storm was coming in.

Perfect, she thought. Neither the Christmas decorations nor the piped-in disco version of "Silver Bells" could dispel her mood. It had been like this every morning since Glen had announced that he wasn't coming home for the holidays. And later, that he wouldn't be coming home at all. He had left her in limbo, not asking outright for a divorce, but making it perfectly clear that he no longer wanted to be a part of her life.

"Madame?"

Lindy realized the waiter was attempting to take her order.

"Toasted bagel," she said without thinking and went back to her ruminations.

And Bill would be arriving sometime that morning. It had seemed like a good idea to invite him to join her for the week. In a few days he would be leaving for Connecticut to spend Christmas with his family, and the company would be on tour by the time he returned to his teaching duties at John Jay College in January. Anyway, it wasn't like she was seducing him. He would have his own room. They were friends. Well, maybe more than friends. Suddenly, she was nervous about spending the next five days with him. What if he pushed her to make a commitment to him? What if he became disgusted with her indecision? What if Glen came back after all?

"So the scuttlebutt is—" Rose lifted a fork of scrambled eggs to her mouth, and Lindy realized that their breakfast had arrived. "That Enrico is unveiling a new line of ball gowns this morning in the vendors' room."

Lindy dragged her attention back to the conversation and breakfast. Biddy was watching her with a worried look. So was Jeremy. Rose arched an eyebrow over a piece of toast.

"Even after what happened last night?" Lindy asked, making an effort to change the focus from her back to Rose.

"Last night was nothing compared to the scene that drove him away in the first place. No one thought that he would ever come back. The man has incredible chutzpah." Rose paused to cut a piece of ham. "He and Luis were setting up a booth in the vendors' room last night, manikins and everything. No slapping dresses on a hanger and shoving them onto a clothes rack like the rest of the poor slobs. But that's all anybody got to see. They hung black drapes around the whole thing before they unpacked the gowns—hermetically sealed from the curious world.

"The hotel security guards finally kicked everybody out around two o'clock. I just happened to be coming out of the Pagoda Bar. Enrico was trying to convince them to let Luis, the Long-Suffering, sit and guard the dresses through the night. Wouldn't want anybody getting a peek before the big day."

"Or do to him what he did to Felicia Falcone last night," said Lindy.

"I'm sorry I missed it," said Biddy. "I'm hanging around from now on."

Jeremy frowned at her over his coffee cup.

Biddy smiled at him, then champed down on her jelly donut and chewed with gusto.

Lindy looked down at her toasted bagel and wondered if a plate of scrambled eggs or a donut would entice her appetite back to normal. "It's a gorgeous dress," she said. "And that turquoise, incredibly rich. The other dresses were so over-the-top, no subtlety anywhere. And those cutaway midriffs and slit skirts, ugh. I always thought of ballroom dancing as the ultimate romantic activity, but—"

Rose and Biddy both gave her a look. Jeremy bit his lip and looked out the window.

"Well, besides *that*, but you know what I mean. This is all so, I don't know, circusy."

"It is getting more and more out there," agreed Rose. "That's what happens when you make everything a competition. But there are still a few tasteful couples on the floor if you know where to look. I'll point them out tonight."

"I wonder what's happening on the boardwalk," said Jeremy, rising from his chair to get a better view from the picture window.

"What is it?" asked Biddy.

Jeremy shrugged. "Beached fish, maybe."

Rose pointed to Lindy's bagel. "Hurry up and finish. I want to get a ringside seat at the unveiling."

Lindy pushed her plate away. "I'm ready."

"Oops. Round three," said Rose under her breath and nodded toward the door.

Dawn stood just inside the restaurant. She spotted them and rushed toward the table. "Have you seen Katja or Shane this morning?" Without waiting for an answer, she sped on. "No one has seen them. Katja never came back to the suite last night. I thought she might have spent the night with some of the girls from the studio, but they haven't seen her either. And Shane doesn't answer his phone. He's missing ten Pro Am heats this morning."

Rose skewed her mouth toward Lindy and Biddy. "Understudy," she whispered.

"Rusty can't possibly take on any more dances and he doesn't know the routines. Mrs. Perkins refused to go on without Shane. She's threatening to leave and wants her money back. Do you know how much that will cost me?"

The three of them shook their heads.

"The woman's in nineteen heats plus two Showcases. At forty dollars a heat and sixty each for the showcases. You do the numbers."

Lindy started multiplying. Almost a thousand dollars, not including hotel and meals.

From the window, Jeremy said, "Oh, shit."

"I'll wring his pretty little neck when he does show up." Dawn stopped to take a frantic look around. "I can imagine what everybody is saying. I bet Junie is just having a big guffaw over this. Damn him."

Rose immediately sobered and said in an uncharacteristically gentle voice, "Maybe Shane's with Junie."

Biddy got up from the table and joined Jeremy.

Dawn finally stopped talking. A look of pain suffused her face. "Junie's in the ballroom." She sniffed, took a deep breath, and brought herself back to speed. "And Enrico is demanding his dress back. How should I know what Katja did with it? I can't even find her. I can't believe she would do this. I've given her everything. She's like a daughter to me. If you see either of them, tell them to come to the ballroom immediately."

"What color did you say that dress was?" asked Biddy.

"Turquoise," Rose and Lindy said in unison.

"Oh, shit," repeated Jeremy. He and Biddy turned to face the others. "There's something turquoise lying in the sand."

"Katja!" screamed Dawn. "Katja!" She spun around and ran toward the door, bumping into a couple just entering the restaurant.

Rose pushed back her chair and took off after her. Biddy, Jeremy, and Lindy exchanged looks, then they, too, rushed to the door.

They took the stairs down one flight to the Casino level, which opened onto the boardwalk. Dawn was ahead of them, running as fast as her four-inch platform mules would allow. They caught up to her at the exit door.

Rose grabbed her. "It might not be—"

Dawn pushed her away and threw herself against the door. Cold air blasted them from outside and wind whistled through the opening. Dawn staggered backward. She grabbed the handle and held on. Then suddenly she was outside and Rose was right behind her.

"Oh, shit," said Jeremy. He hunched over and pushed through the door.

Biddy looked at Lindy. "Here we go again." And she followed Jeremy.

Lindy hesitated. Bill might show up at any minute, and he wouldn't be happy if he found her standing over a body. But then again maybe it was just a beached fish. Wearing a turquoise dress? Not likely. Well, she wouldn't know until she saw for herself. She followed the others onto the boardwalk.

She immediately began to shiver. The temperature must have dropped ten degrees since yesterday morning. A fine mist hung in the air. She hugged herself and looked down the boardwalk. To her left stood the pier, closed for the season. Next to it a set of steps led down to the beach. A bundled figure stood on the sand, surrounded by blue shopping bags and hundreds of seagulls. Is that what Jeremy had seen? A blue shopping bag?

Across from her, chair taxis were lined against the railing, but there were no cab men. She turned to the right. A hundred feet away, a concrete ramp zigzagged down to the beach. A group of people huddled together at the edge of the wooden walkway, peering over the rail.

Lindy heard a scream and saw Jeremy and Rose pulling Dawn away from the ramp. She started to run. The wood was slick with mist and her feet nearly slid out from under her.

She squeezed through the crowd until she could grasp the railing. She looked down—and gagged. Partially hidden in the corner between the ramp and the boardwalk was the turquoise skirt of Katja's ball gown. It was covered with sand and seaweed, and the wet, discolored fabric clung to her legs. The dress was open down the back, where someone had cut the zipper free. She was still wearing her dance shoes.

Lindy leaned closer, peering at the shoes. Katja's feet were hideously misshapen and swollen. Lindy swallowed back her bagel. Thank God the girl's face was hidden. It was bad enough having to see her feet.

Had Katja slipped on the slick platform and fallen over the rail? Hit her head on the concrete ramp? She couldn't have drowned and been washed back to shore. The tide never rose this high. Anyway, the dress would have been wetter and more mangled if she had been tossed about in the waves. And she would have lost her shoes.

Lindy realized with horror that she was already unconsciously looking for clues to what had happened. She had to stop. This was none of her business. Still, she couldn't take her eyes from Katja's feet. They seemed so unnatural.

She felt someone come up behind her. She knew who it was without having to look and she cringed. If he had only been a little later or a little earlier. Why did it seem that there was always a death when they were together?

"For once," said Bill, "I'd like to spend a few days with you without a body coming between us."

She turned to face him. He was wearing a dark overcoat, but he was hatless and his hair whipped in the wind. He nailed her beneath his look, the blue of his eyes a brilliant contrast to the gray surroundings. She shivered, suddenly feeling the cold seeping past her sweater and slacks.

"I don't even know these people," she said through chattering teeth.

He opened his coat and drew her inside it. Lindy swallowed, momentarily distracted from the gruesome scene below her as his body heat began to warm her.

Dawn screamed. "Help her. Please help her! She might still be alive. You've got to help her."

Lindy twisted inside Bill's coat in order to see what was happening. Three hotel security guards were leaning over Katja's body. One was carrying CPR equipment and he began setting it up. The other two pulled Katja from beneath the ramp and turned her onto her back. Abruptly they straightened up, then backed away from the body. There was a gasp from the growing group of spectators, the sound of someone throwing up. Lindy felt Bill shiver.

"Goddammit, goddammit, goddamnit," he rumbled through clenched teeth.

Dawn screamed at the top of her lungs, then fainted. Jeremy swept her up and deposited her on a nearby bench. Biddy's face was blanched of all color.

Dreading what she might see, Lindy looked down at the body. She sucked in her breath in disbelief. Looked again. It was not Katja.

The open eyes of Shane Corbett stared up at them. Red lipstick had been slashed across his mouth, a hideous burlesque of a woman's makeup. His hair was crusted with blood and sand. Something was moving in it. Sand crabs. Lindy swayed and felt Bill's arms tighten around her.

Behind them, cars screeched to a halt, doors slammed, and local police officers rushed to the scene.

Lindy dragged her eyes from Shane's hair. Sand covered his face, chest and bare arms. A splotch of damp, darker than the others, almost black, spread across the bodice of the dress. Not water, not seaweed. Blood. She knew it must be blood, but from where? There was no tear in the fabric that she could see. His head? Wouldn't dripping or even gushing blood form an elongated pattern down the dress, not such a round stain?

She strained against Bill's arms. She wanted a better look, but he held her against him. She knew he was looking, too. Taking everything in. And she knew too that he was thinking the same thing. This had been no accident. Lindy dragged her eyes from Shane's chest only to have them anchor on his feet, thrust obscenely into those dancing shoes.

"His feet," she stammered.

"Crushed," answered Bill.

She jerked against him. "How?"

"By someone with a baseball bat or similar weapon." He sighed. "Probably after they finished bashing in his head."

The city policemen dismissed the security guards and began moving people away. Bill stepped back, pulling Lindy with him.

One of the patrolmen stopped at the bench where Dawn sat slumped against Rose's shoulder. "I'm afraid she, uh, he's dead, ma'am. Were you acquainted with the deceased?" he asked in a voice meant to be gentle but failing miserably.

Dawn nodded.

The policeman flipped open a notebook.

"Could we do this inside?" asked Rose. "It's really cold."

The officer looked down at the beach, then nodded. Rose helped Dawn to stand, but she pulled away, looking frantically around. "Where's Katja? What has he done with her? You've got to find her."

"Just come inside, ma'am," said the policeman. "And tell me about this other person."

Before they could move, Lindy saw Enrico, followed by Luis, burst through the casino doors. He made a beeline toward them, sliding the last few feet and knocking people out of his path. He grabbed the railing with both hands and shook it until it rattled. "My dress," he bellowed. "That bitch. She's ruined my dress." He tore his hands from the railing and covered his face.

Luis stared down at the beach, his face constricting into a mask of horror. Then his fingers touched his lips and he slowly shook his head. Mechanically he reached for Enrico. Enrico flung him away. Luis fell against the railing.

"What are you doing out here? You're supposed to be guarding the booth."

Luis jumped away and rubbed his ribs.

"While you're out here gallivanting all over the boardwalk, somebody is in there stealing my designs. It isn't enough that this baggage killed herself wearing an Enrico original, but you leave the rest unguarded. Can't I trust anybody? Why don't I just give my designs away? Hmm? Shall I stand on the street corner, and say come one, come all, Luis is out on the boardwalk looking at a drowned rat? Steal a few dresses before he gets back."

"I'm sorry, Enrico. But look, it isn't—"

"Get inside."

"Of course. I'm sorry." Luis backed away, then turned and ran back into the hotel.

A patrolman who had been staring at Enrico stepped forward. "If you would accompany us inside, sir," he said.

Enrico turned on him. "How long will it be before I can have my dress back?"

Bill shook his head.

"I don't even know these people," Lindy said defensively.

"Uh-huh."

"We just arrived yesterday." She stopped talking and frowned at him. "How did you know where to find me?"

"Heard it come in over a security radio while I was checking in. I knew you'd be right in the thick of it. I just followed the crowd."

Biddy and Jeremy walked over to them.

"Just in time," said Jeremy, reaching past Lindy to shake Bill's hand.

Lindy realized how ridiculous she must appear wrapped in Bill's coat and arms. She moved away.

"I hope you don't think we plan these things just for you," said Biddy.

"With anyone else I might start developing a complex." Bill gave Lindy a pointed look and motioned them toward the hotel. "I seem to be the only one dressed for the weather."

"We saw the discovery of the body from the restaurant window," said Lindy.

"And just had to come down and investigate," said Bill.

"It's not like we had a choice," Lindy snapped. "Dawn is a cosponsor of the competition. She was with us and she thought it was one of her dancers."

"And was it one of her dancers?"

"Yes, but the wrong one," said Lindy.

Chapter
Five

"So which one was it supposed to be?" asked Bill as the door closed behind them and they were engulfed in warmth. It was stifling after the brisk sea air.

"It wasn't *supposed* to be anyone," said Lindy, annoyed at his attitude. "But Katja is missing. It's her dress. And poor Dawn thought it was her lying dead on the beach."

"She's the one who was having hysterics? She seems more upset about this missing girl than she did about the poor devil in the dress. Is she some sort of relation?"

"They're very close," snapped Lindy.

"Oh, one of those."

"Not one of those," she echoed. "Dawn is Katja's mentor. A mother figure. Not everything in this world revolves around sex."

Irritation flickered across Bill's face. "Are you going to bite my head off every time I ask a question?"

"Only if you keep acting like a condescending twit," she countered, then bit her lip. It must have been the shock of seeing Shane dead on the beach that was making her so disagreeable.

Bill look duly chastised. She could feel him distancing himself from her.

"I'm sorry," she said quickly. "It isn't you. These people are so intense. It tends to rub off on you."

Bill shrugged out of his coat and draped it over his arm. He ran his fingers through his hair, brushing it off his forehead. "Were you first on the scene?"

Lindy shook her head.

"Then you don't have to stay for the questioning." He paused. "Do you?"

She shook her head again.

"Then could we get some coffee and let the police get on with it?"

"Sure." She let him guide her away from the group, just as Rusty Lonigan ran across the casino headed for Dawn. Behind them, Enrico's voice rose in anger. Dawn wept loudly. All the while, slot machines whirred and rang without pausing. No one even glanced away from the rolling pictures at the group of people being questioned by the police.

They went into a coffee bar at the far side of the casino. A few minutes later, they were chatting comfortably like always, even though Lindy had to bite her tongue not to keep bringing up the subject of the possible murder. She knew that Bill was aware of her effort. He was like that. Confronting and backing off. Supporting and challenging. Getting angry and . . . She shifted her attention before she went any further down that road.

She looked at her watch. "Enrico is showing his collection in a few minutes. Do you want to go?"

"Might as well," said Bill with a sigh of resignation. "God forbid that a little thing like murder should stop a fashion show."

"How can you be sure it was murder and not a simple accident?" asked Lindy even though she had thought the same thing.

"I just know. Wait and see."

They stepped out of the elevator to a blast of cha-cha music from the Imperial Ballroom and a blast of Christmas carols from the Pagoda Bar. The hall was already filled with practicing couples. The dancing was more stationary than it had been the night before, and it was easier to maneuver their way through the couples.

"What are they doing?" asked Bill as Lindy led him toward the ticket table.

"Latin, I think," said Lindy.

"Hmm," said Bill.

The ballroom was already crowded. They stopped for a second to watch couples banging out shapes to a popular mambo. "Hmm," Bill said again and guided Lindy toward the group that waited at the door to the dealers' room.

Rose motioned them over to where she and Jeremy and Biddy were standing near the front. Luis was at the door, arguing with the guard.

"Now what?" asked Lindy.

"It seems that Luis left his dealer's badge in the booth last night. And the doorman won't let him in until it opens at ten."

"Yikes! Enrico will be furious."

"Yeah. If anything happens to those gowns, Luis will be an inkblot with string tie." Rose shuddered.

The door opened and Luis rushed inside; everyone else crowded in behind him. The room was filled with booths, crammed together between narrow aisles. Dealers were busy setting up racks of second-hand ball gowns, displays of dance shoes, jewelry, dance CDs, vitamins, and hair products. Luis ran down a center aisle to the far end of the room where dark curtains hung from a metal frame. Barely parting the panels, he slipped inside.

"Better get a move on. When the news about the you-know-what hits the ballroom, it'll be standing room only." Rose muscled her way forward, the others following behind.

Just as they reached the booth, excited whispers rippled through the room. The crowd parted and Enrico walked toward the booth in long stately strides.

Someone nearby said sotto voce, "His Majesty, the Queen," then started humming "Pomp and Circumstance." Another voice said, "Shut up, Vincent."

Enrico took his place in front of the booth and scrutinized his audience. An expectant hush fell over the group. He didn't speak, but with a triumphant look, stepped aside. "Luis," he ordered. But Luis didn't appear. The curtain didn't move. Enrico waited, while everyone held their breath. Then with a disgusted sigh, he took the edge of the drape and fixing his audience with a superior gaze, pulled it aside.

The audience gasped. A moment of shocked silence, then agitated murmurs filled the room. Lindy could only stare, Bill was frozen beside her, she heard Rose stifle a cry, and Jeremy's "Oh, shit."

Instead of an array of gorgeous ball gowns, there were only shreds of torn fabric, hanging from overturned manikins, their heads and arms wrenched off and thrown to the floor. Jagged pieces of fine silk, Chantilly, and Italian lace littered the carpet.

And in the midst of the destruction was Luis, on his knees, frantically gathering up scraps of fabric.

Enrico continued to smile even as he registered the expressions of horror on his audience's faces. His mouth froze in that position, while above it, his eyes transformed into disbelief. Slowly he turned toward the booth.

Luis looked over his shoulder and began to sob, the sound echoing through the room. He scrambled to his feet, pulled one of the manikins upright and futilely attempted to drape pieces of fabric back onto its broken body, only to have it fall to the floor again.

Then everyone began talking at once. Only Enrico stood immobile, staring at Luis and the remnants of gowns that would never be displayed.

Lindy's throat tightened. She wanted to burst into tears, for Enrico, for Luis, for herself. For all those whose dreams had been destroyed. She felt Bill's hand go to her shoulder, and she grasped it without thinking.

Beside them, Biddy was shaking her head, her fingers pulling at her hair. Rose stood perfectly still, her face composed, as her eyes filled with tears.

With a roar, Enrico turned on the crowd, his eyes wild and accusing. He pinned first one person, then another beneath his gaze. He raised clenched fists into the air and lunged at the crowd. There was a communal gasp as people threw themselves from his path.

"Who?" he cried. "Which one of you did this?" Everyone backed away. Only Luis's muffled sobbing broke the silence. Enrico whirled around. "It is your fault." He ran toward Luis, grabbed him by his necktie, and pulled him to his feet. Luis made choking noises and clawed at his throat.

Bill pushed Lindy away and moved toward the two men, but Rose was standing closer. She leapt forward and grabbed Enrico's wrist. He yowled and his fingers opened spasmodically. Luis fell to his knees and crawled away from Enrico. Then he scrambled to his feet and, pushing the spectators aside, he fled from the room.

"I'm sorry," said Rose. She reached toward Enrico, who stood mindlessly rubbing his wrist. He jumped away and glared at her. Then he took a breath, lifted his chin, and without looking left or right, he walked slowly out of the room.

Talking broke out again as soon as he left.

Rose grimaced. "I hated to do that, but things were getting out of hand."

"Right," said Bill. "Nothing like a little martial arts to put things in perspective."

"God, who would do such a thing?" asked Biddy.

"Somebody who's going to be in big trouble," said Rose and cracked her knuckles.

Lindy heard Bill's intake of breath. "I think we'd better get to rehearsal," she said quickly.

"You go ahead, I'll be there in a few minutes," said Rose. She stepped into the booth, knelt down and began to pick up what was left of Enrico's comeback.

"Let's leave her to it," said Jeremy. He ushered the others toward the door.

"I have to pick up my bag in the lobby," said Bill. "I never finished checking in. Where are you rehearsing? I'll come over later."

"The Cathay Cabaret Theatre," said Lindy.

"I bet Jeremy just loves that."

"Not his idea of high art," agreed Lindy. "And I don't think Biddy's told him that we're playing between *Tangos de Argentine* and *Formation Fixation*, which, if it's what it sounds like, won't make him any happier."

"Sounds like a marching band," said Bill.

"That's what I'm afraid of."

The tango company was just finishing its rehearsal as they walked into the theater. The Ash dancers were already warming up around the room, using chairs and tables as barres. Rebo's leg was supported on the back of one of the banquettes. He motioned Lindy over. "How come you didn't tell us the wannabe was coming? We saw you come out of the elevator earlier. *Quelle supris.*"

The wannabe, the name Rebo had given Bill and the rest of the company had adopted. It was just a joke, but it was cruel. Mainly because it was true. Bill loved her. He had told her so. And here she was, stuck in limbo, married and not married, neither fish nor fowl. Afraid that she might love him, too.

"Does this mean he's the gonna-be?" asked Juan with a grin.

Lindy scowled at him.

"We'll take him if you don't want him. He's yummy."

"And he can cook," said Rebo.

"And he has his own hair," added Juan.

"He's straight," said Lindy.

"Lucky for you." Rebo waggled his eyebrows and turned to stretch his other leg.

Lindy sat down next to Jeremy and sighed. "What else could possibly go wrong?"

"I'm trying not to think about it," he said. "I just hope they catch whoever destroyed those gowns."

"Yeah. And whoever murdered Shane Corbett."

Jeremy frowned at her. "Are you sure it was murder?"

"Bill said so."

"Damn."

"My exact sentiments. What happened after Bill and I left?"

"With the police? They cordoned off the area after they reamed out the security guards for moving the body. They asked Dawn some questions. That took some time. She kept saying that Shane kidnapped Katja and they had to find her. They finally convinced her to give them Katja's address in Cherry Hill and her parents' address in Brooklyn. Then they let Rusty Lonigan take her to her room. They've put out a whatever-it's-called for Katja. They wanted to interview Enrico, but he refused to talk until after his showing." He shook his head. "I'd hate to have to confront the man after what just happened. They were searching the beach when we left. That's about all." He lifted his eyebrows. "How'd I do?"

Lindy smiled. It felt good. "You're a veritable storehouse of information. You'll make junior detective yet."

He immediately sobered. "You don't want to get too used to this murder business, Lindy. It's giving me gray hairs and I don't think Bill was happy at all."

Lindy bristled. "Bill isn't my boss, you are." She took a breath and started over. "Not to worry. I wouldn't do anything to change one golden hair in your gorgeous head. I'm staying far away from all things murderous." And with that intention resounding in her mind, she called, "Onstage."

They were performing Jeremy's *Gershwin Preludes*. The 1930s costumes and the theme of changing partners coordinated perfectly with the ballroom theme. It even drew on ballroom vocabulary.

The piece was in the active repertory and the rehearsal went smoothly. Everyone was relaxed and confident, and not averse to mixing business with a little fun. Every time she stopped the music to make a correction, Rebo and the boys broke into parodies of the ballroom competitors, dipping each other perilously close to the floor, and swiveling their heads as they stalked along the floor in an exaggerated tango position. Jeremy burst out laughing more than once, and even Peter could be heard chuckling from the lighting booth. No one had learned about the murder yet, but she knew it was only a matter of time.

Rose came in halfway through the rehearsal but went straight to the costume room. Bill didn't return. Lindy found herself wondering what he was doing.

She cut them loose a few minutes early, hoping to avoid the formation team that would be coming in to rehearse after them. They met them at the door as they were leaving. Jeremy watched them pass by, carrying oversized dress bags, lacquered hair fitting their heads like helmets.

"Should we—" he began.

"No," chorused Biddy and Lindy together and pulled him out the door.

Chapter Six

"So where is he? He just got here. You'd think he would at least invite me to lunch." Lindy stabbed at the cheese-covered *soupe l'oignon* that had just been delivered by room service.

Biddy looked at her sympathetically. "Did you two have a fight already?"

Lindy shrugged. "Not really. But he acts so superior sometimes."

"Well, he was a New York detective before he was a professor. Maybe he has the right to be."

"That's not the point."

"Then what is the point?"

Lindy shrugged and looked at her soup. "I guess I'm just having some, uh, self-esteem issues as they say in the burbs."

"You?" Biddy guffawed, then frowned. "You're serious?"

Lindy nodded. She was mortified to feel her eyes fill up with tears.

"Criminy. You *are* serious." Biddy pushed her plate away and leaned forward on her elbows. "Okay, out with it. This is about Glen, isn't it?"

Lindy nodded again. "What did I do wrong? I just don't get it. I'm thin, I dress well, I look good, right?"

"I think we've had this conversation before," said Biddy, but her voice was gentle.

"Is it because I embarrass him? Does he think I'm just some dumb dancer?"

"Oh, please. You know this isn't about you. Men do these things when they start losing it. It's called a midlife crisis."

"Women have midlife crises, too. They don't divorce their husbands. They just go back to work." Lindy tried for a smile. It was a pretty unsuccessful endeavor.

"Well, if you ask me, more women should ask for divorces."

The telephone rang. Lindy jumped up to answer it, thankful for the interruption. She listened intently for a few minutes, then hung up.

"That was Rose. She's with Dawn. The police are looking for Katja. I guess Dawn is yo-yoing between being afraid she's dead and being afraid that the police are going to charge her with murder."

Biddy nodded and dropped her napkin over her chef's salad.

"What are you doing?"

"Getting my shoes," said Biddy. "That's why Rose called, right? Dawn needs our help."

"Well, she *is* Rose's friend. And let's face it. It's going to be devastating for her one way or the other."

"Bill isn't going to like this."

"Then he should have stuck around to help."

They both started lacing up running shoes.

"So what do you think happened to Shane?" asked Biddy, standing up and running her fingers through her unruly hair. "And what about Enrico's dresses? Do you think the two are connected?"

"Must be, right? It's too odd of a coincidence not to be."

Biddy nodded agreement. "It doesn't look too good for Katja. Either she's dead or in hiding. Which means that either some unknown person killed both of them or she killed Shane for leaving her and slashed the dresses to get back at Enrico for accusing her of stealing the designs for Felicia."

"It seems like Felicia had more of a reason for slashing the dresses, tit for tat as it were," said Lindy.

"But how could anyone get to the dresses? Rose said the dealers' room was locked all night."

"I don't know. I suppose somebody could have hidden until everyone left for the night."

"Possibly," said Biddy. "Let's go." She opened the door and stuck her head out.

"What are you doing?" asked Lindy, grabbing her bag and coming up behind her.

"Making sure Bill isn't out there. His room is just down the hall."

The hall was empty and they hurried toward the elevator. The doors opened and a man stepped out. Biddy and Lindy slunk back like two guilty conspirators. The man nodded and went on his way.

"Whew," said Biddy and stepped into the elevator. Lindy followed reluctantly behind. She was thinking about Bill. How he wouldn't like what she was doing. And how he and Glen were alike in that respect. Only Glen called it dabbling in disaster. It was an affront to his ordered view of the world and he was embarrassed by it. Bill only cared for her safety. She hoped. And it was stupid to compare Bill's attitude to her husband's. It was stupid to be comparing them in any way. But still, if Bill was worried about her, why did he make himself scarce as soon as he got here? The doors opened onto the fifteenth floor and Biddy pushed her into the hall.

"Stop thinking about Bill."

"How—Oh, never mind."

Rusty Lonigan opened the door, frowned at them, then nodded them inside. Dawn was pacing back and forth, systematically crumpling and spreading out a soggy Kleenex. There was a pile of mangled tissues on the table. She jumped when they entered and rushed toward them.

"Please say you'll help me. Rose says you're good at this kind of thing. The police think Katja murdered Shane. I just know they do and it's ridiculous. She's a sweet, kind girl. It's a conspiracy. That's what it is. But I didn't think even Junie would resort to something like this."

She had pushed them back across the room until they were standing against the door.

"Dawn, get a hold of yourself." Rusty took her by the shoulders and led her back to the table. He sat her down and handed her a glass of water, then shook a pill out of a prescription bottle. "Take this. It will take the edge off. We all know how special Katja is to you, but you won't help things by getting hysterical." He shot Rose, Biddy, and Lindy an apologetic look. "And you can't expect these ladies to get involved."

Dawn pushed his hand away. "I've got to find Katja. I'm sure she's terrified. Can you imagine what it must feel like? She's Russian, for God's sake. She's probably used to the Gestapo knocking on doors in the middle of the night and dragging people away, never to be seen again."

Rusty patted her shoulder. "The Gestapo was German."

"You know what I mean. The KGB or something. She might rather kill herself than be taken by the police." This last statement ended on a wail. Dawn yanked another Kleenex from the dispenser, applied it to her eyes and crumpled it into a wad.

There was a knock at the door and Dawn bolted out of the chair with an accompanying shriek. "Katja!" She stumbled over the edge of the coffee table and fell headfirst across the couch.

Rusty opened the door and Junie Baker stepped inside. "I just heard about Shane. It's all over the ballroom. This is terrible, just terrible."

In the light of day, Junie looked much older than he did in the ballroom. His hair was dyed black and shined with gel, but it was thinning at the hairline. His face was puffy, and it looked like he was wearing pancake makeup. A red cummerbund was stretched tight over his waist beneath his tuxedo jacket.

He crossed the room to where Dawn was sprawled across the couch. Dawn scrambled into the far corner and glared at him. "What have you done with Katja?"

Junie threw his hands in the air. Dawn cowered.

"You silly Gumbacher. Get a grip. I haven't done a damn thing to that chubby Pagach. I told you the girl would cause trouble. And now look what she's done." Junie started to pace. It must be a family (or ex-family) trait, thought Lindy.

"She hasn't done anything," moaned Dawn. "She trusted me, trusted Shane. She's a victim of circumstance. Your circumstance." She drew in her breath for another onslaught. "You did this. Don't deny it. You took Timothy and you planned to take Shane." Her mouth trembled spasmodically. "You've probably already had him."

Junie flinched, then looked hastily at the others before turning back to Dawn. He grabbed her wrist and yanked her off the couch. "You don't know what you're talking about. And I'll thank you not to cause any trouble. You couldn't keep Timothy because you paid him shit and couldn't find him a decent partner."

"He could have had Katja," Dawn said defensively.

"I said a decent partner. You think just because you took her in and treated her like a princess, that you could make her into a good dancer? I don't care if she came direct from the Kirov, the girl can't dance. And follow? Ha. That's a joke. It would take a bulldozer to move her across the floor. I can't believe that you've let yourself be snowed by some silly little Russian blini. I don't even know why we let them in the country. They've taken over the whole damn ballroom business. They're wrecking it. And if they can't win fair and square—"

Here Dawn interrupted him with a "Ha" of her own. "You lamebrained, left-footed idiot. You think Felicia and Timothy had a chance against Shane and Katja? I don't care how many judges you have in your pocket. Even they wouldn't be able to keep them from winning."

"And if they can't win fair and square," Junie repeated before she could take a breath to go on, "they'll win any way they can. She knew Shane was dumping her. Timothy and Felicia didn't have a chance against Shane and anybody, but Shane and Felicia would have been the next world champions. So your chubby muffin murdered him."

"You cretin," screamed Dawn. "You *were* going to put him with Felicia. So why did you steal Timothy away from me? What do you need him for? Does he know what you're planning?"

"I'd say it was a moot point at this juncture," said Rusty, finally moving to stop the argument. "Shane won't be winning any titles now."

"Thanks to Junie," cried Dawn. She threw her hands over her face and sobbed.

"What the hell's that supposed to mean?" asked Junie. "It's not my fault."

"I bet you killed him. Sure. *You* killed him. And now you're trying to take Katja from me. Well, you can't have her, you hear? I'll never let you have her."

"*Me* kill him? Give me a break."

"That's enough," said Rusty, glancing uneasily at the fighting couple.

"I would have taken Shane, he's talented, but I don't want that Kreplach," yelled Junie. "I swear, I don't know what you see in her. Or any of those other poor schnitzels that you keep taking in. Get a life, Dawn. You pour your whole soul into those ungrateful ballroom bitches. They take you for everything they can, and then they say sayonara."

"A virtual smorgasbord of epithets," whispered Rose.

"It's your fault," cried Dawn. "If you had only let me—"

"Oh, shut up. It's water under the bridge. Nobody was holding a gun to your head. Go find a husband. Adopt a baby and keep it the hell away from the ballroom business."

Dawn screeched and began pummeling his chest. "You want everything I have."

He threw her hands away and backed up. He strode across the room and stopped at the door. "Not everything," he said and slammed the door behind him.

For a moment no one spoke. The room seemed to reverberate with residual anger.

"He bad-mouths the Russians," whimpered Dawn. "But he marks them just like everybody else." She threw herself into the closest chair and sobbed.

Lindy glanced at Biddy. Her expression hadn't changed throughout the entire confrontation.

"Close your mouth," whispered Lindy.

Biddy's mouth snapped shut, but her eyes stayed wide and unblinking.

Rose went over to sit on the arm of Dawn's chair. Rusty stood behind them, looking worried.

Dawn reached over the back of the chair and grabbed his sleeve. "Junie probably wants my studio, too. Promise me you won't let him buy us out."

Rusty made reassuring noises.

"Promise me."

"Junie already has his own studio just down the road."

"Four point eight miles down the road," Dawn said. "I want to start a suit against him as soon as the comp is over. First thing Monday morning."

"Dawn," Rusty began.

"First thing Monday morning. Promise me."

With a sigh, Rusty nodded his head. "I promise. Are you satisfied? We'll start proceedings first thing on Monday."

She turned to Rose. "And you and your friends will help me find Katja, okay? Okay?"

Rose sighed. "The police are already looking for her."

"They won't find her."

"Do you have any idea where she might have gone?" asked Lindy in spite of herself. She really didn't want to get involved with this, even for Rose's friend. She wasn't sure that Dawn was completely sane.

Dawn looked at her in amazement. "Of course not." She pulled herself out of the chair and pushed back her hair. "I really need to get ready to go to the ballroom. Thanks for coming." She grabbed a makeup case off the dresser and went into the bedroom.

Rose, Lindy and Biddy stood looking after her. Rusty smiled apologetically and closed the door to the bedroom. "She'll calm down eventually. Thanks for coming." He led them to the door. "But I don't think you really need to worry about Katja. She'll show up when she's good and ready." He glanced back at the bedroom door. "Some people never learn."

They walked in silence to the elevators. Rose pushed the down button.

"That was weird," said Lindy. "Think you can translate what just happened?"

Rose shrugged. "Your guess is as good as mine."

"And what about Katja?" asked Biddy. "Dawn seems a tad obsessive about one of her employees, don't you think?"

"It goes beyond employee with Dawn." Rose paused. "Look, here it is in a nutshell. Junie danced her until she was too old to have children. Then he dumped her for another man."

"Ouch."

"So she's always trying to make daughters out of the girls she trains."

Biddy frowned. "Poor Dawn."

Lindy shot her a concerned look. Years ago Biddy had loved a dancer named Claude. He finally came out of the closet only to die of AIDS a few years later. Biddy was the only one who didn't desert him. Now she was in love with Jeremy, who was about as ambivalent about his sexual identity as any man Lindy had known. Was Biddy afraid that the same thing would happen to her?

"But hell, people go on with their lives," said Biddy. "It's stupid not to. Right?"

"Right," agreed Lindy.

"Not Dawn. She's spent the last ten years looking back and hating Junie. Well, actually, we know what it is really."

"She's still in love with him," said Lindy.

"You got it," said Rose. "Sad, isn't it?"

Lindy's mouth was suddenly dry. How awful to be stuck in the past, tied to a man who no longer loved you. She swore in that instant that she wouldn't become like Dawn. She would no longer try to hold on to Glen, to their shared past. She would let go gracefully and get on with her life, like Biddy had done.

"So we don't really think Junie killed Shane?" asked Biddy.

"Why would he?" asked Rose. "If half the scuttlebutt is true, they were lovers, and Junie was planning on making him and Felicia the next *champeens.*"

"Could he really do that? What about the other judges?" asked Lindy.

"Well, you have to be good, but at the top there's not always a big difference in ability. That's where the politics come in."

"And Junie's a bigwig?"

"Yes. But so is Dawn. My guess is that this will be a fight to the finish."

"I certainly hope not," said Biddy and shivered. "All we need is another murder."

"But now Dawn doesn't have a couple. How can she compete?" asked Lindy.

"Well, she does have other couples, just none as good as Shane and Katja. But she'll figure out a way to screw Junie if she can. Because now he doesn't have a winning couple, either."

"What about Timothy and Felicia?"

"She's good," agreed Rose, "but Timothy has a family to support. Competing is an expensive business. Every gown out there costs upwards of three thousand dollars, and weekly coaching at a couple hundred dollars a pop, plus entrance fees. As Dawn would say, you do the numbers. Timothy has to teach too many hours just to make ends meet. He could never fully commit to competing."

"So now, neither of them has a winning couple," said Lindy.

"But what was all that railing against the Russians?" asked Biddy. "Is Junie some kind of xenophobe?"

The elevator arrived and they stepped inside.

"Nah. It's just that the Russians have virtually taken over the ballroom business. They work hard and study hard. And they're good."

"But not very tasteful, if what we saw last night and in the hall this morning is any indication," said Lindy.

"Hey, they do what they're told, and it's American coaches telling them what to do. They just perfect what's been around for years. Only on them, it's clear enough to see how really grotesque it is."

They reached the eleventh floor, just as Bill stepped out of the second elevator. All four of them jumped guiltily.

"Oh," said Lindy. Then she peered at him. He was wearing an overcoat and his hair was damp. "Where have you been?"

"Around."

"Oh."

Bill cleared his throat. He was going to lie to her. He always cleared his throat when he was going to stretch the truth. She felt immensely disappointed. What didn't he want her to know?

"I know some people here," he said vaguely.

"Oh," she said again. She couldn't seem to think of anything else to say. And she was certainly not going to ask him whom he knew. It might be a woman. Maybe that's why he didn't want to tell them where he had been. Maybe that's why he had agreed to spend the week here in the first place. She got a sinking feeling that had nothing to do with Bill's prevarication. It had to do with feeling rejected. But she didn't have a right to feel rejected, did she? She was still tied to Glen. But not wanted by him. She swallowed. She was afraid she'd burst into tears if she tried to speak. Yuck. She was as nuts as Dawn.

"I took the liberty of making a reservation for dinner, that is, if you're free."

"Huh?" Had he just invited her to dinner? Well, that's why he was here after all. So they could spend time together. So where had he been all day? Not with her. He probably felt obligated to take her to dinner to make up for ignoring her all day. "Sure, if you really want to."

Bill frowned. Biddy frowned. Rose frowned.

"I mean . . . that would be great."

"Biddy, why don't you and Jeremy meet us for a drink around six?"

Lindy looked up. He didn't want to be alone with her. Had he invited them to dinner, too?

"Sure," said Biddy. "We were going to meet anyway at the Lotus Lounge on the eighth floor."

"Six o'clock?" suggested Bill. "You, too, Rose."

"Thanks, but I have a heavy date with the boys at the casino."

Bill stopped at a door halfway down the hall. He gave Lindy a questioning look, then slid his key card into the slot and went inside.

As Bill's door closed behind him, Biddy took Lindy by the sleeve of her sweater and pulled her down the hall. "What is the matter with you?"

"Where has he been?"

"Bill? You heard him. He was visiting with friends."

"Maybe."

Rose rolled her eyes, waved her fingers in good-bye and turned down an adjacent corridor.

Biddy opened their door. "So what are you going to wear? I hope you brought the little black number that some good friend with impeccable taste made you buy."

"I brought it," said Lindy, wondering now why she had.

Chapter
Seven

Lindy and Biddy arrived at the Lotus Lounge a few minutes after six o'clock. The eighth-floor bar was far removed from the raucous world of the casino—serene and virtually empty. They stepped through an oval entrance into a room so dark that it was impossible at first to see anything more than the flicker of wall sconces ahead of them.

Lindy started in surprise when a small Oriental man stepped out of the shadows and made a low bow. He took their coats and handed them to another shadowy figure, a pencil-thin woman in a black Mandarin pantsuit, who carried them away.

Lindy and Biddy followed him beneath a mirrored ceiling that reflected their images back like phantom butterflies. They passed a dark wooden bar, shined to a gleaming finish. Only two of the upholstered stools were occupied.

He led them between two japanned screens, decorated with giant nacre lotus blossoms, then through a maze of more screens to a small alcove where Bill and Jeremy sat at a black lacquered table. Here, too, the mother-of-pearl theme was repeated in large lotus flowers on the walls and tabletop. He bowed once more and was gone.

"It's like being inside a Chinese puzzle box," whispered Biddy. "We should have left bread crumbs to find our way out again."

Both men stood up.

"You look lovely," said Bill as Lindy sat down in the chair he held for her.

"Divine," agreed Jeremy.

"Thanks," she said. Tonight she had worked at it, and she was pleased with the results. She was wearing the black DKNY dress, bought during one of Biddy's therapy shopping sessions, and matching sling-back heels that accentuated her high arch. She had bought the dangly gold earrings two years ago with Bill in mind, but had never worn them—until tonight. She pushed aside the niggling question that had begun plaguing her as she dressed for dinner. She wanted to impress Bill, but did this mean she was the worst kind of tease? Or that she was ready to reciprocate his feelings—if his feelings toward her hadn't changed? She felt a nervous flutter in her stomach and glanced at him.

He was looking awfully enticing in a dark gray suit. His hair was brushed away from his face, a faint part down the middle. She watched it with interest, wondering how long it would take before the first strand fell across his forehead. He caught her looking at him and his eyes narrowed in question.

"You guys look good, too," she said.

A waiter appeared and poured wine into two more glasses, placed them in front of Lindy and Biddy, then he, too, was gone. Lindy picked up her glass. Its deep burgundy shone in the light from the brass lantern that hung above the table. Bill's choice. He liked good wine. She had been surprised when she first met him. Tall, lanky, wearing an old hunting coat and faded jeans, and reeking of cigar smoke. He had seemed so large and overbearing and loud. Not someone you'd expect to have refined tastes. But he did. And he wasn't loud, he just had a resonant voice. He dressed well when the occasion called for it, and though tall and angular, he carried it with a supple grace.

Then she noticed that the others had raised their glasses. She must have missed the toast during her mental rambling. She raised her glass to theirs and took a sip.

Silence fell around the table. Bill was studying his wineglass. Well, that was normal. Probably considering the quality of his choice—or else he didn't want to look at her. Things didn't seem to be going right between them, but she didn't know why.

"I think rehearsal went well today," said Biddy, breaking into the silence.

"Yes," agreed Jeremy. "But I'm concerned about Rose. I hope she's not going to get too involved in Dawn Gilpatrick's troubles."

Biddy and Lindy exchanged a quick look.

"Is she?" asked Bill, looking at Lindy, then at Biddy.

Simultaneously, they picked up their wineglasses and took a sip.

"Okay, out with it."

"Actually we were with Dawn this afternoon," said Biddy.

Lindy saw Bill's jaw tense. She jumped in to explain before he lost his temper. "Rose asked us to talk to her. Just for moral support. Dawn thinks Katja is hiding because of her experience with the Soviet police."

"She was involved with the KGB?" asked Jeremy.

"I don't think so," said Lindy. "It's just Dawn's perception of why she might have run away. She also accused Junie of killing Shane. But she blames Junie for everything that isn't right with her life. It's pitiful."

"I suppose she asked you to investigate," said Bill.

"She just asked us to help her find Katja. She's frantic."

"Goddammit, Lindy. I want you to stay out of this."

She frowned at him. "Why are you so down on me? Dawn just asked us to keep an eye out for her friend. What's the harm in that? Do you think I would meddle in a police investigation?"

"Have I ever accused you of meddling?"

The wine turned sour in her stomach. No, he hadn't. Glen was the one that thought she was a meddlesome amateur, an embarrassment to his standing in the community. She was angry at Glen, not Bill. But she was taking it out on Bill, and he didn't deserve that.

"No, of course not. I guess I'm just a little oversensitive these days."

Bill gave her a long look, so long that Lindy began to fidget.

"Did it ever occur to you that I worry about you?"

"Thanks," she said. "And I appreciate it. But you needn't worry. I can take care of myself."

"Lindy, the person who did this is sadistic. Murdered a man, dressed him in a ball gown, then crushed his feet to fit into shoes four sizes too small for him. A person like that would not have the least compunction about offing anyone who got too close."

A frisson of unease skittered across her shoulders and up her neck. "How do you know Shane wasn't wearing the dress and someone mistook him for Katja?"

Bill retreated behind his cop face, as Rebo called it, and toyed with his wineglass.

"You mean Shane might have been some kind of cross-dresser on his way for a night on the town? That's pretty far-fetched," said Biddy.

"I know," said Lindy. "And he couldn't have worn it, even if he could fit into it. The zipper was broken. The killer must have known it was Shane all along. Killed him and dressed him afterward, like Bill said."

Bill didn't respond. Everyone lapsed back into silence. Shane Corbett's body lay among them like an uninvited guest.

Lindy sipped more wine. That explanation was fine as far as it went, but Bill didn't know about the zipper being broken. Something else must have alerted him. Had he seen some detail at the beach that she had missed? It was possible. Bill had been a detective before he left the NYPD to teach criminology. He hadn't lost those skills.

Lindy narrowed her eyes at him. "Did you come up with this hypothesis by what you saw this morning or have you been doing your own investigating?"

Bill cleared his throat.

"And don't bother to lie. I always know when you're not telling the truth."

"You do?"

She gave him an exasperated look. "Yes, I do." She wasn't going to tell him how she knew. He would practice lying until he could do it without that telltale rattle in his throat. So that's where he had been all afternoon, talking to the police. She felt relief and exasperation at the same time. "Isn't it time we were going?"

Jeremy and Biddy stood up. They were dressed for dinner, but Biddy hadn't mentioned that they were joining Bill and her. She hoped they weren't and immediately felt guilty. Nonetheless, she was relieved when Jeremy told them he was taking Biddy to Dock's Oyster House.

"Oysters?" Lindy widened her eyes at Biddy. Biddy raised hers to the ceiling.

"It's a famous restaurant," said Jeremy defensively.

They wound their way back to the front room. The check girl handed their coats to Bill and Jeremy. Lindy watched Jeremy help Biddy into her coat, his hands lightly resting on her shoulders when he had finished. It was a casual, fleeting gesture. So like Jeremy. No hugs or kisses, at least when anyone was around. And yet it was so intimate, so romantic.

They parted in the lobby. Jeremy and Biddy got into a cab. Bill handed a ticket to a doorman dressed in livery that reminded Lindy of the monkeys in *The Wizard of Oz*. There was a spring of mistletoe in his lapel.

"You shouldn't make fun of Jeremy," said Bill.

Lindy sighed. "I know. But it's so sweet. I mean, he's worldly and jaded and so repressed."

"All the more reason."

She cast a sidelong glance at him, then slipped her hand into the crook of his arm. "You're right, of course." The Dragon punctuated her statement with a snort of smoke.

"Thank you—both," said Bill, trying not to smile.

"You're welcome. Now would you like to tell me where you were today?"

Bill gave her a blank look.

"Shall I guess?"

Still no answer.

"At the police station." She gave him a smug smile. God, she hoped that was where he was and she wasn't going to have to listen to any confessions of another kind. She waited.

"I went to the police academy with Andrew Dean. He ended up in Atlantic City. I haven't seen him in years. I just dropped in to say hello."

"I knew it. Do they have any leads? Have they found Katja? Is she alive? Are they going to charge her with murder?"

The Honda pulled up at the door; Bill tipped the valet and helped her inside. As soon as he got in, he turned to Lindy and said, "Put on your seat belt."

Bill turned the Honda into the street. Lindy waited for an answer to her question, but Bill didn't say a word, just concentrated on his driving. Finally, she leaned back in her seat, resigned to wait.

A fine mist of rain coated the windshield and reflected in the Honda's headlights as they drove along the city streets. It was cozy and warm in the car, the windshield wipers arcing in a rhythmic swish-swish, Bill sitting beside her. The urgency of murder gradually faded away as they left the casino lights behind them.

"Where are we going?"

"To a restaurant that was recommended to me." Bill glanced sideways at her, then returned his gaze to the road.

Hmm, thought Lindy. One far away from town. Was he trying to escape the eyes of curious company members or the distraction of murder?

"By your old police academy buddy?"

"As a matter of fact."

"Are you going to tell me what he said?"

"He said that it has excellent food, a good wine list, and an old-world atmosphere."

"Not about the restaurant, about the investigation."

"Nope," said Bill, his eyes intent on the highway.

"Oh, come on."

Bill sighed. "If I tell you what I know, can we forget it for the next hour or so?"

Lindy flinched at his tone of voice. "Okay."

He took a breath. "They haven't found Katja, dead or alive. Right now, they're looking at locals as the possible perpetrators. Slumming seems to be a favorite pastime with some of the casino guests, and there have been several high-profile murders because of it. The casino is pressuring the ACPD to stay away from its clientele. It isn't good for business. There's an uneasy alliance between the town and the casinos. It's a sticky situation."

"But they don't really think it was a local."

"The ACPD doesn't want it to be a local. It makes the city look bad. They're going through the motions to appease the casino owners, but they haven't backed off the search for Katja. She's a good suspect. It was her dress. She was the last one seen wearing it. She and Shane had argued publicly the night before. And she's gone on the lam." He shrugged.

"Dawn will be devastated. She never had children of her own, and she thinks of Katja as a daughter."

"Someone is always devastated in cases like this."

Lindy took a close look at his profile. It gave nothing away. Bill rarely did. But his words were filled with feeling. He had once told her that he hated destroying peoples' lives. But that wasn't why he had left the force. It was because his wife, Claire, had wanted better things than a policeman's salary could give her. He had left the force to teach, and she had divorced him.

Lindy sighed. "Any chance of finding a witness?"

"The boardwalk is deserted at this time of the year. Especially at night. It's dark. It's cold. The ramp shields the view from most of the hotel windows. I don't know, and that's all I know."

"What about the murder weapon? That's what the black splotch across the front of the dress was. Blood, right? If Shane was stabbed or shot, there should have been torn fabric and there wasn't. But all that blood didn't come from his head wound, did it?"

"God, you're scary sometimes," said Bill. "You're right, but don't ask about the murder weapon. It's part of the confidential report. That's all I know about the entire case, so don't ask any more questions."

He slowed down, then turned the Honda into a driveway marked by a hanging blue sign. Lindy recognized it as an exclusive restaurant she had read about in the *Guide to Atlantic City*. It was a rustic, stone and clapboard inn. Bill stopped the car beneath a canopy at the front door. The valet held an umbrella over their heads as they walked up the front steps.

Lindy shivered. "Pretty nasty weather, if you ask me."

"Nor'easter season," said Bill and led her inside.

While Bill checked their coats, Lindy took in her surroundings. The restaurant was warm and lit with a mellow light. An open fire roared in a large stone fireplace at the far end of the room. It was only seven-thirty, but already the restaurant was doing a lively business. The maitre d' led them through the dining area to a secluded table. He pulled out a chair for Lindy and she sat down.

Laughter sounded from across the room. She looked over and sucked in her breath. Rusty Lonigan and Junie Baker were getting up from the table.

"I wonder what they're doing here."

Bill flicked a glance over his shoulder. "Who are they? I saw the redhead in the casino this morning, but not the other."

She gave him a brief account of Rusty and Junie. "Rusty and Dawn are about to sue Timothy Saunders for breaking his contract. And Dawn is afraid Rusty is about to sell out to Junie. She made him promise not to. Rusty and Junie were both in her room today and they didn't even seem to like each other. So why would they be having dinner together?"

"Maybe they're attempting to come to a gentleman's agreement," said Bill. "Going to court can be an expensive venture."

"Hmm, I wonder."

"Well, don't. Just try to enjoy dinner and eat something for a change."

Lindy looked down at her dress. Did he think she was too thin? She had finally gotten back into a size six after two years of constant dieting. She had shed even more weight once she discovered that Glen wanted to leave her. *Was* she too thin? Her hand went to her cheek. She had heard it often enough at her health club. When you reached a certain age, and Lindy guessed that she might be coming close, you had to decide between face and butt. A good body meant a wrinkled face, a good face meant a wide butt. Surely, she hadn't arrived there yet. She was only forty-something. And she felt twenty-five most of the time. She was in her prime.

"Lindy?"

She looked up. "Yes?"

His eyes met hers. "Nothing. I just wonder what it would be like . . ." He trailed off.

"If we hadn't met over a murder?" she guessed.

Bill shrugged.

She reached across the table and took his hand. "We would probably never have met at all. Anyway, we're a pretty good team." She looked at her hand and snatched it back as she realized the implications of her words.

A waiter appeared. Listening to the specials and ordering wine covered her discomfort, but Bill was still watching her intently when the waiter left.

"Did you know that to be a licensed private investigator in New Jersey you just have to fill out a form and pay a fee?"

"Don't even think about it," said Bill.

"I think I would be a good PI," said Lindy only half in jest. "I mean a rehearsal director is always looking for clues. I have a 'good eye' as they say in the business. And dancers know how to think on their feet. Look at the success I've had in applying the same techniques to the crimes we've been involved in."

"You've been damn lucky. And I've aged ten years."

Lindy frowned. "That's what Jeremy said. That I was giving him gray hairs. Not very flattering."

Bill smiled.

"Not funny."

"We just don't want you getting hurt."

"That smacks of condescension."

"No, it doesn't. It's called concern. Now stop trying to pick a fight."

"I'm not."

"Yes, you are. You're mad at me for having professional clout that you don't."

"I have my own kind of clout," she returned. "I'm a natural at this investigation business. People tell me everything." She gave him a meaningful look. "Most people."

The rest of dinner passed with her trying to find out Bill's theories on who had killed Shane Corbett, and Bill adroitly changing the subject. By the time they had finished, they had run out of general things to talk about and had wandered into that other taboo subject: what Lindy was going to do for Christmas. She hadn't told anyone that Annie was staying in Geneva to play with the local orchestra, or that Cliff was going home with his new girlfriend to meet her parents. That Lindy would spend a quiet, peaceful day—alone. It was too pitiful.

She was on her way to a full-blown depression when they stepped outside into a night of gently falling snowflakes.

"Wow," said Lindy. "I didn't think it snowed at the seashore." She lifted her face to white petals that melted as they touched her skin. The magic of it made her momentarily forget murder and the prospect of a lonely holiday.

By the time they reached the hotel, it was snowing in earnest. The flakes formed a curtain of white that swirled in front of the windshield. Snow even blew in under the portico of the hotel, whipping about their ankles and stinging their faces as they got out of the car.

"This is fabulous," said Lindy. "A white Christmas at the beach. Does it snow over the ocean?"

Bill smiled. "I don't suppose looking out a window would satisfy your curiosity, would it?"

She smiled back. "Nope."

"I didn't think so. We could take a walk along the boardwalk, but not in those shoes." He nodded toward her sling-backs.

"It'll only take a minute to change. What do you say?"

"Okay." Bill took hold of her elbow. "But we're only going to look at the snow."

"Of course."

Chapter
Eight

A few minutes later, Bill trundled Lindy past the casino and into the moonless night. He had changed his suit for jeans, boots and a navy blue car coat. Lindy was impressed. She hadn't planned to leave the hotel during the week and had only managed jeans, sneakers, an extra turtleneck sweater, and Biddy's down vest beneath her suede jacket. Both of them were hatless and as soon as they stepped outside, Lindy's ears began to burn from the frigid air.

The boardwalk was lit by Victorian street lamps that carved cones of light into the darkness and captured the falling flakes of snow in suspended animation. The lampposts were adorned with hanging mermaids, sea horses, wreaths and candy canes, all threaded with colored blinking lights.

The melting snow transformed the chevron-patterned planks of the boardwalk into an ice rink, and they skidded across it to stand at the rail and peer out at the ocean. Lindy could hear the waves crashing onto the beach and caught an occasional glimpse of sea foam. But mostly it was dark, the snow disappearing into a black abyss of ocean.

They stood side by side, not talking. After a few minutes, Lindy's eyes slid toward the ramp where Shane's body had been found. It seemed such a forlorn place in the deep night. She and Bill were the only people on the boardwalk. No one else had even come out to see the snow.

She glanced up at the windows in the hotel, hundreds of them looking out over the shore. She counted upward trying to discern where her window was. She had looked out of it when she went to change, but the angle was wrong. No one from that side of the hotel would have seen any altercation at the ramp. Her gaze panned across the front of the building. But what about the rooms on the north side of the hotel? Someone could have looked out of one of those windows and seen what had happened.

She longed to ask Bill if the detectives had put a time on Shane's murder, but she had tried his patience too much that night.

"Stop it," said Bill. He walked her in the opposite direction from the scene of the murder. They stopped near the set of steps that led down to the beach. Ahead of them, the pier, closed for the season, jutted out over the water. Abandoned rides, stripped of everything but their infrastructure, rose skeletonlike out of the darkness: the tower of some flying whirling ride, the humps of a roller coaster, the naked curve of the Ferris wheel shorn of its cars. Concession trailers were shut tight and pushed together inside a chain-link fence. Cotton Candy, Philly Cheese Steaks, Fries, Ice Cream, abandoned now except for the gulls that made their nest in the chinks and corners. Lindy tried to imagine the pier lit up and crowded with people, riotous music, and shouting and laughter. But the image escaped her. All she could see was the bleak, forgotten outlines of a better time.

"Scro-o-o-ge," Lindy moaned in a ghostlike voice. Then she shivered, spooked by her own joke.

A movement on the other side of the rail made her jump back into Bill. "What's that?"

Bill put his arm around her. "Stray cat, stray bum, certainly nothing we want to encounter up close."

"Too big for a cat," said Lindy. "It must be a person. He shouldn't be out in this weather. It's freezing. Why doesn't he go to a shelter?"

"Are there no workhouses . . ."

She cuffed his chin. "Smart-ass."

Bill smiled and pulled her closer.

But she pushed away and looked up at him. "What if he was here last night, too? He might have seen who killed Shane." She slipped out of Bill's arm and started toward the steps to the beach.

Bill grabbed for her. "And maybe he's the one who killed Shane. I'll notify Andrew tomorrow."

She stopped with her foot on the top step and shivered as the shadow scuttled away. She had the briefest glimpse of a slouch hat pulled low over a hidden face. And a long coat. She thought she recognized them.

"It's not a killer," she said. "It's the Gull Lady." She jumped down the last two steps, then whirled around, squinting into the dark.

"She's gone." Lindy peered along the edge of the boardwalk but there was no place to hide there. To her left, the underbelly of the pier was a black hole, menacing and uninviting. A perfect hiding place. She took a tentative step forward, but she was loath to follow the figure into those concrete pilings. She hoped that Bill would volunteer.

Bill was standing on the top step, looking down at her, his arms akimbo. Snow danced around him like flurries in a snow globe. "Go ahead," he said. "I'll stay here and watch your back."

Lindy glowered at him. He burst out laughing. "Your Gull Lady probably has a nice little nest inside one of those trailers. I wouldn't worry about her."

"But the pier is fenced in."

"Bet you there's a hole in the chain-link somewhere. Hurry up if you're planning to take a closer look. I'm getting cold and might have to leave you here while I go in search of a brandy."

"Okay. You've made your point," said Lindy, giving a last glance toward the pier. "You can buy just for being such a wise guy."

"My pleasure." And leaving the Gull Lady and the snow behind, they returned to the hotel.

Lindy maneuvered Bill through the casino toward the Pagoda

Bar. She knew he would choose one with a quieter ambience, but she hoped to waylay Rose and find out what had been going on while they were at dinner.

The ballroom was just letting out for the night. Tired dancers, carrying dance bags and shoes, headed for the elevators. Clumps of people stood in the hall discussing the marks for the evening.

Lindy perused the crowd, looking for Rose, even as Bill increased their pace toward the bar. There was no Rose to be seen.

The bar was already filled with people from the ballroom. The bar itself was packed three deep, and all the tables appeared full.

Bill said something in her ear, but between the singer who stood at the piano, belting out "Jingle Bell Rock," and the conversations of the patrons, she couldn't hear what he was saying.

Just then she saw Rose sitting at a nearby table. She was waving frantically in their direction.

"Oh, there's Rose," said Lindy. "I think she's saving us a place." She heard Bill groan as she pushed her way through the clump of people waiting to be seated.

"Where have you guys been?" asked Rose as they shrugged out of their coats and sat down. "The rumors are flying."

Bill leaned back in his seat and crossed his arms.

"Oh, don't be such a poop," said Rose. "We're getting good at this."

Lindy flashed her a warning look, but Rose was oblivious. "So do you want to hear?" She leaned forward on her elbows and gave Bill a challenging look.

Bill leaned forward on *his* elbows and returned her a look of his own.

Lindy bit her lip to keep from smiling.

A waiter came to take their order.

"Murder is a serious business," said Bill steadily as soon as the waiter had left. "It's permanent."

"Yeah," said Rose. "I know. I worked in Vegas, remember? It happened all the time."

Bill stifled an expletive.

"So anyway, it seems that everybody but Katja and Dawn knew about Junie and Shane."

"Right," said Bill.

Rose frowned at him. "What?"

Bill shrugged. "If everyone else knew, it's likely that they did, too. I would hazard a guess that it's hard to keep secrets in this atmosphere." He gave Lindy a pointed look.

She looked away as a bolt of insecurity jarred her. Was he accusing her of being a gossip? Or talking about their relationship?

Rose shook her head. "Katja seemed genuinely dumbfounded when she overheard those girls talking, didn't she?" She gave Bill the condensed version of what had happened in the ladies' lounge. "And Dawn had just found out when we arrived. She was fuming."

"That was yesterday?" asked Bill.

"Yeah," said Rose, suddenly cautious. "But don't get any ideas. She was plenty mad, but more at Junie than anyone else."

"We saw him and Rusty having dinner tonight," said Lindy.

Rose's eyes widened. "Shit." She looked from Lindy to Bill and back to Lindy. "Did it look like Rusty was telling Junie they were going to sue him?"

"They looked pretty friendly, if you ask me."

"Damn. I hope Dawn isn't right about Rusty wanting to sell out to Junie. That studio is about the only thing she has in this world. God. Junie's stolen her top teacher, would have stolen her best dancer if he hadn't gotten killed. And if he takes her studio, that'll finish her." Rose sighed, then glanced at Bill. "What?"

Bill didn't answer, but Rose seemed to get the message. "No way. Don't even think it. Dawn's whiny and spiteful, but she's not a killer."

"I didn't say a thing," said Bill.

"No, but I saw that look."

The waiter returned and placed brandies before Lindy and Bill. Rose's drink, something called a Flaming Dragon, came in a giant bowl-shaped glass and was cherry red. The waiter placed it on a napkin in front of her, then with a flourish struck a long-stemmed match, and the drink burst into flames.

Lindy jumped. Rose watched, mesmerized. Bill broke into a wide grin. The waiter smiled and bowed his way to the next table.

As soon as the flames died down, Rose touched the glass with her fingertip, then stuck her finger into her drink. With a shrug, she lifted it to her mouth and took a swallow. "Whoa," she said with an expulsion of air. Bill burst out laughing.

Lindy leaned forward, but she had no chance to return to the subject of murder, or to tell Rose about seeing the Gull Lady on the beach. She saw Rebo, Juan, and Eric heading their way. They crowded around the table. Rebo waggled his eyebrows at Lindy over Bill's head. She widened her eyes back at him, telegraphing him not to make any jokes.

He stuck out his bottom lip in a pout. "You guys been out hiking?" he said, looking at Lindy and Bill. "I thought you were going to dinner."

"We did," said Lindy. "Then it started snowing, so we took a walk on the boardwalk." She finished the statement in a mumble, suddenly embarrassed about the implications of a midnight walk by the ocean.

"And?" asked Rebo hopefully.

"And then we came here." Lindy could hear her voice getting tighter. She risked a look at Bill. He seemed to be watching someone at the bar.

"I wish you two would get on with it. This is taking longer than a soap opera."

Lindy's stomach flipped over. How could he say something like that in front of Bill? She risked another glance at Bill, but he wasn't listening. She glared at Rebo.

"And speaking of soap operas," he continued blithely. "Why didn't you tell us about the murder?"

"Yeah," said Juan. "We had to learn about it from some ballroom boys."

"Not good for our image as happenin' kind of guys," said Eric. "Definitely a bust."

"You," said Bill, "had better steer clear of whatever's happening."

Rebo threw his hands up, warding off an imaginary blow. "At ease, bulldog. We'll leave the moonlight walks to you." He grinned impishly at Bill. "We just came to say good night. We're headed into town for some fun."

Lindy opened her mouth to argue, but before she could say a word, Bill said, "Well, be careful." He signed the tab, stood up and looked at Lindy. "Ready?"

Everyone around the table broke into grins, while Lindy flushed to the roots of her hair. She grabbed her coat off the back of her chair and followed Bill out of the bar.

"You did that on purpose," she said as soon as they got to the elevator.

"It was too good to pass up. And since I seem to be the source of so much entertainment, I didn't want to let them down." The elevator doors opened and they stepped inside.

"I'm sorry," she stammered. "They just . . ."

"I know. It's okay." He leaned against the wall, and they were silent all the way to the eleventh floor.

As they walked down the hall toward their rooms, Lindy began to panic. Would he stop at his room? Ask her in for a nightcap? No, they passed his door and he hadn't even slowed down. They stopped at her door, and Lindy fished in her jeans pocket for her key card. Would he take it from her and open the door? Would he follow her inside? Bill didn't move. Lindy pushed the key card into the slot and opened the door.

She turned toward him. He still hadn't moved.

"Good night," she said.

"Good night." He didn't move away and didn't move toward her, just stood there.

"Well, good night."

"Good night." This time Bill stepped back and Lindy closed the door.

"Jeez, how many good nights does it take?" asked Biddy from where she was propped up in bed. She was wearing her glasses. A pencil was stuck through her hair and a blue spiral notebook was lying facedown across her stomach. A can of ginger ale was open on the bedside table. "I was wondering whether I should dive under the bed or what."

Lindy threw her coat and vest on the bed and struggled out of her sweater. She threw it over the coat and vest, then flopped down beside them. "God, what am I going to do?"

"Do you really want me to answer that for you?"

"It was rhetorical." Lindy sat up. "And anyway, I know what you'd say."

Biddy took off her glasses and laid them on the bedside table. She fluffed up her pillow and straightened the covers over her knees. Then she looked at Lindy.

"I'm scared. What if Glen changes his mind? What if he shows up again and wants me back? What if I've forgotten how? I've only made love to one man in the last twenty years—and to nobody since July. What if I make a really big mistake and Bill gets hurt?"

Biddy stared at her. "Since July? Not even when you went to Paris in September?"

Lindy shook her head.

Biddy took a swig out of the soda can. "Let me see if I can do this in order. One, if Glen changes his mind, he's shit out of luck. Two, you haven't forgotten how. It's like riding a bicycle—sort of. And as far as either one of you getting hurt, you're adults, you'll survive."

"But—"

"You've known Bill for how long? Two years. He kissed you on the second day and you've had him on hold ever since. Do you think that's fair? You're getting older by the minute and so is he." She stopped long enough to take another drink of soda.

"We're only forty something. That's not so old. I consider myself a hot babe."

Biddy sputtered and soda came out of her nose. She grabbed at the tissue box on the table and buried her face in a wad of tissues. Dabbing at her nose, she said, "Maybe so, but you've got to fan the fire if you don't want the flames to go out."

"Let's talk about something else." Lindy flopped back on the bed and threw her arm over her eyes.

"How about what I learned when Jeremy and I stopped by the ballroom on our way back from dinner?"

Lindy lifted her elbow and peered out at Biddy. "What did you learn?"

Biddy flipped the notebook over and ran her finger down the page. "Well, Katja is still missing. A lot of people are saying that she killed Shane. They all saw her wearing the dress. And one girl said that she saw Katja in the hall, carrying the dress. Katja told her she was on her way to return it to Enrico." Biddy pulled at a curl of hair, thinking. "But maybe she didn't return it."

"Wow," said Lindy. She was glad that Biddy had already started taking notes about the murder. Biddy was a lot easier to work with than Bill. She stamped down on that thought and concentrated on what Biddy had said. "Do you think she could kill Shane and dress him in her gown?"

"That's the talk. Well, half the talk. There's another contingent that thinks Enrico killed both of them, Shane and Katja. They think Katja's nude body is going to wash up on shore before the week is out."

"How gruesome. But Enrico? That's ridiculous."

"Is it? He's got a big temper and he's strong. Look at the way he grabbed Luis. I was afraid he was going to break his neck." Biddy pulled the pencil from her hair and began to write.

"He loved that dress. He would never destroy it."

"Not even if he caught Shane and Katja slashing the others?"

"Why would they do that?"

Biddy shrugged. "I'm just telling you what people are saying."

"You saw how upset he was when he recognized the dress on the beach. And when that curtain opened. That horror wasn't faked."

"So what do you think?"

"I don't know. I get the feeling Bill thinks it's Katja and Dawn, but I just don't know."

Biddy looked up from her notebook. "Because he was dumping both of them for Junie?"

"I guess."

"I thought Dawn was planning on luring him back with the promise of appearing in the movie." Biddy tapped the pencil on the notebook. "I don't guess there would be any reason for Junie to kill him."

Lindy thought it over. "No, it doesn't make sense. Why would he bother? He's probably had a string of lovers. He dumped Dawn and Vincent, and they're still around."

"Around and bad-mouthing everybody. Those are two bitter people." Biddy scribbled something in her notebook. "How about Dawn or Vincent? Or Dawn and Vincent?"

"Hmm, I guess it's possible, if highly improbable. She's a ditz and he's a drunk."

"Not exactly a winning team. So who else is there?"

"Bill says they're looking at locals, but they're hoping it will turn out to be one of the hotel guests."

"Good, because that's who I've got on my list."

"Bill also said to stay out of it."

"That's what he always says."

Lindy sat up and rested her elbows on her knees. "I know. But this time is different. I can feel it. It's like he's angry with me. It's not my fault Shane was killed."

"Did he say it was?"

Lindy sighed. "No, he just thinks I'm incompetent."

"No, he doesn't."

"He must. Because while he's telling me to butt out, he's been talking to the police. Every time I ask him something about the case, he closes up. And he's been a grump since he got here. I don't know what's wrong with him."

Biddy hummed a pitch, then sang, "He just needs a little love in all the right places" to the tune of a similar country-and-western song.

Lindy groaned. "How did we get back on the subject of Bill? I thought we were making a list of murder suspects."

"Don't look at me."

Lindy pulled a pillow off the bed and threw it at Biddy. Biddy caught it and tucked it behind her head.

"So who else do you have?" asked Lindy.

"Well, if we try to tie it in with the slashed dresses, we have to include Felicia. Some people are saying she sneaked in and slashed the gowns to get back at Enrico for humiliating her in the ballroom."

"Hmmm."

"We don't know who else might have had it in for Shane. But we could throw in Luis, Tim and Rusty just to round out the numbers."

"And their motives?"

"I haven't gotten that far. I just got back before you did."

Lindy found herself wondering if Jeremy and Biddy had stayed in the ballroom or gone to his room before she came in for the night. Then she wondered if Bill's room was the same as theirs and what he was doing now.

"What? Did you think of something?"

"No, I was thinking about something else."

"So do you want to talk about murder suspects or your lack of a love life?"

"Neither." Lindy heaved herself off the bed. "I want to go to bed." She stripped off her clothes and threw them in the bottom of the closet. Then she climbed into bed.

Biddy threw her pillow back to her.

Lindy stuck it beneath her head and closed her eyes. "I don't know why I can't stay focused on one thing at a time. I contemplate murder, and Bill and Glen creep into my head. I think about them and I'm interrupted with thoughts of murder."

Biddy reached to turn out the lamp. "Not to worry. It just means you're a multitasked kind of girl."

"Or a flake."

"Well, there's that, too." Biddy flipped off the light. "Good night."

Lindy heard her chuckling as she drifted off to sleep.

Chapter Nine

L indy awoke several times during the night. An idea was forming in her mind that wouldn't let go. As soon as she saw the slit of light shining through the separation in the drapes, she got out of bed. She tiptoed past the sleeping Biddy, crossed to the window and peeked outside.

It was early. There was no evidence that it had snowed the night before, though the beach was windswept and dark gray clouds hung heavy in the sky.

Lindy shivered, then tiptoed back across the room and took her clothes from the floor of the closet. For a stupid moment she thought of a shower and makeup, then mentally kicked herself for her vanity. If she was lucky she could get out and back again without anyone seeing her. And who she planned to talk to this morning wouldn't care if she looked good or not.

She slipped her key card and a twenty-dollar bill into her jeans pocket and poked her head out the door. All clear. She let the door click quietly behind her and she hurried down the corridor to the elevator.

The casino was noisy, but not crowded. A few people sat at the tables and slot machines; most of them looked like they had been at it all night.

The whirring and clanging of the machines, the drone of muzak, the gold-painted columns, the hanging banners, and the red and white lights that chased each other around the ceiling looked tawdry by day.

A cocktail waitress passed by, taking her time, a half-filled tray of glasses balanced on one hand. She wore a red plush miniskirt trimmed in fur, black fishnet stockings and a bored expression.

A maintenance crew, dressed in the blue uniforms typically worn by Chinese workers, wielded a cherry picker ladder through the oblivious gamblers. One of them climbed the ladder and began replacing a burned-out lightbulb. Another, surrounded by yellow cones, was mopping the few bits of floor not covered in carpet.

There was no sense of time in the casino and no clocks anywhere. It could be midnight or noon for all anyone knew. Lindy looked up and down the aisles of slot machines. Seeing no one she knew, she headed for the door that led outside.

She pushed at the door. At first it didn't open, and she was afraid it was locked. She threw her weight against it. It moved a few inches, then the wind snatched it open and propelled her outside. She stumbled against the gust and caught hold of the door. Clinging to the handle, she forced it closed.

The boardwalk was deserted; not even the most dauntless chair men were out today. The snow had left a slick sheen of ice on the surface of the boardwalk. Bending her knees and ducking her head into the wind, she shuffled flat-footed across the surface. Her progress was ridiculously slow; her feet were tractionless, and the wind pushed her from side to side like a sailboat tacking across the water. At last she managed to skate over to the rail and hang on with both hands.

She peered up and down the beach. She wasn't going to interfere with an investigation, she told herself. She was just curious. She might not even find whom she was looking for, but she felt compelled to try. She wasn't sure why she felt compelled, though she had a suspicion that it had something to do with proving herself to Bill. And she was feeling braver in the morning half-light than she had the night before. She freed her hand from the railing and reached into her pocket, checking to make sure the twenty-dollar bill was still there. Money was more likely to inspire talk than the most intensive police questioning. She was pretty sure that the police didn't bribe witnesses.

She squinted into the wind and had to brush tears away from her eyes. Far down the beach, she saw what she was hoping to see. A bundle, almost as round as it was tall, stood facing the ocean. The Gull Lady. Her hat was tied on with a scarf and the hem of the long coat lifted with each gust of wind. Her feet were hidden by blue plastic grocery bags that snapped in the wind. A flock of gulls crowded around them and swooped to grab morsels of bread that she threw into the air.

Lindy edged her way along the rail until she reached the steps that led to the beach. She stepped off the boardwalk and slid to the bottom, holding on to the rail for dear life.

The wind was even stronger here, and the sand blew into her eyes and stung her cheeks. She pulled her jacket close and burrowed her face into the collar. Then bracing her shoulders into the wind, she began fighting her way to the Gull Lady.

She trudged slowly across the beach, her shoes sinking into the sand with each step. Her thighs began to burn and her lungs ached from the cold air, but the figure of the Gull Lady never seemed to get any closer. She hoped no one was watching her progress from any of the hotel windows. She must look ridiculous. And if Bill found out what she was doing, he'd be furious.

She was about fifty feet away when the woman bent over, gathered up her bags, and began to totter away down the beach. The gulls followed her, their claws pricking the sand, their shrill cries eerie against the crash of the waves. One took off with a flap of wings but was swept back to land.

Lindy's shoes filled with sand, slowing her down. Frustrated, she watched the distance between them increase. After a few yards, the Gull Lady once again dropped her bags and reached inside. She threw pieces of bread into the air. They flew back in her face as the wind shifted.

She turned away and was suddenly facing Lindy. She stood frozen for a moment. Lindy slowed down, not wanting to frighten her. But she frantically gathered her assortment of bags and waddled off down the beach.

"Wait!" shouted Lindy, but her words were snatched away by the wind. She cupped her hands around her mouth. "I just want to talk to you," she cried. "Please wait. I just want to talk." The Gull Lady didn't slow down or turn around.

She was heading for the pier, and Lindy was afraid she would disappear as she had the night before. "I have money," she called. The Gull Lady paused, and Lindy hurried forward. But before she could reach her, the Gull Lady vanished into the shadows beneath the pier.

Lindy hesitated. She had no desire to follow her beneath it, even in the daylight. She stopped several feet away from the pilings, leaned over and peered beneath the pier. There was no movement, no human shape, just shadows that led into darkness. She stepped cautiously forward, then squatted down. "I won't hurt you. I just want to talk."

Not a sound except the cry of a persistent gull who had followed them to the pier and the waves crashing in the distance. Taking a deep breath, she stepped closer, while her body raced with adrenaline. She was scared. No doubt about it. It had seemed like a good idea, lying in her warm bed on the eleventh floor. Now she wondered how she had ever thought she could get information from this elusive person. And why she thought she had to try.

But she didn't want to admit, even to herself, her real reason for doing this. It wasn't about finding a murderer, though that would be a coup. It was because Bill had laughed at her the night before. Standing there so smug. *I'll watch your back*, knowing full well she didn't have the courage to go after the Gull Lady in the dark. He thought she was a coward, a silly, bumbling amateur, sticking her nose where it didn't belong. Well, he would change his attitude when she discovered something useful today.

She braced one hand against the rough cement of the pier. Then she scrunched down her head, bent her knees, and stepped beneath it. It was dark and dank. "Hello?" she called. "Hello-o-o." She listened for a sound. Heard a rustle that made her jump and hit her head on the planks of the foundation. "Are you there?" Her voice sounded hollow and flat.

There was movement in the shadows, and the smell of cheap whiskey assaulted her nose as a bulky shadow loomed before her. Not the Gull Lady. Something more ominous. It moved silently toward her, then split apart. There was more than one of them. She would have screamed, but fear closed her throat.

Now there was a shadow on each side of her. In a burst of panic, she turned to run. An arm rose up, blocking her way. She shrank back and whirled in the opposite direction. The other man jumped in front of her, so close that his breath was hot on her face and the smell of booze and unwashed flesh made her gag. She inched away, step by cautious step, her knees threatening to buckle. They pressed toward her, backing her deeper into darkness. She stumbled over something lying in the sand. A gruff cackle of laughter rose up at her feet, and she jolted forward, straight into the disgusting arms of her pursuers.

Retching, she pushed through them. She stumbled mindlessly, hunched over like Quasimodo, and was surprised when she burst into light, clean air. Still she ran, scrambling on all fours, using her hands to keep from falling facedown in the sand. A stitch tore through her side. She stopped, bracing her hands on her knees, and whooped air. She knew she should keep running, but she couldn't seem to get her body to stand upright again. She felt the two creatures step out from beneath the pier. She spun toward them, and her feet melded with the sand.

They wore ragged coats and knit hats. Two unwashed scowling faces leered out at her from stringy, matted hair. They didn't come any closer, but kept partially hidden in the shadows. It made them appear even more sinister.

She was trapped, ankle deep in sand, unable to move, unable to take her eyes off them. Were they going to kill her? Could she outrun them? Oh, God, why hadn't she brought Rose with her?

"What'dja want?" growled one of the men. She couldn't tell which one.

"I . . . I just wanted to talk to the Gull Lady."

"You p'lice?"

"No. I'm staying at—" She broke off before she said she was a guest at the hotel. They might think she was worth robbing.

"I work at the hotel," she amended. "A man was killed and they think my friend did it." There, that was a plausible excuse for being here.

The larger of the men stepped forward and pointed a filthy glove at her. "We don't know about no killing. You'd best git."

"I will," Lindy agreed. "But if any of you saw who did it, you should tell the police."

"Don't take no shit from the p'lice," said his partner.

"Maybe the Gull—"

"Git." They both raised their arms and Lindy fled. She could hear their hoarse laughter as she stumbled across the sand. She didn't slow down or look back until she reached the stairs to the boardwalk. She stopped to get her breath, feeling braver now that she had put some distance between them and was out in the open. She looked back toward the pier, but there was only sand, the gulls and the pier.

Damn. So much for her great idea. She had botched it. Instead of finding an eyewitness, she had scared the Gull Lady and pissed off her friends, if that's what they were. They would never come forward now.

Dejectedly, she climbed the steps, skirting the icy patches, holding the railing. She stepped onto the boardwalk and this time she did scream when a man stepped into her path. Wrapped up against the weather. Only big teeth showing beneath his smile.

"Hey, lady. You look like you could use a ride."

Lindy drew breath, ready to run.

"Only fifteen dollars all the way to the Taj Mahal."

Slowly, comprehension worked its way past her panic. She saw the sedan chair parked at the side of the boardwalk. One of the chair men had come out today after all. He was standing in front of her.

"Thanks, but I was just taking a walk on the beach."

The man shrugged, pulled a pair of earphones over his knit hat and went to lean on the rail.

Lindy followed him and motioned to him to remove his ear-phones.

"You change your mind?"

"No, but maybe later. Are you here every day?"

"Seven days a week, hell or high water."

"How late do the cabs run?"

"In winter? Until ten o'clock or so."

Not late enough to witness Shane's murder, she thought. "Maybe later," she said. But the chair man had readjusted his headphones. He was immersed in his music, tapping out the rhythm with invisible drumsticks.

She slid her way back to the hotel entrance and fought the door until she was inside again. The blast of hot air brought a painful burn to her face and hands. All that time, effort, and fear, and all she had gotten was windburn. Maybe she *was* incompetent, just like Bill thought.

Nothing had changed in the casino, except that the maintenance crew had moved the ladder to another light fixture. She made it back to her room without being seen by anyone she knew. Biddy was gone. The message light was blinking. Ignoring it, she stripped out of her clothes and jumped into a steaming shower.

Forty-five minutes later she was heading toward the Rickshaw Café. She was starving. Nothing like a morning walk on the beach to bring on an appetite.

Rebo, Juan, and Eric were sitting at a table for four near the entrance. Rebo grinned and motioned her over. His face fell as soon as she reached the table. He shook his head and turned to the others. "Nope."

Lindy sat down in the chair next to him and opened a menu. "Nope, what?" she asked as she looked over the egg selections.

"The wannabe was here earlier looking for you. Couldn't get a reading off him. Had his cop face on. But you. Damn."

"What?" she asked again.

"We were hoping the wannabe wasn't the wannabe anymore, but alas." Rebo lifted the back of his hand to his forehead and sighed. Then he straightened up and frowned at her. "What is wrong with you? If I had that long, tall New Yorker asking me out to dinner and taking me for romantic moonlit walks on the beach, I would have had his ass by now."

Juan sputtered. Eric groaned. Rebo looked embarrassed. "You know what I mean."

"Yep," they agreed and burst out laughing. Lindy concentrated on her menu. Finally she looked over the top of it. "I can't believe you said that. Right here in a restaurant filled with people."

"I didn't mean it like that . . . exactly." Then Rebo burst out laughing, too.

"Jeez," said Lindy and ordered bacon and eggs from the waiter.

"So where *is* Bill?" she asked, hoping it wouldn't bring on another onslaught of bad jokes and speculations about her sex life.

"Don' know," said Rebo. "Just said he'd be gone for a while and he'd see you later."

"Hmm," said Lindy as a plate was placed before her. She made a face. Eggs definitely sounded better than they smelled.

"But the police are here, showing a picture of that girl who disappeared around. Asking if anybody had seen her."

"And had anybody?"

"We did," piped in Juan.

Lindy put down her fork. "You did? When?"

Rebo gave Juan a look. Lindy gave Rebo a look.

"Well," said Rebo, after what sounded like a resigned sigh, "it was yesterday morning. We were, uh, coming in from, uh—"

"A night on the town?" Lindy suggested.

"Right. Anyway it was about four o'clock and we saw this girl get into a car."

"Did you see who was driving?"

"She was. I mean, the valet brought it around. He was getting out and she got in. I remember 'cause he had this great smile. Anyway, we think it was her. Looked like her."

"Did you tell the police?"

"Yeah," said Juan. "And that's when the wannabe told us to mind our own—" Juan let out a yelp and frowned at Rebo across the table.

"Bill told you what?" she asked.

"Hey, here comes Rose," said Eric. Rose was heading their way, dressed in a purple-sequined sweater and black jeans. She was holding a take-out bag in one hand and a shoe box in the other. Rebo pulled a chair over from the next table.

"Splendiferous," he said, giving the sweater the once-over.

"Bought it in the vendors' room last night," said Rose and sat down. "When in Rome . . ."

"I may have to get me one," said Rebo.

"Better hurry. They're going fast." She turned to Lindy. "The police are back. I just finished breakfast with Dawn. I guess they kept her *forever*, according to her, asking about Katja and also about her, Dawn's, relationship with the deceased." Rose lifted both eyebrows. "Now she thinks the police suspect her of murdering Shane."

"Oh, great," said Lindy.

"Well, hell, it'll give her something besides Junie to kvetch about."

"They don't really think she did it, do they?"

Rose shrugged. "I guess they're taking all comers until they can narrow down the number of suspects."

"I thought they were concentrating on a local perp." Lindy shifted her attention to Rebo and the boys. "Evidently it's the in thing to go slumming in town while visiting the casinos. Sound familiar? People have been killed. It's possible that Shane was murdered while he was out on the town. Get my drift?"

Eric, Juan and Rebo nodded dutifully and stood up simultaneously.

"We already got the lecture from the wannabe," said Juan.

"So where are you going?"

"We got the day off 'cause we had to rehearse yesterday," said Rebo. "Gotta hit the slots. When you're hot you're hot."

Lindy frowned at them. "Don't lose all your money."

"Yeah, okay, sure." In a minute they were gone. Lindy watched them pay the cashier and hurry out of the restaurant.

"What's with them? Normally, they would be asking a million questions about what was going on."

Rose cocked her head toward Lindy. "Don't get mad."

"About what?"

"I think Bill put it to them this morning. Dawn and I were having breakfast when he came in. He talked to them for a while. Didn't sit down. Just stood hulking over them." Rose shrugged.

"Damn. He's got a lot of nerve. It's not like we enjoy getting involved in all these murders."

"Right."

"But when we're forced into it, we do a pretty damn good job of getting results."

"I'm with you. And anyway, Dawn, nutcase though she be, is an old friend. Katja is either dead or the number-one suspect. Either outcome will be devastating to her. I'm sticking, Bill or no Bill."

Lindy sighed. "I don't know why he's so uptight all of a sudden."

Rose stood up and gathered her shoes and takeout. "He needs to get laid and so do you."

"Jeez. That's all anybody thinks about around here," said Lindy. She signed the check and pushed her chair back.

"Not me. I'm thinking we ought to find out who slashed up Enrico's dresses. That was really a piss-poor thing to do. And I bet it's connected to Shane's murder."

Lindy grabbed her bag. "Then let's go check out the ballroom. Do a little light eavesdropping and interrogation. At least we can find out if Katja really did return the dress."

Chapter
Ten

The ballroom was filled with people. On the floor, women in skimpy, shiny dresses were being led through a cha-cha by men in black shirts and tight trousers. It was only ten o'clock, yet everyone was dressed as if it were cocktail hour.

"The competition and the casino have a lot in common," said Lindy as they walked inside.

"Game of chance?" guessed Rose.

"That, too. But I was thinking that it doesn't matter what time of day it is, what the weather is, what is happening in world events, it's timeless in here. No matter when you come in, it's always the same. There could be an invasion outside, and no one would miss a beat."

"I think the term you're looking for is 'self-absorbed.' So where should we start?"

"Well," said Lindy, "since we can't talk to Katja and you already talked to Dawn, maybe we should start with Luis and Enrico. Do you think they're still around?"

Rose looked over the crowd. "Not in here. I can't imagine Enrico would want to show his face after what happened. He won't be making any big comeback now." She sighed. "What a terrible thing. Why does it seem like really talented people are always getting the shaft?"

"Spending too much time doing art and not enough doing politics?" Lindy looked out over the dancing couples. Number 211 was on the floor again. Today he was pushing a skinny woman in low-heeled shoes through her steps, all the while grimacing at the judges. Her iridescent skirt was slit up one side and the bodice was low cut and sleeveless. The skin under her arms wiggled every time she took a pose. Next to him another teacher looked bored. Next to him, a bouncy couple seemed to be having the time of their lives.

"Maybe," said Rose. "Speaking of talented people, look at number 110."

Lindy looked over the couples, past Rusty Lonigan, who already looked as though he'd been dancing for hours. At the far side of the floor was the couple Rose had pointed out. She was a heavyset older woman. Her hair was pulled into a high French twist and was streaked with gray. She wore a knee-length dress with a fringed hem, low cut in front, but long-sleeved. She moved her bulk with ease and kept in time with the music. "She looks better than the others," Lindy agreed. "And her costume is flattering."

"Just my point. Now watch her teacher."

Lindy watched. The woman's partner was young. His hair was brushed back and gelled just like all the other men on the floor. But he was completely attentive to his student. He held her firmly but didn't wrestle her into position. He smiled encouragingly at her, then flashed the audience a smile as if he were lucky to have such a partner.

"That's a good teacher," said Rose.

"I can see. Too bad the others don't take a few tips from him."

"Sure is. But there are others like him. You just don't notice them with all the shenanigans going on out there." Rose shrugged. "Well, I didn't mean to get us off track, but I just didn't want you to think that it was all glitz and politics." She looked over Lindy's head and murmured, "Well, well, well."

Lindy turned just in time to see Felicia Falcone pass by, carrying the dress she had borrowed for the final. She was headed toward the vendors' room.

"Feel like doing a little shopping?"

"At least some light browsing," said Lindy. "Race you to Gowns by Marie."

"You think she's tied up in this?" asked Rose as they entered the vendors' room and stopped inside the door.

"I don't think we should discount anyone at this point," said Lindy. "If the murder and the slashings are linked together—and there is the fact that Shane stole a pattern from Enrico for the dress she was wearing—Felicia is as likely a suspect as any other."

"Yeah, but wouldn't she have killed Enrico instead of Shane? That had to be so humiliating, having your dress ripped off in front of the whole ballroom."

"But then why did Katja run? She can't really be afraid of the police. This is the United States, for crying out loud."

"Seems far-fetched," Rose agreed. "Maybe she witnessed it, recognized the murderer and really is afraid for her life. That might make her panic and run."

"I guess. But somehow, it doesn't seem as simple as that. I mean, how did the murderer get the dress? Biddy heard that someone saw Katja returning it to Enrico. And if she did, that implicates Enrico or Luis."

"No way. Someone must have broken in after they left. I saw them leaving, remember? And I saw the guards lock the room afterward."

Felicia was standing in front of the Gowns by Marie display. She was talking with a woman who was in the process of rehanging the dress she had borrowed. Behind her a metal clothes rack was stuffed with colorful gowns, crammed together like Day-Glo sardines. Lindy thought of poor Luis and the manikins that would have displayed Enrico's new line of dresses. Too artistic for their own good? Or on the wrong side of the political power struggle? And could any of this lead to murder?

They sauntered over to a booth that sold jewelry: big dangly earrings of bright paste stones in every imaginable color, rhinestone collars, and hair barrettes of eclectic frou-frou. Two women sat behind the table munching on corn muffins and drinking tea from a red plaid thermos.

Rose picked up a pair of starburst, topaz earrings and showed them to Lindy, while keeping one eye on Felicia.

One of the women stood up, brushing crumbs from her hands, and smiled attentively.

"Just looking," said Rose. The woman sat back down and resumed her conversation.

They moved on, feigning interest in the displays while listening to Felicia complain to Marie about the loss of her dress. At the back wall, Luis was gathering the last of the tattered garments and putting them into a trunk. He moved slowly, respectfully.

An internment, thought Lindy, and her throat tightened. "Shall we see if he'd like some help?"

Luis looked up when they approached but went back to his packing without speaking. Rose knelt beside him and picked up a piece of fabric. She looked at it for a moment, then gently folded it and placed it in the case. Taking her cue from Rose, Lindy moved quietly to do the same. The three of them worked side by side for a while without speaking.

"They must have been beautiful," said Lindy. "We're so sorry."

"Thank you," said Luis. His words were barely audible, thick as if he were drowning.

"Do the authorities have any leads?"

"They're talking insurance." He laughed sharply, a sound caught between a cough and sob. "Insurance. As if these gowns could be replaced."

"Can't you make more?"

Luis tightened his lips and looked at her with a curiously sardonic expression. "I," he said, "didn't make them in the first place. Enrico will not allow anyone to construct his gowns but himself. I do the decorations."

Lindy blinked. Was it bitterness she heard in his voice? And if it was, what should she make of it? She glanced at Rose. Rose pulled one corner of her mouth down into an exaggerated frown.

"But do they think they can find the person who did this? Are they trying?"

"They said it would be too difficult and that if they were so valuable, we shouldn't have left them unattended."

"This room was locked at night," said Rose, standing up and towering over the other two. "I saw the guard lock and check the door to the ballroom when you left Sunday night."

"Which is why they think it was done during the setup. As if someone could come in and tear our lives to shreds without us noticing. Anyway, we didn't start setting up until late that night. Most of the vendors were finished by the time we started. It was supposed to be a surprise." He pushed himself stiffly to his feet and looked around the room. "They were fine when we left for the night. I was here first thing the next morning. It opened for vendors at nine, but the guard wouldn't let me in because I had inadvertently left my badge in the room overnight. Except for that few minutes on the beach, I was waiting here right by the door until it opened at ten." His checks reddened as if he were reliving the put-down he had received from Enrico for leaving his post. "But if these people heard or saw—or did—anything, they aren't telling. I should have been here."

"I hope Enrico isn't blaming you for what happened."

Luis barked out a bleak laugh. "Of course he blames me. Who else can he blame?"

Lindy pursed her lips. "Who do you think did it?"

"I don't know. Enrico thinks that they must have been in on it together. A conspiracy. He's made a lot of enemies over the years. You can't be as good as he is without inspiring jealousy." He sighed. "They drove him away once and now they're doing it again. Why will he never learn? I told him not to come back but no-o-o, he had to have the final burst of glory. Some glory."

He picked up a black three-ring binder opened on the table. Inside a plastic page cover was a photograph of a woman wearing a midnight-blue gown with jewels like stars swathed across the front.

"Is that one of your—Enrico's—dresses?"

"Yes, the portfolio. For all the orders we were going to take." His face crumpled and he fought to keep his composure.

Rose leaned over his shoulder. "May we?" she asked, taking the portfolio from his hands. She turned the page, and the three of them huddled together over the photographs. The next dress was a shimmering gold. The model had just finished a turn and the skirt swirled about her feet. On the third page, a multicolored train swooped backward as the model ran out of frame.

"The Peacock," said Luis. "It was my favorite." A whimper escaped his lips and he slammed the portfolio closed. "Well, no more." He tossed the portfolio onto the top of the case, then reached for a round step stool.

"It had to have happened after you left for the night and before the room opened the next morning. Nothing else makes sense," said Rose.

"Did the guard check the room when he came to close up?" asked Lindy. "Maybe someone was hiding here. He could have waited until everyone was gone, slashed the dresses, and sneaked out afterward."

"The doors don't open from the inside once they've been locked for the night," said Luis. "He wouldn't have been able to get out."

"Doors?" asked Lindy. "How many are there?"

Luis hugged the step stool to his chest, looking thoughtful. "Two, one to the ballroom and one to the main hallway." He lifted his chin toward the opposite wall.

"So do you think it was a conspiracy?" asked Lindy.

"I'm not so paranoid. People in this business can be spiteful. They might steal his designs, but they wouldn't destroy them."

"You must have some ideas about who might have done this," Lindy prodded.

Luis paused and looked past her shoulder. "You might ask her."

Lindy turned and saw that he was looking at Felicia Falcone, who was still in conversation with Marie.

"She's a tough little number," said Luis. "Has to be to have been through as many partners as she has. Not many people would have had the cool to get back on the floor after that scene last night, much less win, and in a borrowed gown no less."

"Vendetta? For Enrico humiliating her in front of the crowd?" asked Rose.

"She stole Enrico's design and then made a cheap copy. She deserved that dressing-down." He smiled self-consciously. "So to speak."

But the other dress, thought Lindy. *Did it turn up on Shane's dead body before or after Katja returned it Enrico?* "Luis, were you here the whole time last night?"

"Yes, like I said, until the guard kicked us out around two."

"And you didn't leave at all?"

He frowned. "No. Except to get some take-out coffee around twelve-thirty. I was only gone for ten minutes. But Enrico was here and everything was fine when I got back. We worked for another hour and a half."

"Someone said that Katja was planning to return the dress to Enrico."

"Well, obviously she didn't. We all saw where it ended up."

"Are you sure?"

Luis's eyes widened. "Of course I'm sure." He plunked the stool down and put both hands on his hips. "Unless you think I ripped up all the dresses except that one, then ran outside with it, asked Shane to put it on, then murdered him." He sniffed. "I wouldn't do that to charmeuse."

Lindy raised both eyebrows at him, waiting for the next step of logic to hit. She saw the enlightenment in his eyes first, then watched it spread across his face.

"Good God. You can ask anybody. Enrico would never do that. Never." He spun away from them and climbed onto the stool. He began yanking the drapery rings off the curtain rod. Drapery pooled on the floor beneath him.

Rose gave Lindy a "Shame on you" look and lifted the drapery from the floor. She folded it over and placed it on the table, then followed behind Luis as he moved the foot stool to another section. She folded the next piece and laid that on the table, and then the next. No one spoke, but Lindy was busy thinking. What if Katja had returned the dress while Luis was out for coffee? Could Enrico have hidden it and then taken it without Luis noticing? Had Enrico murdered Shane? But why?

Luis and Rose had reached the back of the booth. It was slower going here because the curtain rod was flush against the back wall. They were halfway across when the last piece of a drape fell, leaving the wall exposed.

Lindy stared at the wall, her thoughts on murder put on hold.

Rose slowly straightened up, then looked back at Lindy, her eyes round. Behind the curtain was another door. And unlike the other two doors, this one had a release bar that would open it from the inside.

"Good Lord," said Lindy. "Where does that lead to?"

Luis threw out his hands, palms up. "I don't know. I forgot all about it." He stepped toward it and reached for the release bar.

"Wait," Rose and Lindy ordered at the same time.

Luis jumped back and looked at them in alarm. "What? I'm just seeing where it goes."

"Did the security guard check this door when he closed up for the night?"

"No. It was covered over with the drape." His fingertips went to his cheeks. "You think they used this door?" He expelled an Italian expletive, then pushed the door open.

"Wait," Lindy said futilely. "There might have been fingerprints," she said to herself—since neither Rose nor Luis was listening. They had already gone through the open door.

At least Bill couldn't yell at her for this. She knew better than to touch anything at a crime scene. She also knew that she shouldn't be thinking about Bill while Rose and Luis were out there destroying possible evidence. She followed after them, catching the closing door with the tip of her shoe to hold it open. She looked out onto another hallway. Not carpeted and chandeliered, but plain walls painted in institutional green. Linoleum floor. A service corridor.

"Maybe we should ask security to check this out," said Lindy.

Rose rolled her eyes. "Take it from experience. If it ain't the Crown jewels, the hotel will try to get off paying the insurance. Active investigation implies that the joint ain't safe, if you know what I mean."

Lindy knew exactly what she meant. It would be just like the Connecticut hotel staff that had turned from helpful to hostile when they learned that their guests were being investigated for murder. She sighed. "Okay. But let's do this methodically. I'm going to close the door. See if you can get back in."

She stepped back into the room and moved her toe from the door. Slowly it swung shut and Lindy heard the click of the lock. The door began to rattle.

"It's locked from your side," came Rose's muffled voice.

Lindy used her elbow to push against the release bar, and the door opened onto Luis and Rose. Lindy bit back a smile. There was nothing funny about the situation, but the two of them looked so silly together, Rose at six feet and Luis barely five-six, that she couldn't help it.

"Now what?" asked Luis, coming back inside.

Lindy studied the door. "No one could have come in while you were setting up. No one could get through without disturbing the drapery; you would have seen them. They must have already been inside. At least we know how they got out."

"Then we'll never find out who did this." Luis slumped against the wall and pushed his hands into the pockets of his black trousers.

"Do you remember which vendors were still here when the room closed?"

Luis shrugged. "Some of them. There were only a few."

"Then go ask each one if they saw anything at all. Take a pencil and pad and write it down." Luis frowned but pushed himself away from the wall. He rummaged through a soft, black leather briefcase, pulled out a notebook, and walked away.

"That was just a little obvious," said Rose as soon as he had gone.

"Well, I figure that there are three most-likely scenarios. One, Katja never returned the dress, which means she murdered Shane; or she returned the dress while Luis was out getting coffee and Enrico took the dress and murdered Shane. Or she was on her way to return the dress but ran into Luis in the hallway and gave it to him."

"And Luis murdered Shane? Get a grip. Why?"

"I don't know. I'm just trying to follow the dress trail—forensic couture. Any way you look at it, I wanted Luis out of the way while we search the hallway."

"Got it." Rose pushed the door back open then stopped. "If this corridor only leads to the kitchen or something, how are we going to get back in?"

Lindy looked around. "We can stick a wedge of paper—" Lindy and Rose exchanged looks. "The culprit didn't have to hide in here all night. He could have planned this in advance. Just wedge the door and bide his time."

"You mean the door was already rigged when Luis and Enrico set up?"

"It's possible."

"But wouldn't they have noticed that the door was ajar?"

"Not if the opening was small enough." They both looked around the floor for a piece of paper or wood or anything that might have been used to keep the door open. The floor was spotless.

"Hold on a sec," said Rose, peering at the latch. "Just call me Sherlock. Check it out." She pointed to a place midway up the door, close to the lock. A tiny scrap of something adhered to the metal.

"Tape," said Lindy.

Rose touched it with the tip of her fingernail. "Double-back," she confirmed.

"Found on every dress strap, inside every dance shoe . . ."

"And even holds on broken nail tips in an emergency."

"And I was hoping for a piece of hotel stationery with a room number written on it."

"Well, at least we know how it was done," said Rose. "We just have to figure out who and why and if it had anything to do with Shane Corbett being murdered."

"Is that all? Come on. Let's check out the hallway."

Chapter
Eleven

They left the stool propped against the door and went out into the corridor. They followed it to the right toward the sound of clanging pots and pans. Several yards later, the corridor divided at right angles. The right half ran straight along the side of the vendors' room and the ballroom. At the far end, two dancers in tuxedos were leaning over an ash can, hot-boxing cigarettes. One of them stabbed his cigarette into the sand, blew out a lungful of smoke, and sprayed Binaca into his mouth. Slipping the tube back into his jacket pocket, he strode across the hall and swung open a door. Music blared for a second, and then the hall was silent again.

Lindy and Rose took the left branch and were immediately enveloped by the pervasive smell of roasting meat mixed with the sweet odor of dish detergent and steam. Food trolleys were lined up against each wall. Clean ones with spotless white table coverings on one side; used ones, waiting to be cleared, on the other. The dredges of casseroles and scalloped potatoes, left from the previous evening, clung to the sides of the warming dishes. One held a flat pan filled with dirty silverware, stacks of crusting plates and cups, and a pitcher filled with greasy coffee remains.

"Dead end," said Rose.

Lindy stopped at a large trolley that held a cutting board of congealed roast beef. An assortment of carving knives was lined up beside it, the juices from the meat coagulating on the white cloth beneath them. She shivered.

"Or maybe not," said Rose, looking at the knives. "Think we can nab one of the busboys for dress mutilation?"

Lindy pulled her gaze from the knives and turned slowly to look at Rose. She tried to swallow but her mouth was dry. "Or murder."

"Murder? I thought Shane was hit on the head."

"He was, but that wasn't what killed him. Damn him."

"Shane?"

"Bill. There was blood on the bodice of the dress, but no damage to the dress. That's how they know Shane was killed before he was put in the dress. He died from a chest or stomach wound. I guessed that much. But Bill wouldn't tell me anything about the murder weapon. Confidential, he said. That smug, officious—Damn him."

"Give the guy a break, Lindy. He loves you and he's trying to keep you safe."

Nonplused, Lindy asked, "How do you know that?"

Rose made a disgusted noise. "In words that an erudite teenager could understand—Duh."

The door to the kitchen swung open and a thin black man in a white, stained jacket came out.

Rose and Lindy jumped in surprise and so did he. His eyes narrowed suspiciously. "If you're looking for the ladies' room, you came out the wrong door. Go back in the ballroom, straight across to the other side. That door leads to the guest hallway." He grasped the handles of the trolley containing the knives and began to push it toward the kitchen.

Lindy and Rose exchanged looks. Rose's expression held a question. Lindy shook her head. If Shane really had been killed with one of these knives, and it was beyond a long shot that he had been, it would be cleaned long before they could convince anyone to listen to them. She watched the door swing shut behind the dishwasher.

"I don't even know that he was stabbed," admitted Lindy. "Maybe he was shot."

They backtracked along the corridor, past the dealers' room to a set of double doors across the hall. They weren't locked. Lindy pushed one side open and they stepped into a large room, divided by an accordion wall. Round dining tables were covered in white tablecloths and set with flatware and napkins. A speaker's podium and microphone were placed at one end. Other than the wallpaper, gold background with blue fish swimming through fantastic wisps of green seaweed, there was no indication of the Chinese theme—just a generic banquet room.

On the far side were two double doors. Rose let out an expansive sigh. "And behind door number three . . ."

"Is yet another hallway, probably an offshoot of the main one," finished Lindy. She led Rose back into the hall and continued to follow it around a corner where it ended at a service elevator. And to the left, another door.

Rose opened it. "Surprise. It's a hallway," she said and let it close.

"Well, whoever it was had his choice of exits, that much is pretty darn clear," said Lindy.

They retraced their way back down the corridor to the propped-open door. Rose pushed the stool out of the way and the door closed. "Well, at least we found out how the slasher got in—and out. But we still don't know if there's a connection between the slashings and the murders. Let's surmise."

"All right. You first."

"Thanks a lot." Rose crossed her arms and leaned against the wall.

Lindy pulled up the stool and sat down. Her knees stuck up by her shoulders, and she had a flash of Peter sitting on a stool in a Connecticut theatre, accusing Jeremy of murder. She stood up.

"What? Think of something?"

"Nothing helpful," said Lindy.

"Then I suggest we go surmise over lunch."

"We just finished breakfast."

"I ate hours ago and more of your eggs went back to the kitchen than went into your stomach."

"Eggs are nasty."

"So how about a chopped liver on rye? The Dynasty Deli? It's around here somewhere."

"Ugh," said Lindy, but she followed Rose back into the ballroom and out into the corridor. They were heading in the direction of the elevators and a site map posted there when Lindy saw a group of girls gathered around one of the benches that lined the hallway. A ball gown was hanging from the mouth of one of the guardian figures.

Two men dressed in dark suits were standing in front of them. One was asking them questions. The other was writing in a notebook.

"The police," said Lindy.

"Sure looks like it."

Lindy and Rose waited at a distance, trying unsuccessfully to hear what was being said. Finally, the notebook snapped closed and with a nod, the two men walked away. The women remained silent, watching until the detectives took the escalator and disappeared from sight. Then, they broke into excited chattering. Not in English, but another language—Russian.

"The Russian community is pretty tight, isn't it?" asked Lindy.

"Like a thumb screw," agreed Rose. "Though we can't really call them Russian anymore. Russia is just one of countless, changing countries now." She shrugged. "But they're Russians to us."

"Us and Them? Ballroom continues the cold war?" asked Lindy.

"They stick together. It's a tight-knit group. And they're winning."

"It's all about winning, isn't it?"

"That's the general idea," said Rose.

Lindy pressed her fingertips to her temples. "So, they could be hiding Katja. Protecting her, maybe?"

"If she's still alive," said Rose. "Let's go see what we can find out. But be indirect. They'll clam up if they think you're after something."

Lindy nodded. They sidled up to the group. Not one of them looked up, just continued to talk among themselves.

"Hi," said Rose nonchalantly, at least as nonchalantly as Rose was capable of. The talking broke off to dead silence. Rose looked chagrined. She sat down on the carpet next to a girl sponging a pair of satin shoes with a mixture from a cardboard coffee cup. She watched the procedure for a minute, then said, "I always dye my shoes with tea. Gives the best color, doesn't it?"

The girl looked up at her but didn't answer. Finally she give a brusque nod and returned to wiping her shoes. Another girl was sitting on the bench, sewing a strap onto a magenta and purple dress. The chiffon skirt draped over her legs.

"That's a great shade of magenta," said Rose, nodding toward the dress. That girl glanced up but said nothing. "Perfect for your complexion." After a moment, the girl said, "Thank you," and went back to sewing.

Not very friendly, thought Lindy. But who could blame them? If half the things people said about them got back to them, they had the right to be defensive. Or maybe they just didn't understand the language.

Lindy sat down on the edge of the bench. "We're here with the Jeremy Ash Dance Company. We're performing in the show Sunday. Rose used to make ball gowns." She indicated Rose, who smiled winningly at the girls. Lindy had to fight not to laugh out loud, but she noticed that their interest pricked up.

"I make my own dresses," said the girl. Her accent was heavy, but her syntax correct.

"You made this?" asked Lindy. "It's wonderful." Well, it wasn't wonderful, but it was a lot better than some she had seen. "I saw another one I liked, Monday night. It was turquoise."

There was no comment to this so Lindy pressed on. "I forget the name of the girl who was wearing it." No response. "Do you know which one I mean? They say that her partner was killed. Right here at the competition."

Dead silence except for something that sounded like a cat's hiss from the girl who was dying her shoes.

"Katja Andreyevsky," said another girl who was leaning against the wall, barefoot and holding her shoes in her hands. "Bitch."

"Oh?" asked Lindy. "She wasn't nice?"

A sharp look from the girl with the magenta dress, and the girl puffed air through her lips and dropped her shoes to the floor. Lindy watched them bounce on the soft carpet. "Not nice," the girl said despite another sharp look from the girl on the bench. "She is—" She stopped to rattle off a clipped series of words to the girl on the floor.

"Stuck up," she translated.

"Stuck up. She thinks she is too good for us. But look at her now. No partner. No dress. And in trouble with the police."

"Elena," hissed the other two girls.

Elena shrugged. "I do not care. Katja is not one of us. She wants so badly to be an American. Let her. It will get her nowhere. She is a stupid girl. She should have stuck"—confusion flickered across her face—"stuck up to us."

"You mean she should have stuck to her own kind." Lindy supplied the translation for her, while the tune from *West Side Story* rippled through her mind.

"Yes."

Lindy took a deep breath, trying to figure out how to keep the conversation rolling. Gossip was gossip in any language, and most people would indulge in it if given half a chance. "Full of herself," said Lindy.

"That is right. She is too filled up with herself. Always filled up with herself," Elena repeated, obviously liking the phrase. "She turns her back when we try to talk to her, and walks away with her nose in the air."

The other two girls made noises of agreement.

Unlikely they were hiding her, if this was the general consensus.

"As if she doesn't remember her own language or has lost her ear-ring—hearing," added the girl.

"They say she is dead," said the girl on the bench, shaking her magenta skirts and moving on to the second strap.

"Those men who were just here?" asked Lindy.

The girl flashed her a disgusted look but didn't answer.

Elena hissed air through her teeth. "They were policemen. They tell us nothing. We tell them nothing. We show that we do not understand their questions." She shrugged and made an exaggerated frown.

"They asked if we knew where she was staying," said the girl on the bench. "Why bother to answer? Of course, we do not know. She would not come to us for help."

Elena bent over and put on her shoes. "And if she did, we would not understand what she was asking. It is very easy not to understand." She flashed teeth at them, then walked away on her toes, stopped to bend her knees, then continued on her way into the ballroom.

"You told the police you didn't know where she was?" asked Lindy.

The girl on the bench shrugged. "We tell them nothing. We did not understand what they were asking." She gave Lindy a dismissive look and went back to her sewing.

Lindy and Rose said good-bye and walked away.

"So what do you think?" said Rose. "Do they know where she is and won't tell? Or do they think she is dead and don't care?"

"Either way, I don't think they'll be telling us. Talk about an Iron Curtain."

The doors to the ballroom opened. People poured out into the hallway and dispersed in different directions.

"Told you it was lunchtime," said Rose. "There's Rusty. He looks pooped." Rusty walked toward them, drinking from a large paper cup. Sweat glistened on his face and as he reached them a drop of it rolled off the tip of his nose and into the cup.

He patted his face with the back of his sleeve. "I don't guess you've seen Dawn today."

"Not since breakfast," said Rose.

"Oh, she had time for breakfast. Lucky her." He stopped to drink from the cup. "I'm sweating my butt off out there. She could at least assume an appearance of interest and come to the ballroom long enough to compliment the ladies on their dresses. Or something. I guess it would be too much to ask for her to remember to meet the movie people. They should be checking in about now." He let out an exasperated sigh. "Someone should meet them."

"Here she comes," said Lindy. Dawn rushed out of the ballroom, saw them, and came running over.

"She's alive," she said. "Someone saw her leaving the hotel Monday morning. I'm so relieved. And another stroke of luck. The Hollingfords are getting a divorce. I'm sure I can get Danny Hollingford for Katja. He's a perfect height for her. Have you heard anything about it?" She looked at Randy for a response, but continued before he had a chance to answer. "I asked him to meet me for lunch. If I make the offer good enough, maybe he'll relocate. He could take over Timothy's students. Then I'd be able to keep an eye on the partnership—"

Rusty exploded. "Damn it to hell, Dawn. This obsession is getting to be too much. The girl is probably dead. You can't just make decisions about hiring without consulting me. And you have to meet the movie people." He grabbed her wrist, wrenched it around and looked at her watch. "Ten minutes ago."

Dawn's free hand slapped her cheek. "The movie people. I nearly forgot. Katja and Danny Hollingford will be perfect as Fred and Ginger."

Rusty sputtered.

Rose latched on to Dawn's elbow. "We'll go with you to the lobby." She gave Rusty a sympathetic look. "Take a break. We'll get her there."

Dawn didn't stop talking even after Lindy and Rose ushered her into the elevator; she merely switched her attention from Rusty to them. "If only Katja was here to meet them. "I know they'll love her."

Rose and Lindy stared at the elevator doors and let her talk.

Chapter
Twelve

It was easy to spot the movie people. Three men and a woman stood in a tableau beneath the golden dragon, looking mildly put out and very important. It was a toss-up as to which one of them would blow smoke first. The dragon alone seemed unperturbed with his situation.

The tallest of the men, silver haired and swathed in a near-to-floor-length fur coat, passed leather gloves from one hand to the other. Producer? Next to him was a heavyset man with a wide, light gray beard and flowing white hair that sprang from a bald pate. Rimless glasses magnified twinkling blue eyes, and Lindy would have thought of Santa Claus if he hadn't been vigorously complaining to the woman next to him, tiny as one of his elves but much too nervous—the production assistant. Which would make him the director. And the slight man with shaggy hair and intense eyes that roved the lobby must be the cinematographer.

Not a slouch group, thought Lindy as she and Rose propelled Dawn toward them.

"Harold," Dawn cooed, disappearing into the tall man's fur coat. "Lovely to see you." They gave each other air kisses, Dawn standing on tiptoe to reach the vicinity of the man's face.

"Mission accomplished," said Rose. "Now, can we have lunch?"

"Not yet," said Lindy. She had just spotted another group of men standing off to one side. She knew instinctively who they were even if the dark suits and short haircuts hadn't announced their profession. She recognized the top of the head that stood above the others.

Bill looked up just in time to catch her eye. A flicker of a frown crossed his face when he saw her. He spoke quickly to the man next to him and strode toward her. She had already started off in their direction, Rose beside her, and they met halfway across the lobby.

"Cut off at the pass," whispered Rose as they came to a stop in front of Bill.

"I see you've been busy this morning," said Lindy dryly.

"I was looking for you earlier," answered Bill.

"Uh-huh." She flicked a glance at the detectives. The group broke up and began dispersing through the lobby. Only one man stayed behind and he was looking their way. He smiled when Lindy caught his eye. She turned back to Bill. "Giving them the benefit of your expertise?"

Bill took a slow breath before answering, and Lindy imagined him counting to ten as he exhaled. She didn't know why she was being so mean to him. Was she really jealous of his professional clout? Or was she just taking her hurt out on him, since Glen was far away in Paris? Maybe everyone was right and it was just sexual frustration. She took a slow breath to match his.

"Well, I guess I'll go have lunch," said Rose. She turned away.

"Oh, no, you don't," said Bill. "Not so fast. I want to hear what you girls have been up to this morning."

"Should have stuck around," said Lindy. "And you'd know." She bit her lip. She really needed to get a grip on herself. She was going to drive Bill away and then where would she be? The detective was walking their way; he was still smiling.

"Your friend's awfully chipper considering this is a murder investigation," said Lindy.

Bill turned around. "Ah, Andrew." He turned back to Lindy and Rose. "Andrew Dean, Rose Laughton and Lindy Graham of the . . ." Lindy missed the rest of the introduction. *Graham*, Bill had intro-

duced her as Graham. Well, of course he would, it was her professional name after all, but it rang differently this time. Was she no
longer going to be a Haggerty? Lose the husband, lose the name?
Well, Graham had been good enough once and it would be again.
"We were just going to lunch," Bill finished.

Andrew Dean held out his hand. Lindy shook it. "How do you
do?" She smiled brightly. Probably too brightly. She turned down
the wattage. There, self-confident, not flighty.

Andrew Dean's smile increased as hers decreased. It put her immediately on guard.

"Having any luck in your investigation?" she asked.

Bill narrowed his eyes but forbore saying anything. Detective
Dean shrugged. He was a slightly built man with faded blond hair
and pale eyelashes. "We're asking questions on the outside chance
that somebody saw something the night of the murder or knows the
whereabouts of this Russian girl."

"Well, the Russians aren't talking," said Lindy, taking a step forward and turning toward the detective, effectively cutting out Bill's
involvement. "Your men talked to them this morning. I don't think
they learned much. But they talked to Rose and me. They don't like
Katja. Said she was stuck up and that they wouldn't help her." She
tried to hide her satisfaction, when Dean's eyebrows rose. "You
might try talking to the Gull Lady. She's always on the beach. I tried
to ask her some questions, but she ran away."

Dean took out a notebook. "I think I know who you mean. I'll
put someone on her."

Lindy heard Bill expel another long breath behind her.

"I really have to run," interrupted Rose. "See you later." She
took off toward the elevators.

Dean watched her leave, then turned back to Lindy. "Anything
else you think I should know?"

Lindy ignored the hint of amusement in his voice. "You do know
about the designer dresses that were destroyed. Someone came in
through the service corridor. Kept the door unlocked with double-
back tape." Lindy felt a flicker of unease and against her will she

turned to include Bill. "I tried to keep anybody from touching it, but Luis was too upset to listen."

She felt Bill's tension and knew he was barely containing his exasperation. She was going to catch hell as soon as Detective Dean was gone. She turned back to Dean. "We're not sure it has anything to do with the murder, but it's something to pursue."

"Lindy—" Bill began.

"I know. The hotel has its own security to deal with that, but they're not doing anything about it." Bill took her elbow. His fingers dug into her skin. She winced and pulled away. "Well, someone should. It was an awful thing to do and—"

"I think it's time to have lunch," said Bill. "See you later, Andrew."

The detective nodded, then dipped his chin to Lindy. "Thank you, Miss Graham. You've been very, uh, enthusiastic." He walked away, smiling.

Lindy stared after him, not knowing whether to be embarrassed by his condescension or mortified that he had called her "Miss." So she turned on Bill. "If you're not going to be supportive, why don't you just butt out?" She regretted her words the moment they were out of her mouth.

Bill's face lost all expression. A great technique for masking his feelings, but she knew the barb had hit its mark, and she felt awful.

"Sorry. I didn't mean that."

"You invited me. Do you want me to leave?"

"No. Of course not. It's just—I just want you to respect me."

Bill shook his head. "How could I not?" He turned her toward the elevator and they stared at the closed doors. She thought of Shane that first day glaring at the elevator as they waited for it to take them to the ballroom. What had happened to him? She was vaguely aware of Dawn's voice nearby. Talking about Katja and how perfect she would be for the movie. Lindy glanced to her left. The movie people were standing beside her looking politely blank. Both elevator doors opened. The movie people and Dawn took one; she and Bill stepped into the other. The doors closed, the elevator started upward.

"I know you think I'm out of my league," said Lindy, controlling her voice, not daring to look Bill in the face. "I never went to college. I was too busy learning steps and living in studios and theatres. But I've seen the world and I've read. Just because I work in a profession based on youth, beauty, and—and good feet, doesn't mean I can't think."

"Lindy—"

"I may not be as smart as you, but I do okay. I'm well respected in my own field."

"I know you are."

"And don't tell me I'm having a midlife crisis. I'm not." The last word wobbled out and Lindy turned her face away.

Bill grabbed her by the shoulders and turned her around. "You little idiot."

"See?" Her bottom lip quivered and she had to bite it to keep from crying.

He gave her a shake. "Idiot. It's a term of endearment since I'm not allowed any others. I think you're smart. I know you're smart. You don't need a degree to prove it. I think you're beautiful and energetic. You have a unique vision of the world. You care about people. I think you should divorce Glen and marry me."

He stopped. They stared at each other. Then his eyes snapped shut. "Jesus Christ."

The elevator doors opened and a couple stepped in. Lindy had no idea of what floor they were on. The elevator started back down. They could ride up and down forever if one of them didn't move, like a Bunuel movie or Charlie and the MTA.

The doors opened and Lindy stepped out. They were back in the lobby. She heard Bill's bemused laugh and then he escorted her outside.

"Well," she said, "I'm glad we got that settled." She smiled at him. "You look a little pale."

"Lindy—"

"You probably need some lunch."

* * *

They ran into Rose coming out of the Pagoda Bar. "Too crowded. I'm going to the casino to see if I can persuade the boys to take me away for lunch. You're welcome to join us." Before either could reply, she swept them toward the escalator and down to the casino level. They stepped into a din of sounds, lights, and swirling colors. Rose put her hand to her forehead, scanning over the rows and rows of slot machines as they progressed through the casino. "There they are."

At the near end of a row of slot machines, four heads were bent forward in concentration. A waitress deposited glasses at their elbows and wandered off. Lindy, Bill and Rose stopped behind them and peered over their shoulders at the spinning cherries, bars, and lemons.

"Have you guys been here all morning?" Lindy shouted over the noise.

No one looked up, but four heads nodded distractedly, while fingers continued pushing buttons at a furious pace.

"I hope you have money left for rent," she said at the top of her lungs. Her words were drowned out by a loud siren. Lights began flashing farther down the row. Coins clanked into the trough of a machine while the grandma in the white quilted coat scooped them into a plastic coin cup.

Everyone watched mesmerized until the clanging and wailing stopped.

"Not fair," groused Juan. "She just got here." He slid off his stool. "I guess I've had enough. I think I already spent my paycheck."

"You're not giving up already?" Rebo finally looked away from the row of unmatched pictures in front of him. His shaved head glistened in the colored lights. "Lindelicious. Didn't hear you come up."

"Just stopped by to say hello. We're on our way to lunch."

"First, check out my new do." Rebo snatched a hat out of his pocket and pulled it onto his head. It was a green visor held in place with a band of green sequins. He turned his head right and left to give Lindy the full effect.

"You look like a chocolate bonbon on a plastic doily," said Juan. "Good enough to eat." He smacked his lips.

Rebo grinned and pulled Lindy toward him. "And the wannabe is looking awfully fetching. Are you sure you don't want to share?"

Lindy rolled her eyes.

"Didn't think so." He turned back to the machine.

Lindy looked over his shoulder and frowned. "Where are the arms?"

"Mama, this is the twenty-first century. They don't have arms anymore. You just push a button. You can play three machines at once and not build a bicep."

"They have a few one-armed bandits for the old fogies along the back wall," volunteered Eric.

"Thanks," said Bill, taking Lindy's arm. "But the old fogies aren't staying."

"I didn't mean you," Eric said in a voice that sounded like he expected Bill to throttle him on the spot.

In the background, the quilted-coat lady had whipped out a cell phone and was yelling into the receiver. "Ritchie. Forget the new suit I told you I'd lost. Go buy two."

"We're going to lunch," said Lindy.

"Have a nice time," said Rebo. "We have to stay here."

"Uh-huh."

"We're on a stakeout. Check out the craps tables."

Lindy looked around. She wasn't sure which ones were the crap games. "What am I looking for?"

"Him." Rebo pointed to one of the tables where Vincent Padrewsky was pushing a stack of chips into the center. "He was here when we came in and has been losing ever since. He's down to his last hurrah. Want us to question him?"

"About what?" asked Lindy at the same time Bill growled, "No."

Ignoring Bill, Rebo turned toward Lindy. "About where he was the night the dresses were slashed."

"Too late," said Rose. They looked to the table, where the dealer was scraping the pile of chips away from Vincent. Vincent slid off the stool and slouched away. Rose sat down next to Rebo and reached across to take one of his chips.

"Hey, if you win with that, half of the pot is mine."

Rose slid in the token. Seconds later, coins were dropping into the trough before her.

"Damn," said Rebo, pushing his visor back to get a look at the winnings.

"Come on," said Bill. "Get your coat. I know where we can have a quiet lunch."

As they turned to leave, sirens and bells blared again and a familiar voice yelled, "Hello, Ritchie . . ."

A few minutes later, they were driving south along the beach. It was raining and the sky was ominously gray. The Honda was buffeted by unexpected gusts of wind.

"Where are we going?" asked Lindy.

"To see Lucy. I thought we could use a break from the hotel."

"Lucy?"

Bill glanced across the seat at her. "We can have lunch there."

Lucy. So he did know a woman in Atlantic City. Lindy had always wondered what his women friends were like. It looked like she'd be finding out pretty soon. But the thought of sitting over lunch while two old friends reminisced about the past, or worse, the present, made her grow cold. Was he punishing her for what had happened in the elevator? Was he trying to make her jealous? Could she compete with Lucy?

By the time Bill parked the car, Lindy had worked herself into a funk. He turned off the ignition and they sat, waiting for the rain to let up. Lindy stared through the windshield but could see nothing but four gray columns in a grassy square through the curtain of rain. At the first letup, they ran across the gravel to a small white house. Bill didn't stop to knock, but swung the door open. He and Lucy must be really good friends. Damn.

Lindy stood in the doorway while she brushed rain from her face and jacket. Then she looked up at her surroundings and blinked—

several times. They were in a gift shop, and Bill was buying tickets from a teenage boy behind the counter.

"I thought we were going to Lucy's," said Lindy.

"We're here." He led her over to a casement window and peered out.

In the yard was a . . . Lindy leaned forward, then followed the gray columns upward. "It's an elephant," she exclaimed. A giant elephant.

"Meet Lucy," said Bill with a pleased smile. "A tour starts in five minutes."

"In 1881 James Lafferty Jr. commissioned Philadelphia contractor William Free to build something that would attract tourists to land he owned along the beach," the boy explained as he led them up a spiral staircase in one of Lucy's legs. "She's six stories high, cost $25,000 to build and was moved from her original site in 1970."

They stepped onto the wooden floorboards of Lucy's interior, a large square room studded with windows—twenty-two in all, their guide informed them. While their guide talked to a couple with a sleeping baby in a front pack, Bill and Lindy climbed a short flight of steps into Lucy's head. Her eyes were two portholes, and they stood side by side looking out to the gray sea beyond.

"You know what I like best about you," said Lindy, keeping her eyes focused on the distant horizon.

"I'm glad there's something," said Bill.

"There's lots, but I really, really like the way you take such pleasure in simple things: a good dinner, carving pumpkins, looking at the sea." She sighed and finally turned to look at him. He was still looking out his porthole and she took a minute just to enjoy the view. He glanced over his shoulder. "Hungry?"

Yes, she was.

Chapter Thirteen

They ate lunch at a nearby restaurant that looked over the ocean and spent the rest of the afternoon ducking into art galleries in between downpours, driving through nearby towns looking at architecture and Christmas decorations. Simple pleasures, made more pleasurable by the closeness she felt with Bill.

Away from the hotel, things returned to normal. He was fun and attentive, and Lindy forgot all about the murder investigation that awaited them. But as soon as they stepped into the lobby, the oppressive feeling was back in spades. She tried to fight it. She knew Bill was trying to fight it, too. Neither of them had any success.

"What's on for tonight?" he asked.

"I kind of want to see some of the competition. There's Professional American Smooth. You know, fox-trot and waltz and stuff like that. Timothy and Felicia are dancing. They won Rising Star, Sunday night. And there's something called Theater Arts, like old adagio teams, I think. You know, 'Who ordered the ballerina' lifts and—"

Bill raised his eyebrows.

"Who ordered the ballerina. The girl sits in the guy's hand, and he lifts her over his head."

Bill still looked skeptical.

"Like a waiter. Get it?"

"Oh. Who ordered the ballerina. Got it."

"And Rose says we might see a Flying Donut."

"Definitely not to be missed."

"You want to go?"

"For a while, anyway."

"Great. It starts at eight."

She left him at his door and went to change.

At eight o'clock, Bill and Lindy sat down at one of the Stepping Out tables. Rose was already there, as well as Biddy and Jeremy. Lindy saw the two men exchange wry glances as they sat down. Jeremy was a talented, tasteful choreographer who put everything into finding just the right movement to complement the music. Bill enjoyed the theatre, but Lindy didn't think either of them would put up with competitive dancing for long. Rebo, Eric, and Juan were sitting at the next table. And beyond them, Kate, Andrea, and Paul sat at a table with several Stepping Out students.

"Where are Mieko and Peter?" asked Lindy. "I've hardly seen them this trip."

Rebo, ears always on the ready to snag or relate a piece of gossip, leaned over. "We think Peter and the Ice Maiden are getting it on."

"No," said Lindy. "Really?" She looked over to Paul and Andrea, who were now a couple privately as well as on the stage. But until last winter, Andrea and Peter had been in a relationship. Now, they had both moved on. *Change partners and dance with me*, thought Lindy. Looking around at the company members, she counted three such relationships. Andrea and Paul, Biddy and Jeremy, Rebo and Juan. There were probably more that she didn't know about. It was common. With so many days together in rehearsal, in the theatre, and on tour, relationships at home tended to corrode and new relationships were made on the road.

She looked at Bill. Everyone was waiting for them to become an item. And she was tempted. God, how she was tempted.

There were so many couples competing in the American Smooth

Division that they had to be divided into two qualifying heats of eleven couples each. Even so, the floor looked incredibly crowded. Within the first few seconds of the first dance, two couples ran into each other, knocking one of the men down and causing a third couple to trip over them. Fortunately no one was hurt, but they had to stop to rearrange the couples into three heats instead of two. The competition started over again. Lindy caught Bill stifling a yawn. At the end of the first round, she stifled a yawn.

"Did you guys eat?" asked Jeremy. "At this rate it will take all night to get to the final. There's time to grab a quick bite."

"Count me in," said Biddy. Biddy could knock back extraordinary amounts of food and was still as thin as a sprite. Even Lindy had stopped having to count carbs and calories, thanks to her impending divorce.

"Anyone else?" asked Jeremy, looking around the tables.

"Nah," said Rebo. "We're doing Spandex glut out tonight. Anyway, we lost most of our per diem at the slots today."

"A few days as a starving artist should teach you about the evils of gambling," said Jeremy. Of course, he'd be advancing them all money tomorrow. He was a softie, but instead of encouraging them to take advantage of him, that made them fiercely loyal.

They went into the Pagoda Bar and Grill because it was close and fast. Behind the main room was a smaller, quieter dining room, dark and overbearing with the Chinese equivalent of Torii gates abutting the walls at each booth. The cabaret singer was muffled by the beaded curtain that separated the back from the main bar. Still, it was hard not to hum along with "Walking in a Winter Wonderland."

Bill slid into the booth next to Lindy. She could have moved farther over, but didn't, even when they ended up sitting with thighs touching. She felt herself slipping toward the point of no return. She told herself to move away, then argued that it would look like a rejection. So she frowned at her menu as if it were the most exciting thing she had ever read.

The four of them shared an assortment of grilled meats, fish and vegetables that they dipped into a variety of piquant sauces. Bill ordered a bottle of pinot noir that was a perfect complement to the dishes. No one mentioned Shane's murder.

Lindy felt satisfied and a little sleepy when they retuned to the ballroom. Bill's hand had found its way to the small of her back as they walked, and for the first time, she wasn't afraid that someone might see them.

They passed several nervous couples making last-minute corrections in the hallway.

"Must be the finalists," said Lindy. She looked for number 307. Timothy and Felicia were there. Felicia was wearing a new dress. A tangerine orange handkerchief skirt topped by a black-and-orange-sequined bodice. One of the hair decorations Lindy had seen in the vendors' room was stuck into a lacquered French twist that bordered on the geometric. Hanging two inches from her ears were orange paste earrings that sent a tingle of memory through Lindy's mind. Earrings and the Russian girl, Elena, talking about how Katja had ignored them. *As if she had lost her earring—hearing.* The earrings. Shane had been dressed in the gown and the shoes. The murderer had even added lipstick. Why not the earrings? They hadn't been on his ears, she was almost positive. She cut her eyes toward Rose. They needed to talk—without Bill knowing about it. His hand suddenly felt hard and threatening on her back. She shifted away, and he dropped his hand to his side.

She wished she could explain that it wasn't him, but there were more important things to deal with at the moment. "Hurry up, we don't want to miss anything," she said, hoping to gloss over the awkwardness between them.

"I think I've had enough," said Bill. "I'll see you tomorrow."

"But—" She stopped herself. He was an adult. If he didn't want to be with her, to hell with him. "See you tomorrow," she said and watched him walk away.

"Geez, Lindy," said Biddy.

But it was Jeremy's voice that broke her out of her thoughts. "You're being stubborn. Go after him."

She squared her shoulders and turned to face him.

"Do it," he said before she had a chance to argue. "I'm your boss, remember?" She did remember and she remembered her answer. *Bill's not my boss, you are.* But Jeremy was right. Bill's friendship was more important to her than a hundred murder investigations. She nodded, then followed after Bill.

He was already gone from the corridor. She headed toward the bank of elevators. No Bill. She peeked into the Pagoda Bar, where the singer was bemoaning that she couldn't remember a worse December. Neither could Lindy. Bill wasn't at the bar; maybe he had gone to his room. She wandered back toward the counter of phones that stood between the men's and women's lounges. She'd give him time to get upstairs, then call. And say what? She leaned against one of the Ming guardian figures while she contemplated love, divorce, murder, and competitiveness.

She picked up the house phone and started to punch in Bill's extension. Junie Baker, clipboard in hand, came out of the men's room. Luis came out right behind him.

"How can you be so cruel?" he shouted at Junie.

Junie whirled around and poked a finger into the smaller man's chest. "Shut the hell up, Luis. You're causing a scene. You know what happens to people who cause scenes in this business."

Luis stared at the finger on his chest, then he knocked it away. He leaned into Junie, crooking his neck to look into his face. "I want an answer. The police were here questioning Enrico about the murder. Those interfering women must have told them about the dresses."

He's talking about me and Rose, Lindy thought indignantly. They had been trying to help and this was the thanks they got.

"Was it you who destroyed them? You didn't manage to finish him off all those years ago? So now you had to try again?"

"Keep your voice down." Junie's words were hissed out between clenched teeth.

"I won't keep my voice down," Luis retorted. "I don't care if the whole world knows what you did."

"We'll talk about this later. I've got to judge the final in a few minutes."

"We'll talk about it now. Enrico is upstairs in his room. Crying and crying. It wrenches my heart out. He won't let me in. He thinks they're going to charge him with murder."

Junie's hands flew out in exasperation. Luis flinched back and held up his hands to ward off the expected blow.

"Cut that out. I'm not going to hit you. That's not the way I do things."

"I know how you do things, you despicable—"

Lindy was listening unabashedly. She was sure the couples in the hallway were, too. Junie and Luis were making plenty of noise. Junie seemed to realize this. His hand wrapped around Luis's forearm, and he dragged him across the carpet and into another corridor that ran perpendicular to the main hall.

The couples went back to practicing, and Lindy followed Junie and Luis across the hall. She squeezed behind a strategically placed guardian figure in hopes of hearing the rest of their conversation.

Their voices were muffled and Lindy could only make out a few words. She needed to get closer. Cautiously, she peeked around the statue's head and peered down the hall, just in time to see an EMPLOYEES ONLY door close. She followed, hugging the wall.

This must be the door to the service elevator. She remembered that there was a right angle turn just inside the hallway. If they had moved past that, she would be able to hear them without being seen. If they hadn't, then she would have some serious explaining to do. She knew she wouldn't get any understanding from either of the men if they caught her, but she'd worry about that later.

She cracked open the door just far enough to see a thin rectangle of carpet and wall. The echo of voices told her that they had continued down the hall.

"Here," she heard Luis say. He must be showing Junie the door where the slasher had entered. Good. She could creep as far as the banquet room and hide just inside the door. Then maybe she'd find out what was going on and if it tied into Shane's murder.

"What makes you think I would destroy Enrico's dresses? What could I possibly gain?"

"You're a vindictive bastard. Look what you did to him before. Just because he was trying to protect you."

Lindy pressed herself against the wall and inched toward the banquet room. She slowed down as the possibility of a confession presented itself.

"Bah," said Junie. "He thought he could . . ."

Lindy was at the door now. It was already ajar, but fortunately the banquet room was pitch-black. She squeezed through the opening and leaned forward to listen. An arm came around her waist and snatched her away from the door. At the same time, a large hand clamped over her mouth. Her heart stopped. She struggled to breathe through her nose, and her heart burst into clamoring.

Whoever it was had her in a viselike grip, wedged against his body and the wall. Then recognition began to replace fear. She knew that body.

"Don't say a word," whispered Bill in her ear.

"Wha—"

His hand clamped harder over her mouth. "Later."

She nodded, showing him she understood. Slowly he released his hand from her mouth. It joined the other arm that was restraining her. *Not a bad way to eavesdrop on a murder confession*, some renegade part of her brain noted.

"I have to get back to the ballroom," Junie said. "They've probably sent someone out looking for me. I suggest you do the same. But let me make this plain once and for all."

Simultaneously, Bill and Lindy leaned forward, straining to hear.

"I had nothing to do with the dresses being destroyed. No, let me finish. I wasn't the one who ostracized Enrico all those years ago. Enrico did that by disrupting a major competition."

"Because you betrayed him."

"Bullshit. Okay. I was a little angry. I'll admit it. Nobody wants to be told that their lover is cheating on them. Especially not by somebody who has been a good friend. A real good friend. So I overreacted a little. Enrico overreacted a lot and that's why he had to run off to Italy."

Luis made a disgusted sound.

"And you might as well know. Enrico and I are friends again. So you'd better get used to it."

"Ha. You won't stay friends for long. You never could."

"This time is different. We're both getting older. Can't keep up with those young energetic boys anymore."

"Liar. What about Shane?"

Lindy heard Junie's drawn-out sigh. "Shane was a nonevent. Not that he didn't try, mind you. They all try."

"But everyone says—"

"I stopped listening to what everyone says years ago. I don't have the time or the interest."

"I don't believe you. I'm going to make Enrico go back to Italy. We should never have come here."

"Probably not," said Junie. "But you did."

"You knew we were coming. Oh, my God." Luis's voice held a note of betrayal as well as outrage.

"Don't jump to conclusions. Enrico called me from Italy. He asked me whether I thought he should come. I said it was his choice and that's the last I heard until I saw him in the ballroom Sunday night. Neither of us killed Shane, if that's what you're worried about. We were together that night. Talking over old times. Now I'm going back to the ballroom. For your own good, don't cause any more scenes." Footsteps receded down the hall. An anguished cry from Luis. He rattled the door to the vendors' room. Someone opened it, and he went inside.

Lindy bolted forward; Bill's arms tightened around her.

"Hurry," she whispered. "This would be a perfect time to talk to Luis when he's overwrought and not being careful."

Bill turned her around. Instead of answering, he pulled her back into his arms and she felt herself being kissed. *Wow.* Junie and Luis fled out of her mind and were replaced by wonder. This was even better than the other time he'd kissed her, two years before. She kissed him back. He was warm and all-encompassing. Her hands drifted up his chest, to pull him closer or push him away, she didn't know which. This was all right. This was very all right. This was the way it should be. This was—over.

His arms released her. Where his body had been warm next to hers, there was now cold air. She opened her eyes. Bill had thrown the door open and was striding down the corridor toward the ballroom.

Chapter
Fourteen

Bill was sitting next to Rose at the Stepping Out table when Lindy returned to the ballroom. She sat down in the empty chair beside him. From across the table, Biddy gave her an approving smile.

Lindy pulled her chair close to Bill's. "What were you doing in the banquet room?"

Keeping his eyes on the dancing, he leaned over and said into her ear, "I was in the hallway looking at the door to the dealers' room when I heard them come in. I popped into the closest open door. Imagine my surprise when you popped in, too."

She pulled away far enough to look him in the face. Tango music blared to life and she jumped. Bill smiled at her. "Someone on the inside is more apt to find out what's going on in an investigation. You said so yourself."

She opened her mouth.

Bill placed two fingers over her lips. "I've been thinking about what you said the other night at dinner. About understanding the modus operandi of these people. I was just following your information."

"But you didn't include me." Her jaw was so clenched that she had trouble whispering the words.

"But not because I don't respect you. It's just—you scare the hell out of me."

She frowned.

"I know you're perfectly capable of—" The emcee's voice boomed through the air, followed by applause. He was announcing the finalists.

"What?" She had to yell to be heard.

"I said, you're perfectly capable of tracking a murderer. I admit you're good at it. I just don't want you to get caught in your own trap. I'm not sure you realize how hazardous this business can be."

Simultaneously, she was hit with flashes of being chased through the backstage of a theatre by a demented killer, the ground giving away beneath her feet on a New York mountainside, falling through a trapdoor, being stalked in a deserted forest. It was frightening to be the center of that. But how more frightening to be a bystander, who could only watch, seeing the whole scene unravel, fearing the worst, and not being able to help. She swallowed and touched his sleeve.

"And your last dance, couples, the Viennese waltz." The music began. Dancers swirled across the floor, and further conversation was impossible. Ninety seconds later, the waltz ended as abruptly as it had begun. The competitors left the floor to wait for the final results. General dancing was announced and noncompeting couples took to the floor.

While the music played, chairs were set up across the front of the dance floor and several judges took their places.

"Theatre Arts," said Rose. "What we've all been waiting for."

The first couple was announced. A popular song blasted through the loudspeakers. From opposite sides of the room, a man, wearing black slacks and an open-to-the-waist shirt, and a girl, in an iridescent thigh-length shift, ran toward each other. The man lifted the girl over his head and began to turn. The audience broke into applause and whistles. She slid to the floor and clung to his leg. He grasped her foot and pulled her to standing in a vertical split. The audience cheered again. They separated, and the girl ran toward him. Up she went, over the head, more spinning. More applause.

The first dance ended and another couple replaced them. The music started quietly. The girl was dressed in a dark blue, floor-length gown with a high neck and long dolman sleeves. It was an eye-stopping contrast to most of the costumes Lindy had seen. The couple went through a series of controlled adagio movements, the girl's legs stretching into high extensions. It was obvious that she had been ballet trained.

Halfway through the dance, the music made a sudden shift into a synthesized rock-and-roll beat. The man placed his hands on her shoulders and Voila. The gown was snatched away, leaving the girl attired in a red-, white-, and blue-sequined leotard. The crowd burst into appreciative clapping and yells. The couple's arms shot into the air. With a hip thrust, a shimmy, and a head roll, they strutted to opposite sides of the floor.

"Flying Donut on your starboard bow," yelled Rose over the music. Both dancers ran toward the center of the floor. The girl threw herself into a back bend just as the man swept her off her feet. And somehow, he was holding her over his head, still in her back bend, but now parallel to the floor, hands grasping her ankles, and smiling sideways at them.

Lindy tilted her head, trying to figure out how they had accomplished the feat. The music crescendoed and the man let go. The girl free-fell down his body. At the last minute, his feet opened, and she stuck on his ankles inches from the floor. The audience went wild.

"Shit," said Bill.

Jeremy turned with an unholy gleam in his eye. "That alone was worth the trip," he said.

At the next table, Rebo was jumping up and down in his seat. Eric's hands moved in the air as he tried to duplicate how the trick was done. Kate had grabbed her ankles and was riding sidesaddle in her chair. Lindy was sure she would be seeing Donuts and Variations at the run-through for the movie people the following morning.

There were five other numbers, but none attained the entertainment value of the Flying Donut. Lindy's attention drifted back to the question of Shane's murder.

She scanned the room, picking out those people she knew to be involved somehow with Shane. Rusty was sitting at the next table, surrounded by his students. Dawn was strategically located between the director and the movie producer at a front table. She was talking nonstop, her head moving from one to the other in a verbal tennis match. Her tablemates stared intently at the dance floor.

Junie Baker was chatting with the woman next to him on the dais. Neither was judging this event and didn't appear interested in the dancing. They'd probably seen it all before. Couples kept the same routine for months. The woman wore her platinum hair pulled back to a peak that rose several inches above her head. She was too plump for the gold satin jumpsuit she was wearing. She turned her head and prisms of light glanced off her ears. *Earrings*, thought Lindy. She had to find out about the earrings.

She leaned across Bill and poked Rose. "Earrings," she mouthed. "Was Shane wearing earrings when they found him?"

It took a moment for Rose to draw her attention from the dancing and come up to speed. But at last she shook her head no. Then her eyes widened and Lindy could practically see her mind taking on the ramifications. "Holy cow." Rose cut her eyes toward Bill. "Later," she mouthed back.

Lindy went back to perusing the room but didn't see any of the other major players. Katja was still missing. Hiding or dead. No Luis and no Enrico, who was in his room crying his heart out, according to Luis. *His* room. Did that mean that he and Luis had separate rooms? And did that mean they weren't lovers like she and probably everyone else assumed? And who was the lover that had cheated on Junie all those years ago? Was he still around? And could it possibly have anything to do with Shane or was it just another dead end? Timothy and Felicia were probably outside, waiting for their callback. And Vincent would be in the bar or casino if not in the ballroom.

She wondered where he got the money to hang around competitions. He didn't compete professionally and he had no students that Lindy had seen. It would be easy enough to ask and she would. But somehow she didn't see Shane's murder being about money. Vindictive, Bill had said. Changing partners, Rose had said. When one couple broke up there was a flurry of rearrangements. Lindy had seen it herself. The Hollingford divorce was already sending a ripple through the competitive community. Reshuffle, start again. Rising star. A struggle to the top. Sort of like life, only glitzier.

Finally, the Theatre Arts competition ended and the judges returned to the dais. "And now, what we've all been waiting for," began the emcee. "The judges have asked six couples back to the floor for the final round of the First Annual International Stars Ballroom Competition, American Smooth Professional Division."

At the back of the room, anxious faces awaited the verdict. Timothy and Felicia stood at the front of the group, looking confident. "Couple 139." The audience applauded as the couple took the floor. "Couple number 244." Two-forty-four hugged and rushed to the floor, while couple 210 backed despondently away. Timothy and Felicia were next in line. "Couple three"—they lifted their chins, not looking at each other, but out to the floor, and stepped forward—"sixty-six." Timothy and Felicia froze midstep as the couple behind them jumped into each other's arms and ran past them to the floor. There was a moment of startled silence, then applause.

"Shit," said Rose and caught Lindy's eye. Lindy turned back to Timothy and Felicia. They still stood in place, their smiles firmly in place as if they didn't believe what they had heard. "Couple 382." Another couple hurried past them and finally, without turning or changing their expressions, Timothy and Felicia backed out of the light.

The finalists spread across the floor and took their poses to begin the same four dances for the third time that evening.

"I thought they were a shoo-in with Shane and Katja out of it," said Lindy.

"They were," answered Rose, her voice laced with shock. "Man, it's going to hit the fan tonight. We don't want to miss this. Wow. Holy shit."

Similar responses could be heard at the tables near them. Lindy looked up at the dais. The judges smiled down at the couples. Even Junie was smiling in spite of the fact that his favored couple had not been called back. Lindy wondered if his smile was all show.

"What's going on?" asked Bill.

"Couple 307 was supposed to be in the finals," Lindy explained.

"We just sat here for two hours and it was rigged?" Bill looked incredulous.

"Not exactly rigged, but it's sort of like wrestling; some couples are strongly favored to win."

More general dancing followed. Then the presentation of the Theatre Arts winners. The Flying Donut couple came in first. At last the six finalists for the American Smooth were called back. They lined up across the dance floor. Sixth place, fifth place, then fourth was announced. Each time a couple was called, they air-kissed with the couple next to them before stepping forward to receive a medal and more air kisses from the judges. First place went to couple number 139, Malininsky and something-ova.

Once again they lined up, this time in place order, and pictures were taken. The winning couple began an honor dance. At the end, the lights came on and the judges left the dais. People began to leave the ballroom. Junie walked across the floor, looking completely unruffled, though Lindy guessed he must be furious.

"Come on," said Rose, pushing her chair from the table and standing up. "We don't want to miss this." Lindy jumped up beside her, and Bill stood, reluctantly. They were joined by Biddy and Jeremy, and they all followed Rose into the hallway. Halfway down the hall, Lindy realized they had picked up an extra person. Vincent Padrewsky was walking alongside her. He caught her eye. "Are we having fun yet?" His breath was sour with whatever he had been drinking. The smell of alcohol seemed to exude from his skin. She moved away from him.

Ahead of them, Timothy had stopped Junie at the elevator. A computer sheet was crumpled in his hand. He shook it in Junie's face. "Look at these scores. Lavalle gave us a sixth in waltz and tango. She's never marked us this low before. And Crommerty. He gave us a seventh in Viennese. Viennese. It's our best dance."

"I know. I can't believe it," commiserated Junie. "I just don't know what happened." He shook his head. "Felicia, pet." He motioned her over. She came sullenly forward, and he put a fatherly arm around her shoulder. "I don't know what to say. Maybe your timing was a little off tonight; maybe it was the dress."

"Bullshit," said Felicia. "Bu-u-ll-shit." Her eyes flashed with anger. Then she turned and marched away. Junie looked after her, shrugged, and pressed the elevator button. The door opened, but before Junie could step in, Timothy jumped in front of him, blocking his way.

"Timothy, please, I know you're upset. So am I. But these things happen."

"They sure do. But not on the dance floor. These decisions are made in the judge's lounge. You said if I competed, you'd push me, make sure there would be money in it. I've got kids, Junie. I can't afford this shit."

"And it just keeps getting better," slurred Vincent in Lindy's ear. She saw Dawn rushing toward Junie and Timothy.

"Well, Timothy," said Dawn, coming to an abrupt halt. "What a great career move for you. Now you know what it feels like to be screwed by Junie Baker. I tried to tell you, but you wouldn't listen. And now I'm going to sue your ass." Dawn gave him a toothy smile. "Have a nice night." She turned and marched triumphantly into the Pagoda Bar.

Beside Lindy, Vincent giggled and followed Dawn into the bar.

"You can't let her do this, Junie," cried Timothy. "They're going to take me to the cleaners. You said you'd take care of it. You'd better. And if what everybody's saying is true, that you're planning to buy her out, I want a piece of the action. Make me a partner or I'll make trouble."

"Rumors, Timothy. Merely rumors," said Junie, sounding bored.

"Big trouble." Timothy threw the paper to the floor. The elevator doors opened once again, and Junie stepped inside. The doors closed on a sputtering Timothy.

"Christ," said Bill. "I'd better ask Andrew to put an armed guard on that Baker guy."

Lindy nodded. She was thinking the same thing.

"Interesting," said Jeremy. "I think we'll say good night." He took Biddy's arm and they walked away.

Rose nudged Lindy in the ribs and skewed her mouth to the side. "We'd better intercept Dawn and find out what happened to the earrings. Unless you and Bill have other plans."

"We don't," said Lindy, more loudly than she intended.

"Don't what?" asked Bill.

"Don't want a drink, do we?"

Bill shrugged. Rose shrugged. She passed behind Lindy and whispered, "I'll get the dirt. I'll call later. If you're not in your room, I'll leave a message." She wiggled her fingers. "Night," and she went into the bar.

Bill walked Lindy to the door of her hotel room, waited until she opened the door, and said a brief good night. Much too brief, considering that kiss. Maybe he was having second thoughts. Or maybe he wished he hadn't kissed her at all.

She dumped her evening bag on the bed, slipped out of her shoes, and started to pace. Biddy's notebook was sitting on the table near the window. She picked it up and opened it to the page of suspects.

Was there someone or something she didn't know about? Granted, she didn't know these people, but it was the same kind of closed, incestuous kind of world that theatre was. Everybody knowing everything about each other, lots of angst and carrying on that was quickly dropped when the next scandal hit. It had only been two days since Shane's body was found. Had everyone already forgotten him? There didn't seem to be one person mourning the passing of Shane Corbett. Had they informed his parents? Would a teary-eyed mother or roommate pack up his belongings to take back home?

And that was something else they should know. Who were his roommates? He probably had several. She made a note in the margin of the page to ask Dawn.

Bill hadn't mentioned the police questioning roommates. She looked at the phone. Should she call and ask if he knew anything? *Right, Graham*, she thought. *You know what that will look like.* She looked at the phone for a while. Sat down and made some more notes. Paced. Looked at the phone again. Oh, hell, why not. She rang his room. The line was busy.

Who the hell was he talking to at one in the morning? Andrew Dean. Or somebody else. Maybe she didn't want to know. She waited ten minutes. Called again. Still busy. She slammed down the phone. It rang.

"Hello."

"Damn," said Rose. "I was hoping you weren't there."

"Then why did you call?"

"I mean I was hoping I'd have to leave a message 'cause you were out carousing."

"No carousing," said Lindy and was surprised at the disappointment in her voice.

"Not to worry, there's always tomorrow. But listen to this. I go into the bar and ask Dawn about the earrings. At first, she doesn't remember about loaning them to Katja. Then she gets this funny look and says, No, Katja didn't return them. A second later she gets an even funnier look and says, Yes, Katja did return them. Then she says she can't remember. Then suddenly she does remember that she has to do something and leaves me with the tab." Rose's sigh was audible through the phone. "Either way, it doesn't look good, does it?"

"I'm afraid not," said Lindy.

Chapter Fifteen

L indy lay in bed, looking out at the gray morning. The storm had settled in. Sheets of rain slashed at the window, leaving a dense layer of water across the plate glass. She could hear the gusting of the wind, and even though she was safely enclosed on the eleventh floor, she felt its cold.

Cold—and alone. No doubt about it. The bed next to her hadn't been slept in. Professionalism aside, Biddy had spent the night with Jeremy. Lindy sighed. So she was alone. She could handle it. She'd be damned if she would become like Dawn, tied to the past, blaming her present condition on a man who no longer loved her.

She squinted at the clock by the bed and sat up. 8:10. If she didn't move it, she'd be late for the nine o'clock call. She reached for the phone, punched in the extension for room service and ordered coffee and toast. The coffee to get her going and the toast to soak up the caffeine.

She went into the bathroom and turned the shower to hot. A pile of clothes lay on the counter. Biddy had come and gone and not wakened her. The sight only added to her sense of isolation. No longer the days when one of them would come back in the early morning hours and share all the pleasurable details of the night before.

They were adults now. Biddy was in a meaningful relationship, at last, and Lindy had no desire to make it less meaningful by treating it as a source of entertainment. And Biddy wouldn't expect Lindy to share her pleasurable moments, even if she were to have some. Life changed; it was time to move on.

She climbed into the shower. The hot sting of the jets took her breath away. She let the water run over her back and shoulders, then reached for the shampoo and lathered her hair. Her mind began to stray through a kaleidoscope of ideas. She did some of her best thinking in the shower. She carefully skirted the question of her changed status from loving wife to unwanted wife. It was easier to dwell on the convoluted machinations of the ballroom industry and the death of Shane Corbett.

She carefully replayed the scene on the beach as the room filled up with steam. Seeing the flash of turquoise below the boardwalk. Dawn's hysterical reaction. The discovery that the body was not Katja's, but Shane's, his broken feet, the slash of lipstick, but no earrings. Dawn's convenient memory loss about whether Katja had returned the earrings. Was she covering for Katja or protecting herself? She had certainly thought it was Katja dead on the beach. Enrico hadn't even noticed that it wasn't Katja lying there in the sand. And Luis had looked horrified when he realized the truth.

So where was Katja? Dead? Missing? It was hard to believe that she had disappeared without a trace. But if she wasn't dead, where was she?

She'd have to get Bill to tell her if the police had any leads. That was turning out to be the hardest part of this investigation. Getting Bill to trust her.

She turned off the shower and stepped out, just as a knock sounded at the door. Room service. She must have spent longer in the shower than she realized. Wrapping a towel around herself, she dripped to the door. She opened it a crack, then jumped back into the bathroom and closed the door. He'd have to do without a tip. That was life.

As soon as she heard him leave, she moved into the bedroom and poured a cup of coffee. She stared out the window as she drank it. She and Rose would have to confront Dawn today. Make her tell them what she knew. Hopefully, it would be nothing that they would be forced to pass on to Detective Dean.

And she and Bill hadn't had time to discuss what they had overheard in the banquet room the night before. She had to drag her thoughts from what else had happened in the banquet room. She reached across the table for Biddy's notebook and opened it to the page where she had written down the conversation between Junie and Luis.

Junie had been the cause of Enrico's blackballing years before. Directly or indirectly. She scrolled her finger down the page. *No one likes to be told that their lover has been cheating on them.* Had Enrico been his lover, or had Enrico been the one to tell him? The latter, Lindy thought. They had been friends and now they were friends again, *good friends.* That could be construed in several ways, but considering the players, Lindy thought she knew what it meant.

She frowned. Poor Luis. Did that mean he was about to be ousted as Enrico's lover? Was it possible that he wasn't a lover, but merely a loyal assistant? "The long-suffering," Rose had dubbed him. Maybe he was tired of suffering. But she couldn't see him destroying his life's work, and she couldn't figure out any possible reason that he would have to kill Shane.

Unless . . . Lindy distractedly picked up a piece of toast and took a bite. Could he have conspired with Shane to steal the dress pattern? And then was afraid that Shane would tell Enrico? That didn't make sense. Someone who knew about sewing wouldn't need the actual pattern. They could cut their own from the dress itself. Even she could pull it off if the design was simple enough. And the Russian girls all made their own gowns.

She tossed the piece of toast back on the plate. She was getting off the track. The only thing that tied Luis and Enrico with Shane was that Katja was debuting the new dress. And would a dress be worth killing over?

Possibly, though it seemed a bit far-fetched. But an entire line of dresses. That might be cause enough. If Luis or Enrico had caught Shane destroying the dresses, either might have been angry enough to kill him. But if someone had the turquoise gown, Katja had returned it. So where was Katja?

Lindy drank back the last of her coffee and closed the notebook. She was running around in circles and she needed to get to the theater.

She dressed quickly, black jeans and a chamois skin shirt. Comfortable for rehearsal, even though it was a dress rehearsal specifically requested by the movie people. And rehearsal required sensible shoes. Thank God. Her feet were beginning to rebel at high heels. She reached for her Nikes.

A quick application of makeup, earrings, and a last-minute colorful scarf to throw around her neck left her seven minutes to get downstairs. She grabbed her dance bag and headed for the elevator.

She couldn't leave off the feeling that she was missing something. Love, hate, revenge, greed, fear. Motives for murder recognized as far back as the Greeks and maybe before. And there were plenty of those emotions running rampant through the ballroom community.

Revenge for stealing a dress design. Hate for leaving Dawn. Or Rusty for that matter. Love? Junie said he wasn't Shane's lover, but he could have been lying. Katja? "He said he loved me." Greed. Of wanting a title, or a partner? Fear? Of what?

The elevator arrived and she stepped inside. There were all kinds of fear. Of losing, of winning, of being hurt. Of being alone? Katja, Dawn, Luis. Hell, it could apply to all of them. Even to herself. The elevator and her stomach descended at the same time.

No. She at least was not afraid of being alone. She wasn't looking forward to it, but she would survive it. And anyway, why kill someone if you needed them?

She was wading through a quagmire of possible motives. And motive was fine and dandy as far as it went. She had been an avid mystery buff before real murder intruded into her life. And the stories she had liked were big on motives, not just means and opportunity.

Of course, the writer could make anyone the murderer, he just needed to make sure no one had an alibi.

And if the murder took place in the middle of the night, the way Shane's had, most people would be asleep. And if you were sleeping—alone—you didn't have an alibi.

Motives and alibis. Yuck. At rehearsal, when a dancer was on the wrong foot or missed a lift, she didn't ask for reasons and excuses. She analyzed the problem and she fixed it. She could fix this, too. She just needed better investigative tools. She had only been half kidding when she had mentioned the private investigator's license to Bill at dinner.

Jeremy's dancers, the *Tango de Argentina* dancers and the cast of *Dance with Me* were warming up onstage. Jeremy and Biddy were sitting at one of the tables in the house. Otherwise the theater was empty. Evidently the other participants didn't believe in hour call.

Lindy went up to the stage. Normally she would give company class before a performance, but this was really only a rehearsal for an audience of four. The *Gershwin Preludes* only used seven dancers and they were already warming up on their own. She gave the few notes she had taken during the Monday rehearsal. The dancers went to change into costume and Lindy sat down with Jeremy and Biddy.

Biddy scrunched up her face as Lindy sat down, an expression that said, Yeah, okay, so I stayed out all night.

Lindy smiled. "So how are things going?"

"Fine," said Jeremy. "Rose is finishing up backstage. Peter's in the booth. He got lassoed into doing some simple lighting for the Formation team and the honor dances that will round out the program."

"They're going to do the honor dances today?"

"Yeah, but just the ones that have already won. Rising Star, American Smooth and Theatre Arts. They insisted. Everybody wants a shot at being discovered by the movies. On Sunday they'll add the American Rhythm, International Standard and Latin champions."

"Aren't you the knowledgeable one?"

"One of the sponsors just explained it to Peter, and I was listening. I'll forget all the names before the morning is out."

Other performers straggled in. The dancers from *Formation Fixation* came en masse already lacquered, made up, and wearing their costumes—matching salmon-colored ball gowns for the women and tails for the men. The last to arrive were the individual couples doing the honor dances: Malininsky and partner, the couple who had done the Flying Donut, and Timothy and Felicia. They handed their tapes to the soundman and went onto the stage, which was now empty.

Rose came over and stretched out along a couch on the tier above them. "All ready and raring to go."

At five minutes to ten, the movie people came in, escorted by an out-of-humor Rusty Lonigan. This morning he was dressed in black stretch trousers and a black-and-silver striped shirt. He deposited them at a table that held a coffeepot, mugs and bottles of Evian water, then he detoured to where Lindy and the others were sitting.

"I don't suppose you know where Dawn is?" he asked Rose.

"No, and I didn't see her at the restaurant. But there must be ninety places to eat a bagel around here. Maybe she's running late."

"Maybe she's about to run out of luck. I saw you talking to her last night. Did she seem upset? I mean more upset than usual? She left the suite sometime last night or early this morning. And nobody has seen her at all."

Rose sat up. "You mean she's missing?"

"Probably not missing. But where the hell is she? I called the apartment in Cherry Hill. I thought maybe she freaked and went home. I even called the beach house, but the phone lines are down because of the storm. I could wring her neck." Rusty pushed back his sleeve and looked at his watch. "Damn. I've got to run. Have to be on the floor in two minutes, and there's nobody to hold Harold's hand. It was her big idea to do this movie tie-in, and now she's dumped it in my lap. If you see her, tell her she needs to get her shit together and fast." He hurried out.

"Oh, déjà vu," said Rose. "Wasn't that the same conversation we were having when they discovered Shane's body?"

"Pretty similar," said Jeremy. "I just hope it doesn't have the same outcome."

Rose got up and pulled a threaded needle from where it was stuck through her denim shirt pocket. She handed it to Lindy. "Can you stand backstage with this while I go make a quick sweep of the ballroom? I'll be back before the Gershwin is on."

Lindy took the needle.

"Don't look so panicky. It's like carrying an umbrella. If you're ready to sew, nothing will tear. Back in a flash."

She loped down the tier and past the director's table. Harold watched appreciatively as she ran out the door.

The house and stage lights dimmed. There was no curtain. They could see the *Dance with Me* cast take their places. Bright lights popped on, revealing couples in period costume, lounging on gilt chairs and couches. The men wore swallow-tail coats and held white gloves and top hats; the women wore huge white gowns covered in dazzling jewels, pleats, and ruching. The music began a slightly drunken three-four. They had obviously been out reveling all night. They yawned and stretched in slow motion while lazily singing the delights of sacher tortes, new wine, and the waltz. As the music accelerated, they rose from their languid poses and began to whirl around the stage, at first sedately, then faster and wilder, singing the whole time, until at last the couples fell into a raucous tumble on the furniture. The lights blacked out as they all lifted imaginary wineglasses in a toast to Vienna.

The few people in the audience clapped enthusiastically, except for the movie people. They talked among themselves, pointing to the stage and nodding, or shaking their heads, while the production assistant wrote furiously in her notebook.

"*Viva Vienna*," said Jeremy. "Cute."

"Not cute enough to keep them on Broadway. They closed last week."

The tango company took their places. Lots of flicks and kicks and passionate body rubbing. The lighting was so dark that it was hard to see much. The movie people looked bored. Not what they were looking for.

They perked up during the *Gershwin Preludes*, especially when Paul and Andrea made their entrance.

"They better not be thinking of taking those two away for a movie," said Jeremy. "We've got a tour next month."

"I wouldn't worry," said Lindy. "We'll probably have time to do several tours and a couple of New York seasons before *The Secret Life of Fred Astaire* starts shooting. I can't imagine they have enough material to get a full screenplay."

Formation Fixation was, well, a formation team. And the honor dances were the same dances they had seen the night before.

It only took an hour. The sponsors had kept it short on purpose, so as not to interfere with the last evening's Yuletide Ball for which they had hired a full orchestra. It seemed like overkill to Lindy. Who would want to dance all night after having danced all week?

She was backstage when a message came back to Paul and Andrea that the producer would like to see them. She was surprised at the jolt her stomach took when she heard the request. Her first reaction was to run out into the house and yell, "You can't have them." But of course neither she, nor Jeremy, nor Biddy would stand in the way of them getting a movie offer. They certainly wouldn't try to kill them.

Rose came out of a dressing room, carrying costumes. "Come back while I dry these out."

Lindy followed her down the hall to a wardrobe room that looked more like a salon than a place for sewing and ironing. The floor was carpeted. The clothing racks were stainless steel. In a side room, a gleaming chrome washer and dryer stood side by side. "Deluxe accommodations," she said, looking at the upholstered chairs and Bernina sewing machine sitting on a carved cherry-wood table.

"Dawn hasn't been seen," said Rose. "I asked all over the ballroom. I even tried calling her apartment in Cherry Hill. No answer."

"Should we call Detective Dean? Are you worried?"

"Worried, yes. But I don't think she's been harmed, if that's what you're thinking."

"You think she's absconded? Fleeing the police?"

Rose heaved an unhappy sigh. "That or she's gone to Katja."

"You think Dawn knows where she is?"

"Well, I don't think she killed Shane Corbett, so she must have found Katja."

"Got any ideas about where they could be?"

"Actually, I do. You brought your car, right? How would you like to take a little drive?"

"How little and to where?"

"Dawn's beach house. She used to always spend her holidays there. And it being close to the time to deck the halls, I just happen to have brought my Christmas cards along. I have the address to the beach house in my palm pilot."

"And how far away is this beach house?"

"It's on an island about twenty minutes away. We can find out if Dawn's there and be back in under an hour. And nobody will be the wiser."

"I think that might be obstructing justice."

Rose harrumphed. "What's just about persecuting somebody because she has bad taste in men and hair color and thrives on misplaced loyalties?" She stared fixedly at Lindy until Lindy gave in.

"All right, if we can get out without anybody seeing us. Get your coat and meet me in the self-park lot across the street."

Rose frowned. "You parked your own car?"

"I didn't realize it only cost two bucks to use the valet service. I thought I should start saving money, since . . ." She trailed off.

"Let's go." Rose started for the door. "A word of advice?" she said, pausing to look at Lindy from the doorway.

Lindy nodded.

"Jeremy will never let you starve, but you had better get over your own misplaced loyalties and take that bastard for everything he's worth."

Chapter
Sixteen

B astard? Lindy had never thought of Glen as a bastard. Actually, she didn't know what to think. Sure, they seemed to have gone their separate ways since the kids had gotten older. That was typical in the suburbs. And with Glen's promotion to oversees consultant in Paris and her job with the dance company, they spent less time together than ever before. But bastard?

She hadn't noticed any change in his attitude toward her. It had been too gradual. Everyone assumed he was seeing other women. She had to admit that it was probably true. And she knew with certainty that that was why she was feeling so insecure, so needing to stick up for herself. That stupid remark about not having a diploma. She had never even thought about it before. It boiled down to one thing. She was being rejected, and she didn't know why.

She went for her jacket and took the covered walkway to the hotel garage, then the pedestrian door to the street. She was hit by a pelting mixture of rain and snow. Across the street, she could see Rose hunkered against the Volvo. She hurried across the street, or at least she tried to. She had never felt wind this strong.

She thought about the driving gloves and down jacket that she had left in the station wagon and pushed forward. She fumbled with the keys while Rose waited with her hand on the passenger door handle. She, Lindy noticed, was fully outfitted in padded jacket, mittens, and a colorful pointed knit cap that must have been hand-made in Tibet.

She jumped into the driver's seat and punched the unlock button, then pulled on leather gloves that were stiff and cold. She reached over the seat and exchanged her suede jacket for the ski parka.

"Criminy," she muttered through chattering teeth. The Volvo's ignition caught and she turned up the heat full blast.

"Always check out the weather reports when traveling to a for-eign country," said Rose in a pedantic voice.

"I didn't think I'd being going out of the hotel, so I left the heavy stuff in the car," Lindy chattered back at her. "Which way do we go?"

Rose unfolded a map that took up most of the front seat. "And carry a map of the area," she said. One mitten circled over the paper, then zoomed in and poked a spot on the map. "We are here. Turn right out of the parking lot."

Lindy showed the attendant her registration card and turned right out of the parking lot.

"Take the second left."

She did, fingers gripping the steering wheel as the Volvo skidded around an icy corner. A trash barrel rolled across the street in front of them and Lindy braked, making the Volvo fishtail wildly.

"I hope Dawn's got a heavy car. Mine is really good in bad weather, but this is an ordeal. I hope we don't find her crashed into a tree somewhere."

"Me too. Get onto Pacific Avenue going south. It looks like we have to go over a couple of bridges to get to her."

Oh, great, thought Lindy and hunkered down to the task.

In a few minutes, they had left the large buildings of Casino Row. Sleet turned to snow as they drove past the small shops and houses on the outskirts of town. Broken branches littered the street. Snow was beginning to pile up along the curb, but the street surface was slick with a combination of ice and slush.

It took twenty minutes just to get to the bridge. At this rate they would be gone well over an hour. Lindy slowed down at the approach to the bridge, frowning as she concentrated on keeping the Volvo in the single lane. It didn't occur to her that there should have been more lanes, until she saw the bridge itself. Her eyes widened. Not the four-lane superstructure she had taken for granted, but two narrow lanes that rose into a dense gray layer of fog.

She eased her foot down on the brake and shifted into second, then began inching up the bridge. She almost missed the tiny sentry post at the midpoint. She carefully came to a stop but overshot the tollbooth by several feet. She didn't dare try backing up, so she lowered the window and stuck her head out into the elements.

At first, the booth appeared deserted. She wouldn't blame the attendant for taking the day off. It was a wonder that the little house hadn't already been blown away. The top of the toll booth door slid open and an arm stretched toward her.

"How much?" she yelled.

The voice at the other end of the arm answered something, but Lindy could only make out the word cents. She handed him a dollar. "Keep the change." She closed the window and proceeded cautiously to the other side. She didn't breathe until they were on solid ground again. Except that it wasn't solid. To each side, marshes stretched out as far as she could see, which wasn't very far. Stalks of cattails harpooned the flakes of snow as they drifted toward the water. Billboards stood on stilts in the mud, but their advertisements were blocked by a dense curtain of white.

Lindy hunched forward over the steering wheel. She stared out the windshield, trying to find a yellow line, oncoming headlights, something by which to navigate. The mother in her told her to turn back and let the police look for Dawn. She would have been furious if Cliff or Annie or Glen had tried to drive under these conditions.

And this thought, which should have deterred her from such a rash act, was exactly what sealed her determination to go on. Her children were grown, living away from home and didn't look for her permission anymore, and Glen—well, she no longer had any say in what he did.

"How many more bridges?" asked Lindy.

"Looks like there's just one more. But where in the hell are we? There's nothing out there. Just green stuff, brown stuff, icky stuff and an occasional trailer. Where are all the luxury homes?"

"Packed up and gone to Florida," said Lindy. "Actually I think they're out there. We just can't see them. I can barely find the edge of the road. This is turning into more than a few minutes there and back."

"Sorry," said Rose.

It was so humbly and simply said that Lindy had to force herself to keep her eyes on the road. This was not like Rose at all. She must be really worried.

Ahead, a haze of floating lights came into view. Minutes later, they were driving past storefronts, hastily being closed up and shuttered over by owners bundled up against the cold. A black SUV was idling in a parking space, black smoke puffing out of the muffler as a man scraped a two-inch layer of snow from its windows. Farther along the sidewalk, which was no longer discernible from the street, several cars were blanketed in white, either abandoned to the storm or waiting for more optimistic owners to claim them.

Abruptly, they were past the town and back into the marshes. There was no traffic on the road. They drove in silence, trying to ignore the alien landscape.

A solitary light was the only warning of the next bridge. This time Lindy began braking earlier and managed to stop at the window of the tollbooth.

The window slid open, and she felt a meager wisp of warm air from the space heater inside. The attendant wore a knit cap pulled low over his ears and topped with a red baseball cap. An immense black beard hid his mouth.

"Thirty-five cents," he said. "I hope you're on your way home or planning to stay wherever you're headed. Everybody that can get out already has. I'm closing the bridge."

"Why?" asked Lindy.

Rose leaned toward the driver's window. "We're only going to be a minute. Can't you wait for us?"

The man chewed on his mustache. "Maybe five minutes. She's gonna freeze up and it'll be too dangerous to drive. If you can get back before I get the barricades up and it hasn't gotten worse, you can get back over. Otherwise, hope you got a warm place to stay. Radio says they're expecting six to thirty inches. What kind of weather forecast is that, I ask you? The difference between a pain in the butt and a blizzard." He shook his head. "A blizzard no less," he continued as Lindy handed him the change. "Haven't had a blizzard since '96. You be careful, ya hear?"

A blizzard?

"In that case," said Rose, "can you direct us to Mariposa Lane?"

"Sure. Go to the Getty station and turn left. That's Ocean View. Winds around a bit. Right after the first cul-de-sac make a right and Mariposa should be the next left. It's a short street. Don't get lost, or I won't be here to let you across." The man stepped out and walked to the front of the tollbooth. Lindy could just see the orange sawhorse as he waited for them to pass.

The Getty station was easy to find, though all the lights had been turned off and sawhorses barricaded the entrance. Lindy turned left, hoping that she was on Ocean View, because she couldn't read the street sign.

"Keep your eyes out for a cul-de-sac," she told Rose as they followed the dark meandering street. In the distance, a solitary house had turned on its Christmas lights. Red, blue, green like miniature footlights behind a white scrim of snow.

"I think that was the cul-de-sac," said Rose so shrilly that Lindy jumped and the car swerved. She fought to keep it on the road, pumping the brake as she made the right turn. It was a battle lost before it was begun. The Volvo slid sideways across the street and came to a stop, inches short of a telephone pole.

Lindy and Rose let out simultaneous sighs of relief. Lindy shifted into reverse and stepped gingerly on the accelerator. Nothing but the spinning of wheels. Back to drive, again to reverse. All it did was mire them farther into the snowbank.

She looked at Rose. "I guess we go on foot from here. If Dawn isn't there, we may have to engage in a little B and E. The bridge is probably closed by now, and I don't want to be found frozen behind the wheel tomorrow morning. Grab the cell phone. We'll call Jeremy and tell him where we are. If we can get any reception."

Rose lifted the phone from the dashboard and looked ruefully at Lindy.

"Don't you dare start apologizing," Lindy warned. "I don't think I've ever heard you apologize in the year I've known you. You've got a reputation to maintain." She grinned a grin at Rose that had absolutely no humor behind it. She just hoped Rose couldn't see through it. "Lead on, Commodore Perry."

Lindy locked the car, and she and Rose started on foot down Mariposa Lane. Lindy waited on the street while Rose tramped up to a deserted house to read the address.

"Number fourteen. Dawn's is number twenty-two, so it can't be more than five more houses, right?" Rose turned to look down the street. A gob of frozen snow flew off the point of her hat and hit Lindy square in the face. She jerked away in reaction, and her Nikes slid out from under her. She hit the snow with a grunt of surprise, then she began to laugh. Rose dragged her back up and they fought on, arms linked, into the darkness.

Four houses later, they saw a dim glow of light shining through a picture window. As they moved closer, the shapes of two cars in the driveway emerged before them. Lindy gave herself a mental kick for not asking Rebo what kind of car he had seen Katja get into.

There were no tracks leading to the door. Either this was the wrong house and no one had come or gone since the storm began, or else the snow was piling up at an alarming rate. Lindy refused to even think "blizzard." She was wasting time that she could be spending with Bill on a useless quest to help a completely selfish person. But it was for Rose, not Dawn, and when the dust—or in this case snow—cleared, your friends were the most important things you had.

She poked at Rose's sleeve and shrugged a question at her. They both peered around at the other houses. All were dark. They started toward the light, Rose leading the way. Lindy trudged behind her, ankle deep in snow, her hands numb beneath her leather gloves, her ears and hair matted with freezing snow.

The house was a small cape, not a luxury beach house. There was a gabled roof over the stoop and someone had wrapped tinsel around the support posts. One of the strands had come loose and whipped recklessly in the wind.

Rose knocked on the door while Lindy tried futilely to stamp feeling back into her feet. They waited. No one came to the door, but they heard muffled voices from inside. They leaned closer to the door trying to make out the words against the wind that chuffed behind them. Rose knocked louder and was met with a sudden silence. The light went off.

"That sounded like Dawn," said Rose and reached for the doorknob.

"I hope you're right. I don't want to get shot for trespassing at Christmas. Bill will kill me." She stopped, shocked at her own words. She should have said "Glen will kill me." But sometimes truth had a way of kicking you in the ass when you least expected it.

The door opened to Rose's hand. "Dawn?" she called. "It's just Rose and Lindy. We came to help."

They waited. There was no response. Rose stepped inside before Lindy could stop her. "Dawn!"

Lindy had no choice but to follow. She shoved the door closed and groped for a light switch. She hoped this wouldn't be her last action on earth as she imagined a big burly, beer-drinking man with a shotgun waiting for them in the dark. The light popped on and exposed the two women, huddled together in front of the unlit fireplace, staring back at Lindy and Rose.

"Dawn," Rose said on a deep sigh that was part relief, part exasperation.

She and Lindy stepped farther inside the room. It was warm and smelled faintly of coffee and cinnamon.

Dawn and Katja pressed closer together. The metal fireplace tools clanked as one of them stepped back against them. Dawn let out a cry. Then she looked frantically around the room. "Did you bring the police?" she demanded in a desperate voice.

"Of course not," said Rose. "Randy was worried about you. We were worried about you."

"Randy? Does he know where we are?"

"No. No one knows where—" Rose bit off the rest of the sentence as Lindy shot her a warning look. It was too late.

"Are you sure?" asked Dawn.

Katja was looking from one woman to the other. She hadn't said a word. Lindy wondered if she understood what was being said.

"Yes, but, Dawn, what the hell are you doing? You're going to be in serious trouble. The police are looking for Katja. You can't hide her from them. It's illegal."

Lindy no longer worried about Katja's ability to understand English. Katja glared at Rose with a spark of such violence that Lindy caught her breath. Then Katja crumpled, throwing herself into Dawn's arms, crying like a child.

Dawn fell into an upholstered chair, cradling Katja against her and smoothing her hair. The chair was a faded green, shabby and comfortable like the rest of the furniture: a matching couch positioned at an angle on the other side of the fireplace, a square end table with a fringed lamp and telephone, a scuffed red leather ottoman and an oval maple dining table that stood off to one side. It seemed an odd choice of interior design for a woman who usually decked herself out in spandex and false eyelashes.

But today Dawn's eyes were rimmed with smudged mascara and her face was puffy. She had been crying. Her knit blouse gaped open where a button was missing. She was barefooted. One of her high heels was lying next to the fireplace. The other lay at Lindy's feet where she stood near the front door.

Either Dawn was a particularly sloppy housekeeper, thought Lindy, or there had been some serious shoe activity not too long ago. Had the voices they heard from the porch been voices raised in anger? Had it turned physical?

"Dawn," said Lindy in as gentle a voice as she could muster, "you need to let the police know that you've located Katja."

Katja stiffened, but Dawn held her tight. "That's impossible. They'll think she murdered Shane and, of course, she didn't."

"Then she needs to explain that to them. They'll have translators if she's uncomfortable speaking in English. But you can't keep hiding her. It will only make it look worse."

Katja pushed Dawn's arms away and jumped to her feet. " I-di-en't do eet. I won't go." She looked wildly around the room.

"Don't try to run," said Lindy. "None of us is going anywhere. There's a blizzard raging outside. My car is stuck in a snowbank, and they've closed the bridge to the mainland. Just stay calm and tell us what happened."

Katja shook her head, every muscle taut as if she might bolt for the door. Lindy readied herself to stop her if she did. She felt Rose alert beside her.

"She didn't know anything about it," said Dawn. "And I didn't know where she was until last night. She called me so I wouldn't worry about her. She didn't even know that Shane was dead. She just came here to get away from everything."

"To theenk," interposed Katja. "I came to theenk. It was so horrible. What happened. About the dresses."

An alarm rang in Lindy's mind. Rebo had seen her leaving the hotel before the slashed dresses were discovered. Had she known about them, or had she merely mixed up her noun endings in an unfamiliar language?

"The dress, I mean."

"She was so distraught when I told her about Shane that I had to come to her." Dawn slumped back in the chair and passed her hand over her already ravaged makeup. "Oh, I just don't know what to do."

"You can't turn me in," cried Katja. "They will . . . keel me." She snapped her head toward the picture window. "What was that? I saw something outside. They have come to keel me." Her eyes were wild with fear.

"No one is going to kill you," said Lindy. "And it's just the wind." The lights flickered. For a second, the room went dark, then the lights came on again.

"Oh, damn," said Dawn, heaving to her feet. "This always happens in bad weather. I'd better get out the candles."

Lindy gritted her teeth. "We need to call somebody and tell them we're okay."

"We can't; the telephone is out. There's probably a line down somewhere."

Rose picked up the phone from the end table, while Dawn opened the drawer, looking for candles. "Dead," she confirmed and put it back down. She reached into her coat pocket. Katja cowered back. She brought out Lindy's cell phone and punched in a number. The expression on her face said it all. They were either out of range or the weather was too bad to get through. Lindy felt like crying. She didn't want to be stuck here until the roads were cleared. That could be days away.

"I'm leaving," said Katja.

"You can't," said Lindy. "None of us are going anywhere."

"Oh, yes, I am."

The lights flickered off again. This time the darkness lasted longer. Katja was a mere shadow, moving toward the fireplace. There was a rattling sound.

The lights flickered back on. Katja held the fireplace poker in both hands. "I'm going," she repeated. "Get out of my way." She took a step forward, feinting with the poker. Lindy stepped to the side, but flashed a quick look toward Rose, who was standing between Katja and the door. Together, they would be able to stop her. It would be sure death to flee into the storm.

Katja took slow steps toward the door, the poker jabbing the air. Dawn sobbed in the background, her hands still in the candle drawer.

There was a sudden gust of snow-spiked wind, and Lindy turned automatically toward the door. A figure loomed on the threshold. The four women shrieked as a man stepped inside. Snow clung to his coat and his cheeks and ears were pink with cold.

Damn, thought Lindy. *He's done it again.* Riding in like the cavalry. It was amazing. And it pissed her off.

"Ladies." Bill slammed the door behind him. He addressed the room, but he was looking straight at Katja.

Chapter
Seventeen

"Don't—don't come eeny closer," said Katja, brandishing the poker.

Bill pinned her with a look that had it been aimed at Lindy would have made her squirm. "Cut the accent. I'm not in a very good mood."

"Dawn, help me," Katja pleaded.

"I'm not going to hurt you," said Bill, his eyes shifting between Katja and Dawn. "But you need to put down the poker, Miss Karen Anderson of Millburn, New Jersey."

Katja screeched and lunged at him. Bill merely stepped out of the way, and Katja stumbled into Rose. Rose twisted the poker from the girl's hand as she fell to the floor. Rose twirled the poker like a baton and offered it to Bill.

"Nice piece of choreography, you two," said Lindy, vowing that moment to sign up for a martial arts class as soon as she got home.

Bill's attention shifted to Dawn. "Move your hands slowly from the drawer," he said. "And put them where I can see them."

Dawn didn't move. "But she didn't kill Shane."

"Now, Dawn. Lindy, move away from her." His voice was steady, hypnotic.

Lindy stepped back. Katja screamed at the same time, and Dawn's hand came away from the drawer. Bill lunged toward her, but she was already aiming the pistol at Lindy's midsection. Bill seemed to hover in the air, then stopped dead still.

The pistol was small, but Dawn's hand was shaking so much that the nose of the gun jerked spasmodically in the air. She grasped it with both hands trying to steady it.

"No one move," Bill said quietly, modulating his voice to a soothing pitch that Lindy would never have believed possible. It didn't matter. She wasn't going anywhere. She was trying not to breathe.

Dawn looked wildly around. "Please," she said. "Just leave us alone."

"Dawn," said Bill in the same quiet voice, "you don't want to go out in the storm. The roads are very dangerous. I don't want you or Katja to get hurt."

Lindy wondered why he had gone back to using Katja, instead of Karen. Was she Russian or just a Jersey girl?

Dawn seemed to waiver. The gun stopped bouncing in the air, and Dawn's shoulders sagged.

Lindy wondered if she should try to move away. She was vaguely aware of Rose and Katja near the door, but she couldn't take her eyes off the pistol.

"It ees a trick," shouted Katja. "Hurry, Dawn, we must get away."

Dawn snapped out of her indecision and lifted the gun once again, only this time it was pointing at Bill. "Move out of my way—please."

Bill stepped aside, a controlled movement, but even from where Lindy stood, she could feel the concentration in his body. *Please*, she begged whatever spirits were listening, *Don't let him do anything that will get him killed.*

Katja grabbed coats off a coatrack by the door, and she and Dawn backed out of the house.

Rose moved toward the door. "What are you waiting for? We have to go after them."

"No," Bill commanded. He let out his breath and continued more easily. "Let them go. They won't get far in that car and the bridge is closed. I had to strong-arm—" He stopped when he saw Rose's raised eyebrows. "Verbally strong-arm the attendant to let me cross.

"Are you all right?" he asked Lindy.

She nodded. She was alive and so was he. That was all right.

Bill crossed to the window and looked out. Rose and Lindy moved up behind him. Dawn's car was fishtailing down the street back toward the bridge.

"Stupid," said Bill. "Call 911 and tell them to be on the lookout for a Ford hatchback."

"Can't," said Lindy. "The phone's out and the cell phone isn't picking up a signal."

"Christ," said Bill through clenched teeth. He raked strands of wet hair off his face and looked from Lindy to Rose. "If I thought they could survive the night stuck in their car, I'd leave them out there and let the local police pick them up in the morning."

The lights flickered again. This time they didn't come back on.

"Goddammit," Bill said from the darkness. He pushed past them and headed for the door. "Stay here."

"No," said Lindy. "It's dangerous out there."

"Then come on. You and Rose can protect me."

Lindy and Rose followed him outside, but there was no Honda.

"Where is your car?" asked Lindy.

"Next street. Near the Volvo. That's what took me so long to get here. You weren't in the car. I didn't know which way you had gone. I was afraid you were dead."

They went single file, back toward the main street, wading through snow that was now shin deep. Rose led the way. She was the only one who was wearing boots. Bill and Lindy followed, stepping in her footprints. The wind at least had died down and only a few snowflakes drifted slowly to the ground. Lindy could hear Bill muttering under his breath.

"It looks like it's letting up," she said. Bill didn't deign to answer. Rose didn't even look her way.

They nearly bumped into the cars before they saw them. The

Volvo was just a pile of snow. The Honda was covered in an inch of white powder. They climbed inside, while Bill scraped off the windows. Lindy sat in the front; Rose sat in back with her elbows resting on the back of Lindy's seat.

Bill tossed the scraper into the car and got in. "Put on your seat belts," he said. "And keep your eyes open for a mangled hatchback." Rose slipped back against the seat without a word. Lindy reached for her seat belt.

He threw the Honda into reverse, backed down the street and into the cul-de-sac. Then he shifted gears and drove cautiously toward the Getty station. All the while Lindy and Rose peered futilely out the windows looking for Dawn's Ford. At the Getty station, they turned right toward the bridge. The Honda swung to the side. Bill released the steering wheel as it spun into a skid. Slowly, he guided it to a stop, and they all breathed an audible sigh of relief. Bill hunched over the steering wheel, stretching his shoulder muscles, then he straightened up and they were heading for the bridge.

They were in sight of the bridge and there was still no sign of Dawn and Katja. Lindy thought they must have gotten away. Bill eased down on the brake, but the Honda kept sliding forward. He pumped the pedal. The orange sawhorse rose in front of them. Bill continued to pump the brakes, his eyes fixed ahead. There was a crunch as they hit the sawhorse. It splintered and the car came to a stop.

"Shit," said Bill. "Shit." He hit the steering wheel.

Lindy cringed and crossed her fingers, hoping fervently that the Honda wasn't damaged. She glanced at Bill, but he was looking past her into the marshes.

"What?" asked Lindy, peering into the dark. Then she saw it. A second sawhorse lay on its side on the embankment. Dawn and Katja had not made it across the bridge. The edge of the guardrail had been ripped off, and Dawn's hatchback lay in the marsh. The trunk was pointing toward the sky. The hood was under water. There was no sign of life.

Bill was already out of the car and running across the road. Lindy and Rose jumped out and followed. They stopped at the top of the embankment and looked down.

"Stay back," said Bill. He pushed Rose and Lindy back onto the roadway and ran back to the Honda. He reached inside and the trunk popped open. Seconds later, he was coming back, armed with an industrial-sized flashlight that made a glaring circle against the snow. A coil of rope was looped over his shoulder; he was shoving a plastic shopping bag into his jacket pocket.

"Always prepared," mumbled Rose.

There was a creak. The hatchback wobbled in the mud, then slid farther down into the muck. The passenger door cracked open, then was pushed fully back. A pale face showed over the edge of the car.

"Help," choked Katja. "Help."

"Stay calm," said Bill. "Where is Dawn?"

"She's stuck. And unconscious." Katja grabbed the edge of the car and tried to climb out. The car shifted. She screamed as she slid into the water.

Rose jolted forward. "It can't be that deep. We've got to help."

"We are. But there's no reason for us all to get wet. Stay where you are." Bill shoved the flashlight at Lindy. "Shine it over here." He aimed the beam toward the guardrail. Lindy held it as steady as she could, while he tied one end of the rope to it.

"Help me," cried Katja, sounding hysterical. "We're sinking."

"You're not sinking. Just hold still." Bill yanked at the rope, testing the guardrail. Then uncoiling it as he went, he waded into the marsh.

His progress was slow, the water was over his knees. Each step made a horrible sucking noise. And Katja continue to wail as she clung to the door. Bill skirted the car, trying not to cause it to sink any farther. Before he could reach for Katja, Katja grabbed for him. It knocked him off balance and they both fell against the hatchback. It groaned, seem to teeter, then sank farther into the water.

Bill struggled back to his feet and dragged Katja away from the car. "Stay calm, damn it. I'm going to tie this rope around you. Lindy and Rose will pull you to shore."

Katja became utterly still, her eyes round with fear as Bill tied the rope around her waist. But when he tried to push her in the direction of the embankment, she clung to his neck. He peeled her away and threw her into the water.

"Okay. Pull on the rope. When she's on dry land, throw the rope back, then frisk her. Thoroughly." Keeping a safe distance, he hauled Katja out of the water and gave her a push toward the bridge. Lindy and Rose pulled. She fell, flailing at stalks of sedge. Her face disappeared beneath the water, only to reappear seconds later. She gasped, choked, started coughing, but they kept reeling her in. As soon as she was within arm's reach, Rose hefted her onto the embankment. But it took both of them to get her back onto the bridge.

While Rose searched the shivering girl for weapons, Lindy retrained the flashlight on the car. There was no sign of Bill. Her heart jumped to her throat. "Bill!" she croaked. "Bill, where are you?" She was about to drop the flashlight and go after him when he emerged from the inside of the car. Dawn was draped over his shoulder.

He dumped her across the car. The hatchback sank under the extra weight. Lindy bit back a cry.

"Throw me the rope."

Rose tossed the rope. It hit the car but slipped back into the water. There was another creak from the hatchback.

"Easy, Rose, you're doing fine," said Bill. His words were distorted. Probably because his teeth were chattering. He must be freezing.

Rose threw it again. This time it hit Dawn and rested across her back. "Good g-girl," Bill said and began to tie it around Dawn.

Lindy tried to train the flashlight on the knot, but her hands were shaking so much from cold and fear for Bill that the spot of light danced crazily in the dark.

"Okay, let's see if we can get her out. I can't carry her. Too much weight for the mud. I'll keep her head out of the water. You pull." Rose pulled while Lindy held the flashlight on Bill and the unconscious woman. He was hunched over holding Dawn's shoulders as he tried to guide her toward land. Lindy could tell it was a struggle. He had only managed a few steps when he straightened up. "Goddammit," he yelled.

"What?" cried Lindy. "Bill, are you okay?"

"Lost my damn shoe."

She wanted to laugh with relief, but Bill had started up again and it took all her concentration to hold the flashlight steady. After what seemed an eon, they dragged Dawn on to the embankment.

"Get her into the car. There's a blanket in the trunk," said Bill. He stepped back into the marsh.

"Come back," said Lindy. "What are you doing?"

He didn't reply, just kept moving toward the car. She shined the light after him. He disappeared over the side. The hatchback shifted under his weight.

"Bill!"

There was no answer. She moved the beam about, frantically searching for him. She was vaguely aware of Rose carrying Dawn, a car door slamming, but she couldn't find Bill. She swept the beam over the water. Nothing but grasses and black water.

"Lindy!" The command was sharp. She jerked the flashlight back to the car. Bill was crawling up over the side. "Throw me the end of the rope." He sounded tired and frozen. She laid the flashlight on the ground so that its beam continued to shine in the direction of the car. Her fingers were numb. She didn't know how she would get them around the rope, much less throw it.

There was a cracking sound from the water.

"Lindy. You could hurry."

She looked for Rose, but she was in the car ministering to Dawn. She threw out a prayer and tossed the rope. Bill's hand grabbed it out of the air and he wrapped it around his wrist. Lindy held on to the rope, every muscle tight. Bill pulled himself forward just as the hatchback rolled onto its back. The impact knocked him forward. For a second the rope went slack. In the next second, it was nearly yanked from her hands. She grabbed as hard as she could and the rope burned across her palms before it stopped. Bill was only a few feet away. He took two more steps, flung the rope onto the embankment and collapsed onto the ground. He lay there breathing heavily and shivering.

Lindy moved toward him, but he pushed to his knees and stood up. He was completely wet. His car coat hung heavily from his shoulders, dripping water. He was only wearing one shoe. Lindy burst into tears of relief.

He was shaking with cold, but he stopped to untie the rope from the guardrail. His fingers were clumsy.

"Forget the rope," said Lindy. "We can come back for it tomorrow." She started dragging him toward the Honda.

"M-m-might need it."

"Then I'll get it. You get in the car where it's warm." She shoved him forward, then went back to retrieve the rope, cursing under her breath as she did. The knot was wet and had tightened under the strain. It was impossible to untie. She went back to the Honda on numb feet.

Rose had the heat turned up to full blast. Bill was sitting in the passenger's seat. His coat was gone and Lindy was thankful to see that at least his sweater seemed to be dry. Nothing else was.

"Do you have a knife?"

Bill fumbled with his pants pocket but couldn't manage to get his hand inside it. Lindy moved his hand away and plunged hers into the pocket. She pulled out a Swiss army knife and caught Bill's grin as she straightened up.

"Gr-r-r-r," she said.

She cut the rope from the guardrail and sprinted back to the car. At least it had stopped snowing; maybe they could get back to Atlantic City after all. She threw the rope into the trunk and slammed it down. She slid into the driver's side and glanced at Bill.

"Now what? Should we try the bridge?"

"No."

Lindy swallowed her disappointment. "Dawn's?"

"Yes. You'll have to drive."

Lindy had to fight the urge to bang on the steering wheel. It was probably only four o'clock, but the cloud cover made it seem like night. That meant at least twelve or fourteen hours stuck in a blizzard with a possible murderer and an angry Bill. Well, blizzard or no, they were getting out of here first thing the next morning.

She took one last hopeless look at the bridge and sighed. "I guess there's no other way. I hope you're not too uptight about your car. Here goes." She shifted into reverse and the Honda lurched back.

Bill closed his eyes and continued to shake.

Chapter
Eighteen

Lindy never knew how she managed to get the Honda back to Dawn's house. She was too busy being angry at the stupidity of the situation. Dawn had returned to consciousness during the ride, but no one spoke. The only sounds from the car were sighs, chattering teeth, and the whir of the heater.

She even made the turn into Mariposa Lane and brought the car to a neat stop in front of Dawn's house. She left it in the street, several feet from the curb, where it would have the most likely chance of being extricated the next morning.

Rose and Katja helped Dawn from the backseat. Bill opened the glove compartment, pulled the grocery bag from his coat pocket, and put it inside. It landed with a clunk.

"What's that?" asked Lindy, unable to stifle her curiosity.

"The murder weapon, if my guess is right."

"Dawn's pistol? Shane was shot? Why didn't you tell me?"

"If I don't die from exposure, I will." He shut the glove compartment and reached for his keys. "Pop the trunk, will you?" She did, while Bill locked the glove compartment.

Bill limped around the car, cursing the loss of his shoe. He pulled the flashlight and a gym bag out of the trunk and slammed it shut.

Then he and Lindy trekked after the others across the lawn of snow to the dark, empty house.

At least it was warm inside. It would grow cold quickly with no electricity to run the furnace. Lindy hoped the fireplace was real. She'd burn the dining table if she had to.

Katja and Rose deposited Dawn onto the sofa, while Lindy hung up Bill's waterlogged jacket.

Rose lit candles, placed them in holders strategically around the room, and took one into the bedroom. A few minutes later, she returned with an assortment of clothes and blankets and turned to Bill. "I don't think you'll fit into Dawn's capri pants, but there's a bathrobe on the bed."

Bill lifted the gym bag. "I always travel with a change of clothes."

Lindy raised her eyes at him. Always prepared, right. For sleepovers with beautiful women, she bet.

"For weekends in Connecticut. Sometimes I leave straight from work."

Connecticut. Great. Snowy nights by a warm fire, brandy and . . .

"When I visit my mother." He flashed Lindy a smile.

Damn him. Fortunately, she was too cold to be embarrassed.

He went into the bedroom while they dressed Dawn, and Katja changed. Rose was dry, and Lindy was only superficially wet where she had dragged Bill onto shore. Rose tossed her a pair of black stretch pants, which she accepted gratefully.

"Everybody decent?" asked a voice from the bedroom doorway.

"Never have been," said Rose. "Why start now?"

Bill stepped into the room, wearing jeans, several layers of sweatshirts and a pair of running shoes. He held one battered, mud-covered street shoe in his hand. He crossed to the fireplace and put it on the hearth.

Lindy thought about his coat, his shoes, the trousers and sweater that had been ruined in the water. He'd probably never want to take a vacation with her again.

"How is she?" asked Bill, gesturing toward Dawn.

Dawn roused enough to say, "I'm okay. Thanks for getting me out."

"Hmm. Better watch her for signs of concussion. Any wood for the fireplace?"

"Some kindling in that bucket. Duraflames in the kitchen. Bottom cabinet to the right of the sink."

Turning on the flashlight, Bill went into the kitchen and came back carrying two Duraflame logs. He set one in the fireplace and took a match from the hearth.

"The nice thing about fake logs is that they catch without a fuss. But they don't give off a lot of heat." He tossed on a handful of kindling. "If it gets any colder we may have to requisition a chair or two."

No one protested. The log was soon blazing, looking awfully cheery in spite of the morose atmosphere.

"I'll see if I can find some coffee and a pan to heat water," offered Lindy.

"Look for some marshmallows," called Rose. "We can roast them over the fire and sing 'Kumbaya' while we're waiting to be rescued."

Lindy took the flashlight and went to the kitchen. There were pans and coffee, even sugar and milk. But no marshmallows. She pulled out a rack from the apartment-sized oven and put her stash on it.

When she carried it into the living room, Bill was sitting in the green chair, leaning toward the fire. She knelt down on the hearth and rigged up a makeshift grill by balancing the rack across the fireplace irons. She put the pan of water on to boil.

She stood up and caught Bill looking at her stretch pants. Well, maybe it wasn't the pants that kept him enthralled. She never wore stretch pants. But maybe she would from now on.

"It will probably take a while," she said to him. "Are you okay?"

"Those were particularly comfortable shoes," he replied. He had trouble getting the *particularly* out. His facial muscles must still be numb. She clamped down on the thought that she might have had about that if she had allowed it to get that far.

"Sorry," she said. "I'll buy you another pair. And a jacket, too. What do we do now?"

"Wait for first light and try to make it back to Atlantic City."

"In a blizzard?"

"Doesn't look like a blizzard. The snow has already stopped."

"Famous last words," she groused.

No one spoke until the water had boiled and Lindy passed out mugs of steaming coffee.

"Umm. Chewy just like I like it," said Rose.

Lindy handed a cup to Bill and sat down on the hearth next to his chair.

"Now that we're all cozy," he said, "maybe you ladies will tell me what I missed."

He was met with four blank faces.

"I'd like to ask a question," began Lindy.

Bill shot her an exasperated look, which she conveniently misinterpreted as consent for her to continue.

"What did you mean about Katja being from Millburn?"

"She isn't Russian. Never was. Never will be. Her parents don't live in Brooklyn. Her father works for the county sanitation commission. Her mother is a Jersey housewife."

"It was my idea," said Dawn wearily. "I thought it would jumpstart Katja's career. Everyone's marking the Russians over American couples. I didn't think she should be held back because her name didn't end in -ova."

"Eet would have worked too," interrupted Katja, still clinging to her accent.

"Did Shane know?" asked Lindy. If he had been in on the ruse, then there would be no reason to kill him. But what if he had just found out and threatened to expose them? She saw a quick exchange of glances between Dawn and Katja.

"No," said Dawn. "I thought the fewer people who knew, the better would be the chance of us pulling it off."

"Who did know?" asked Bill.

"Just me and Katja. She answered an ad for teachers about four years ago. She had studied ballet. You practically have to to win these days. After her first day of training, I knew she had a shot at a championship, so we concocted a little story." Dawn sighed and leaned her head against the cushions. "I'm so tired."

Rose flicked an anxious look toward Bill. He stood up and walked over to Dawn. She shrugged away from him. Katja looked ready to attack.

"I just want to look at your pupils. Open up."

Dawn opened her eyes. Bill lifted one eyelid, then the other. "You seem okay. Get some sleep. Rose will wake you up every half hour to make sure you're all right."

Bill took her coffee cup and Dawn curled up on the couch. Rose tucked a blanket around her. Katja took the opportunity to press herself against the opposite corner.

Rose sat down between the two women. "What's going to happen?"

Bill shrugged. "We have to take them back. Then it's up to Andrew and the ACPD."

"But I don't know anytheeng," whined Katja.

He cut off her response with a curt wave of his hand. "Then you tell them you don't know anything. But I wouldn't waste that fake accent on them. They're the ones who told me."

Katja smiled sheepishly at him. Lindy rolled her eyes. Women were always fawning on him. So why had he never remarried? The thought startled her. Her hand jerked and coffee sloshed out of her cup.

Bill darted a glance in her direction, then returned his attention to Katja.

"Sorry," said Katja. "But I've gotten so used to it, it's hard to stop."

"That's why the Russian girls think you're a snob, isn't it?" asked Lindy. "The real reason you ignored them is that you knew they'd catch you out if you talked to them."

"I studied Russian in high school, so I knew a few phrases when I went to work for Dawn. I've got a set of Berlitz tapes at home. But

I'm not good enough to carry on a real conversation." Katja shrugged. "Well, it was nice while it lasted. Do you mind if I get something to eat?"

"Rose will go with you," said Bill.

The two of them went into the kitchen, carrying one of the candles. The sounds of rummaging could be heard a few seconds later.

"Do you think one of them did it?" asked Lindy, after shooting a look to make sure Dawn was asleep.

"It doesn't matter what I think. It's someone else's job to find out."

"But aren't you curious?"

He looked down at her. The look lasted a long time, but Lindy couldn't read the meaning behind it. Finally he said, "Anybody can be curious. But it takes a trained team and long, draining hours of investigation to come up with real answers. And having external influences (Lindy read that as "nosy women") just makes the job more difficult. We're not asking any questions directly pertaining to the murder. Understood?"

Chagrined, Lindy nodded. He did think she was incompetent. "Look, we weren't trying to mess up the investigation. Dawn hadn't been seen since last night. Rose was worried. She and Dawn have been friends for a long time. She just wanted to come out to see if she was here. We were just going to check on her and come right back. You would never have even known we had gone." Lindy frowned. "How *did* you find us?"

Bill cleared his throat.

"Don't you dare lie."

"What makes you think I was going to lie?"

"Trust me. I know."

Bill sighed. "I was just coming back to the hotel, from, uh—"

"The police station where you were talking to your friend Andrew, and?"

He looked away, but not before she saw his suppressed smile, and she knew she had him.

"And?"

"I was coming back to the hotel. I was trying to get there before the rehearsal was over so maybe we could have lunch. But I was running late because of the weather. I had just rounded the corner to the hotel when I saw Rose dressed like a sherpa—where did she get that hat?—headed for the parking lot across the street. So instead of handing my car over to the valet, I pulled out of the hotel and watched. And what to my wondering eyes did appear? You running across the street to meet her. So I followed you."

"You could have caught up to us and just asked where we were going."

"And you would have told me you were going to the mall for panty hose. Unlike you, I can't tell when you're lying."

Sucker punch. She felt like Wily Coyote, one minute running on the cliff, the next hanging in space. "I—I never lie to you. Not intentionally anyway."

She looked at Bill. He wasn't smiling. He wasn't frowning. His face was expressionless. Damn. What had she said this time?

"And you weren't planning to conceal Katja's whereabouts from the authorities?"

"Of course not," she said defensively. "Well, actually I hadn't thought that far ahead. And now it's a moot point."

"Yes, it is."

Rose and Katja returned from the kitchen, carrying armloads of food. Bill shot Lindy a warning look. Rose arranged a plate of crackers, slices of cheese wrapped in plastic, and a jar of gherkins on the ottoman, while Katja took a bag of potato chips and sat down in her corner of the couch.

"Eat up," said Rose. "It was the best I could do. Katja's taste in food is on the Jersey side of haute cuisine." Bill and Lindy declined. From the sofa came methodical crunching sounds as Katja made her way through the bag of chips. Rose sighed, folded a cheese slice into quarters and put it on top of a round cracker. She wandered over to the end table and picked up the cell phone. She punched in some numbers and listened. Then she put it back on the table. "Nothing. Are we going to sit like this all night?"

"You and Lindy can sleep if you want," said Bill. "I'll watch these two. These are the last of my dry clothes, and I have no intention of chasing them through the snow again."

A slow glimmer of a smile lit Rose's face. "I can watch them. You two could—sleep."

"Right," said Bill.

Rose's smile faded. "Just a suggestion. I'll look for some cards or a Parcheesi board."

Lindy glanced at Bill. He was watching Katja like he expected her to bolt any minute. Katja was obliviously munching chips. Her incarceration certainly didn't seem to be affecting her appetite. Dancers were slaves to junk food, it was true, but Enrico was right. She should be dieting instead of stuffing her face with carbs and grease. Of course, if she really had murdered Shane, it wouldn't matter if she was fat. She wouldn't need to fit into a ball gown ever again.

Lindy shifted on the hearth. Butt bones and bricks were not a good combination. If they were going to sit here for hours, she needed a softer seat. Bill had appropriated the only comfortable chair in the room, though he, himself, looked anything but comfortable. There was no question that he had taken charge of this operation.

"I know you're upset with me," said Lindy.

"This just isn't the way I expected to spend our first night together."

"Cards and Parcheesi," announced Rose. She was lugging pillows and a comforter from the other room. She dumped them on the floor and went back into the bedroom. Lindy stared into the livid colors cast by the Duraflame. She didn't look up until Rose returned with another armload of blankets and several magazines. "Just like a slumber party," she said.

"Cut the crap, Rose," Bill snapped.

Lindy glanced toward him. Rose frowned, then slowly an evil smile took its place. It grew until she had to bite her lip and turn away, but not before she sneaked a wink at Lindy.

Lindy pushed up from the hearth and nearly fell, her knees creaky from cold and sitting. She reached for the arm of Bill's chair to steady herself. She grabbed Bill's arm instead. "Sorry," she mumbled, snatching her hand away. She moved to a clear space on the floor and went through a series of stretching exercises. Feeling better, she asked Rose, "Parcheesi or gin rummy?"

They played until the numbers on the cards began to swim before Lindy's eyes. Rose stretched out on the floor by the fire and fell instantly asleep. Bill sat unmoving in the chair. Probably on a slow seethe. Lindy leaned back against the edge of the couch and closed her eyes.

She didn't mean to sleep, but she was yanked from the dark by the sound of someone moving about the room. It was daylight. Bill was putting out the remains of the fire. Rose was folding blankets. Lindy stretched. Someone had put a blanket over her during the night.

"Is it morning?" she asked, stifling a yawn.

"Near enough," said Bill.

"Still no electricity?"

"No."

She looked at the dead fireplace. "I guess we're not making coffee."

"No. You can wake up the other beauties and we'll attempt the bridge."

Lindy sighed and stood up. So he wasn't a morning person. It was obvious he hadn't slept at all. The planes of this face were sharp, his eyes tired. His chin was scratchy with stubble. Not dark and shadowy like Glen's morning growth, but a light brown and, she bet, soft.

She turned away and stared out the picture window, while she stretched the kinks out of her joints and muscles. It was early, the sun just coming up. But it was sun, at last. It sparkled off the field of white that surrounded the house. In the middle of the road, the Honda was bare of snow. There was an area cleared around it. The tires had been fitted with chains.

Bill had been busy this morning, and she hadn't even heard him. Some investigator she was. He could have asked for help. But he hadn't. Too bad. She was good at shoveling snow.

Chapter
Nineteen

The Honda crunched slowly over ice-hardened asphalt. On the sides of the street, snow had piled against trees, bushes, and mailboxes, but it seemed to have stopped at six inches and not the expected thirty, for which Lindy was grateful. They just might be able to get off the island after all.

Twice they had to stop, while Rose and Lindy pushed from behind as Bill guided the car back on course.

The barricades were still positioned across the bridge. The hatchback lay on its back in the marshes, wheels facing the sky like an overturned beetle.

Bill stopped short of the bridge and got out of the car. He walked to the first barricade and scuffed at the snow, then he continued toward the tollbooth. After a few minutes, he turned and slid his way back to the car.

"We'll try it," he said, knocking the snow off his shoes.

"Are you sure this is safe?" asked Lindy.

He closed the door and gunned the engine. Taking that for an answer, Lindy shut up, so she could concentrate on gritting her teeth and clinging to the door arm. The Honda inched forward, the chains clanking beneath them.

With excruciating slowness, they climbed the rise of the bridge, the passengers as quiet and still as dummies in a safety commercial. They passed the tollbooth and started to descend. The Honda lost its grip on the road and began to slide. Bill's hands rested lightly on the steering wheel; both of his feet were steady on the floorboard. Lindy held her breath as he turned the wheel with a light touch. They luged down the incline until Lindy felt the car shudder and the wheels grip the grating of the bridge approach. Then Bill touched the accelerator and the car vaulted onto asphalt.

Lindy let out her breath. "Only one more to go," she said quietly. Beside her, Bill was silent.

The tension Lindy had felt emanating from the backseat soon changed to morose acceptance as they crept along the deserted highway. The rhythmic clank-clank of the chains was hypnotic, and several times she glanced over to make sure that Bill was fully awake.

After an interminable length of time, which had really only been twenty minutes according to the numbers on the dashboard clock, they came abruptly into the town they had passed the night before. And although no one had bothered to open for the day, a single lane had been plowed down the center of the street. Lindy blessed whichever beach dweller had the eccentricity to keep a snowplow.

The next bridge was partially cleared and open. A policeman wearing an orange vest motioned for them to stop. In the backseat, Katja whimpered. The policeman came to the window, and Lindy wondered if Bill would turn Katja over to him. Bill only listened to the man explain that they would have to wait until the two cars ahead of them were allowed to cross. Only one lane was clear. It would only be a few minutes and thanks for their patience.

Lindy raised an eyebrow at Bill. He stared out the front windshield.

They watched the first car slowly ascend the bridge, its rear end drifting from side to side like a fish in slow motion. When it disappeared over the crest of the bridge, the policeman motioned for the next to begin. Bill inched the Honda forward, they waited. At last, they started over the bridge, slowly at first, then with more speed as

Bill's hands played on the steering wheel. On the other side, they passed a truck and a station wagon waiting to be allowed onto the island. The truck bed was filled with bags of rock salt.

Bill kept the Honda in the tracks made by the cars that had preceded them. It was slow going but at least the road was flat and relatively straight. Once they had to skirt a downed power line, cordoned off with yellow tape and guarded by a police car with two Dunkin Donut coffee cups on the dashboard.

Forty minutes later, they came to Atlantic City, and the snow gave way to frozen slush. They drove through town, past trees encased in a frozen armor of ice. Branches had snapped off and were lying ragged on the ground. Windshields were covered in sheets of eye-dazzling brightness. On the sidewalks, bundled people attempted to shovel away a combination of ice and snow. In a front yard, surrounded by reflecting honeycombs of chain-link fencing, children built an ice man and threw dangerous-looking snowballs at each other.

There were no lights anywhere. Stores were dark, even those that had managed to open for business. Ahead of them, however, the lights of the casinos were running at full power, rising from behind the dark, battered town like a jeering Emerald City.

Lindy heard Bill let out a relieved sigh. She reached over and touched his shoulder. Just for moral support. Just as a thank you.

"What do we do when we get back to the hotel?" Rose's voice broke the silence and Lindy and Bill both started.

"We'll take them straight upstairs. No stops. No talking to anyone. Understood?"

No answer.

"I'll call Andrew and the CSI and ask them to meet us in Dawn's room."

At a red light, Bill reached for Lindy's cell phone. He punched in numbers, then left a message for Andrew Dean to call back or to meet them at the hotel.

The cell phone rang as they were turning into the valet parking area of the hotel. Bill listened without a word, then disconnected.

"He said to keep them until he can get over. The city is a mess. No electricity. No water. Accidents. Injuries." He sighed. He was looking bleary-eyed.

The valet took the Honda. Bill retrieved the shopping bag from the glove compartment, and the five of them straggled into the lobby.

Inside the hotel, it was business as usual. Several tourists were having their picture taken beneath the gilt dragon. There was a long line essing its way toward the reception desk. Bellhops moved back and forth with luggage racks, empty and full. The only sign of the storm was one lone Baccarat vase, placed near the entrance to catch an occasional drip from a leak in the ceiling.

It took over an hour before Detective Dean appeared at the door to Dawn's room, accompanied by another plainclothesman and two women in uniform. They had just finished breakfast, which Rose had ordered from room service and charged to Dawn. Dawn ate little, then sat staring out the window. Katja polished off what was left of Dawn's breakfast as well as her own—evidence of a clear conscience, thought Lindy, or incredibly cold blood.

The detectives stepped just inside the door. Dean's eyes widened in speculation. After a brief explanation from Bill, told off to the side out of hearing distance, Dean motioned the two female officers over. "Take them into separate bedrooms. They're not to touch anything."

Katja immediately got up from the table and walked toward the bedroom on the right, but not before shooting a sulky look at Bill.

"Costini," said Dean. The taller of the officers nodded and followed Katja out. He turned to Dawn. "Officer Reynolds will take you into the other room." The second officer, a black woman whose hair was closely cropped beneath her cap, stepped forward.

"But that's Rusty's room," said Dawn. "I can't go in there."

"I'm sure he'll understand," said Dean and flicked his head toward the door. "She touches nothing, clear?"

Reynolds nodded and took Dawn by the arm.

As soon as both doors closed, Dean pulled up an armchair and sat down. He motioned for Lindy and Rose to sit down on the couch, which they did without speaking, just a quick exchange of looks. Bill stood at a distance, looking at the three of them with an expression reminiscent of the hotel guardian figures.

Detective Dean slipped a notebook from his breast pocket and leaned back in the chair while he flipped through pages. "Well, ladies, which one of you would like to start?"

Neither Lindy nor Rose spoke up.

Dean waited. Clicking and reclicking his ballpoint pen. "I could charge you with aiding a fugitive."

"We didn't know they were fugitives," said Lindy, suddenly irritated. "We were just worried about Dawn."

"And why is that?"

Rose and Lindy told the story in tandem, throwing the narrative back and forth between them. They tried to assure the detective that they had not known where Dawn and Katja were. That it had been a hunch. Lindy felt Bill flinch at the word, but she patently ignored him.

When they came to the part of the story when Bill had found them, he joined them on the couch. By that point, they were more than willing to let him take charge. Being questioned by the police was a tiring, unnerving business. Lindy had made statements several times in the past, but she hadn't gotten used to it. She didn't see how anyone could.

Dean perked up when Bill came to the part about Dawn threatening them with the pistol.

"And where is this pistol, now?" asked Dean.

Bill produced the shopping bag. He laid it on the coffee table and opened it to reveal the pistol he had taken from Dawn.

Detective Dean made a moue of approval. "Damn. Murder weapon? It's the same caliber. What happened to it?"

"I had to fish it out of the marshes. Sorry. I had to work with what was available."

"No apologies necessary." Dean shook his head. "Can't believe you of all people are teaching school. You must have left some hole in the NYPD detective squad when you left."

Bill shrugged, dismissing the topic.

Dean stood up. "I'll take those other two in for questioning. Who knows? I might get lucky and hit the jackpot." He lifted his chin to the plainclothesman who was standing by the door. He went into Katja's bedroom.

"But I di-eedn't do anytheeng," Katja protested through the open door.

"Oh, by the way," he said to Lindy. "We found your Gull Lady this morning."

"That's great," said Lindy, trying to ignore Katja's moaning. "Did she tell you anything? See who did it?"

Dean chewed on his upper lip and shook his head. "She's dead. Hit by a piece of flying corrugated tin during the storm. Whatever she knew is gone along with her. However, we did find something interesting in one of her bags. I thought one of you might be able to identify them." He opened a rectangular carrying case and lifted out a small paper bag. He dumped the contents onto the table.

Lindy's mouth went dry. Two earrings. Rows of rhinestones hanging from a blue paste stone. She glanced at Rose, whose mouth had dropped open.

"Don't even think about it," said Bill, emphasizing each word.

"So you've seen them before?" asked Dean.

Lindy nodded. "Or at least ones like them. Dawn loaned them to Katja the first night of the comp."

Detective Dean's eyebrows rose. "Dawn did?"

"Yes, Katja had lost one of hers."

"But there are probably hundreds of pairs like that," said Rose. "They sell them in the vendors' room. You can't be sure they're Dawn's."

"That's true," said Lindy. "They could belong to anyone."

"Maybe this Gull Lady killed Shane for the earrings, thinking they were real," said Rose.

Dean skewed one side of his lips. "Nice try. But it's probably just a case of scavenging. She isn't a credible suspect—no record of real violence except when someone tries to take her Wild Rose away. Though I won't rule out the possibility until we try to lift some prints and run the .38 through ballistics."

"But what about the Gull Lady's friends?" asked Lindy. "They prevented me from talking to her the other day. They must know something."

"Gone to ground. They always do when there's trouble. We'll find them eventually, but I doubt if they'll be coherent enough to make a credible statement."

The door to the right bedroom opened. Katja came into the living room, supported by the female officer and plainclothesman. "She isn't feeling well, sir."

"I don't doubt it," replied Dean.

Katja took one look at what was on the table, and her body convulsed. She covered her mouth with her hand and ran back into the bedroom. The officer followed her.

The hall door clicked open and Rusty Lonigan rushed into the room, followed by Junie Baker. Dean jumped forward to prevent their entrance. Rusty pulled up sharp and stretched to see over the detective's shoulder. "What's happened? Where's Dawn?"

"In here," came Dawn's muffled voice through the closed door of the bedroom.

"Thank God." Rusty started toward the bedroom.

"Just a minute, sir," said Detective Dean.

"Who are you?"

"Detective Andrew Dean, Atlantic City Police Department." He flipped open his ID. Rusty hardly looked at it. "Has something happened to Dawn?" He turned to Lindy and Rose. "I heard that you found her, but I couldn't leave the floor until the lunch break. Is she all right?"

"She's unharmed," said Dean. "But she needs to go down to the station and answer a few questions."

"About what?" Junie broke in.

"Junie? Is that you?" Dawn bolted past the bedroom door. Officer

Reynolds appeared right behind her. She glanced at her superior for instructions. He shook his head. Dawn ran straight to Junie and threw her arms around him. He stood awkwardly for a moment, then patted her back while he looked at the others, obviously wishing someone would take her away.

Finally he pried her arms from around his waist and stepped back. "I told you that girl would cause nothing but trouble. Now are you ready to listen?"

Dawn shook her head and tears flew off her cheeks.

Junie took an exasperated breath. "You'll never learn, will you?"

"That's enough," said Dean. "I'll have to ask you not to talk anymore."

Dawn's eyes flashed at him. "Why?"

Rusty was staring at the table where the pistol and earrings lay side by side. "Because I think they're about to arrest you for murder." He nodded toward the table.

Dawn gasped. "Me? But—" Slowly she turned to see what he was looking at. She shook her head, her eyes bewildered. Then she lifted her chin and in a not-quite-steady voice, said, "Of course. For murdering Shane."

Rusty reached for her. Dean leapt between them. "Before you say another word—You have the right to remain silent . . ."

The recitation continued in a totally still room. Junie was the first to break the silence. "Total bull. She didn't kill Shane. It was her protégé." The word dripped with sarcasm. "Katja Andreyevsky. It had to be. She was the last one seen with the dress. Find her, Detective, and you'll find your murderer."

"We have found her," answered Dean. "They'll both be accompanying me to the station."

Junie turned to Rusty. "Dawn will need a lawyer. Do you have someone?"

Rusty was staring at the table. "I have a student downstairs. He's done some work for us. I'll ask him."

Junie turned to Dawn. "Don't say anything until you have a

lawyer present. Do you understand?" Dawn didn't respond. "Do you?"

"It doesn't matter," she said finally.

"Of course it matters. Do you want to take the rap for that bimbette? She'll let you do it. Don't think she won't."

"I'll have to ask you to leave," said Dean, motioning toward the door.

"What is the matter with you?" Junie yelled past Dean. "If you're in jail, I may just take over your studio."

Dawn's head jerked up and her eyes flashed with anger. But it died instantly. "Take it," she said and turned her back on him.

Junie stared after her, his face full of shock and, Lindy realized, concern. Well, go figure.

Dean motioned to the plainclothesman who was standing at the door. He opened it and escorted a protesting Junie into the hallway. Rusty stayed put. "I have to change for the afternoon's competition. When can I get back into my room?"

"I'll have someone accompany you to get what you need. Then I'm afraid you'll have to book another room for tonight."

"This is outrageous. I had absolutely nothing to do with any of this."

Dean gestured toward the door. "Then the sooner you let us do our work, the sooner you'll be able to have your room back." He waited until Rusty retreated to the hallway, then closed the door behind him. He puffed up his cheeks and blew out air. Then he looked at Dawn, who stood motionless in the center of the room.

"Where's your coat?" he asked.

Dawn flinched. "I'll get it."

"That won't be necessary. Just tell Officer Reynolds which one is yours. Costini," he barked toward the closed door of the other bedroom. Officer Costini stuck her head out.

"Bring Ms. Andreyevsky out and find her coat. I'm taking both of them in."

"No!" wailed Katja from the doorway. "No!" cried Dawn at the same time. She latched on to Dean's coat sleeve. "Please. Leave her alone. She had nothing to do with this. It was me. I did it."

"Dawn, shut up," cried Rose, then shot Dean a contrite look.

"Best to heed your friend's advice," said Dean. He crossed over to the coffee table, wrapped the pistol in the bag, then put it and the bag of earrings into the carrying case.

Officer Costini led Katja to the closet and had her point out her coat. After searching through the pockets and lining, she handed it to Katja. Officer Reynolds did the same with a light pink jacket that Dawn pointed out as hers.

"Dawn," said Katja, "that jacket isn't warm enough. Take your dress coat."

Dawn's eyes flitted from Katja to the officer. Dean stepped in front of the closet and looked inside. "I don't see a dress coat," he said.

"I—it isn't there," stammered Dawn. "I must have left it somewhere."

"Black? With a leopard collar?" asked Dean.

"Yes."

"I believe we have it at the station."

Dawn gasped.

Katja moaned. She turned to Dawn, her face filled with horror. "It was you? Oh, no-o-o," she cried on one long extended breath. "You shouldn't have done it. I know you did it for me, but you shouldn't have done it." She buried her face in her hands and sobbed. Costini escorted her out of the room.

Dawn stared at the space in front of her, while the policewoman helped her into the pink jacket. Then they, too, went into the hallway followed by the plainclothesman.

Dean turned to the others, his expression apologetic. "The suite will be secured by one of the hotel's security teams until I can get a search warrant. We'll search the beach house. I'll have someone return your car, Miss Graham, if you'll give me the keys."

Lindy reached into her bag and handed him the keys. He held

the door for them and accompanied them out. Several people were standing by open doors watching the excitement.

"Think she did it?" asked Bill.

"I don't know. I don't like her," Dean said. "I don't like her one bit." He tipped his head toward Lindy and Rose and strode toward the elevator without looking back.

Chapter Twenty

"Why is everyone so eager to have it be Dawn?" asked Rose despondently as they stepped into the elevator. "You've already convicted her."

Bill raised tired eyes toward her.

"You heard your detective friend. He doesn't like her. But that's no reason to arrest her."

Bill's lips tightened. "He meant he doesn't like her as a suspect. But he has to figure in the physical evidence, and there seems to be a substantial amount. The earrings, the pistol, the flight, and the coat, if it turns out to be hers. If all of the evidence pans out, it will be pretty cut-and-dried. Just let them do what they do." He stopped to stifle a yawn. "I'm going to take a shower and a nap. You two should do the same. And don't do any more second-guessing; don't get into any trouble; don't—"

The doors opened on the eleventh floor. "Don't worry," said Lindy. "We have a rehearsal."

"Good. Go to it. I'll see you around six."

"I noticed that you didn't tell him that rehearsal doesn't start until two," said Rose as soon as the doors closed and they continued downward.

"It gives us just enough time to make a condolence call. Maybe even time for a shower before we have to be at the theatre."

Rose pulled her hat out of her coat pocket and shoved it on her head. "I take it this condolence call is under the pier."

"You guessed it."

Outside, the sun was shining and the slush had begun to melt. Streams of water gushed from the drains of the souvenir shops and meandered across the surface of the boardwalk. Mounds of ice sat in puddles like melting ice sculptures. Soggy newspapers and handbills wrapped themselves around the lampposts. Overturned garbage cans rolled up and down the boardwalk. Except for three idle cabmen lounging against the rail, there was no one in sight.

They climbed down to the beach, then turned left toward the pier. They searched the shadows for any sign of habitation, but only found a makeshift tent of sodden cardboard and disturbed several gulls who had taken up residence beneath it. They picked their way through broken wine bottles back into the open air and stood looking at the deserted amusements.

Back on the boardwalk, they studied the entrance to the pier. The chain-link gate had snapped open. One side sagged beneath the weight of an overturned pretzel trailer. Yellow tape had been laced back and forth through the opening to keep out trespassers.

Rose took a quick look around, lifted the tape, and climbed through. Lindy followed her inside.

A path was cleared down the middle of the pier but to each side, carts and rides and concession stands were shoved tightly together.

"You take the right side," said Lindy. "I'll take the left. Look in windows, underneath trailers. Anywhere someone might be hiding."

They separated but found nothing, no one, except for a feral cat that jumped in front of Lindy as she searched the storage racks of Ferris wheel cars. Together, they climbed beneath the roller coaster and walked among the grids that supported the hills and loops rising above them. Except for the wind that whistled through the steel supports, it was eerily quiet. They frightened another group of gulls huddled close together. They flapped nervously and resettled a foot away.

"It's useless," said Lindy. "There's no one here. The police probably scared them away."

"Now what?" asked Rose.

Lindy shoved her hands in her coat pockets. "Where would you go if you were homeless and your usual hangout had been ransacked by the police?"

"The shelter?"

"Not if you were afraid of getting caught."

"There are probably hundreds of places for them to crash."

"Yeah," Lindy agreed, thinking of the abandoned tent and broken wine bottles beneath their feet. "A liquor store."

"That sounds like lots of fun. AC probably only has a hundred or so." Rose tugged her hat down over her ears. "Well, hell, we have about four hours until rehearsal. Let's see how many we can canvas."

They headed toward town, down a street that dead-ended at the boardwalk, past the entrance of the Grand Pavilion Hotel and the self-park lot. At the next corner, they turned into a street of small restaurants, bars and bodegas. It was hard to believe that this neighborhood was only two blocks from Casino Row.

They stopped at the first liquor store. It was a shabby storefront with a metal gate pushed back from the door. Two smeared plate-glass windows were empty except for a half-lit neon sign that flicked out PACK-G- STO—. Both windows were backed with unpainted plywood. Rose tried the door. A buzzer sounded when they stepped inside.

A man appeared from an unlit doorway at the back. He was of Oriental descent, short and thick, wearing a white shirt rolled up at the sleeves. A tattoo snaked up his left arm.

"Can I help you ladies?" He made no move to help them, just watched as they walked past a soda case and two rows of bottles with names that would have made Bill shudder and came to a stop in front of him.

He leaned over the counter and peered at them. The tattoo rippled across his skin.

Lindy tried not to stare. "Actually, we're looking for someone. Two men who might, um, shop here."

A treble giggle came from unmoving lips. "Oh. You're looking for some fun, huh?"

"No, no," Lindy said hastily. "We're looking for two men who were known to be friends with the Gull Lady. A woman who is always feeding the birds out on the beach."

"Police were already here. I told them. I don't know anything. You go on away. Tell them I still don't know anything."

"But we're not with the police," said Lindy. "The Gull Lady was killed in the storm. We just wanted to pay our condolences."

The man made a hissing sound. "Go away. I am honest man, have honest business. I don't want trouble. Go away."

Rose and Lindy hesitated. He hissed again, and Rose and Lindy bolted for the door.

"That was scary," said Rose when they stopped two doors away. "If the police were there, they've probably hit the other liquor stores, too."

"And if the others weren't any more cooperative than he was, they probably haven't found them."

They continued to walk down the street. Neither talked for a while. Lindy was thinking about the liquor store owner and what he must think of the Grand Pavilion Hotel and it's opulent chinoiserie, when a dirty hand was shoved into her face.

She jumped back, saw Rose taking a defensive stance.

"Have a quarter for a cup of coffee?" whined the person who belonged to the hand.

"Just a minute," said Lindy, digging into her coat pocket.

"Why don't you come over to that grocery and we'll buy you a sandwich?" said Rose.

"Nah, just gimme the quarter."

Lindy handed him some change.

"He'll just buy hooch with it," said Rose. "We shouldn't contribute to—"

"Rose, give me a break. I'll do extra hours at Father Andrews's soup kitchen when I get home." She pulled a dollar from the other pocket. The man reached for it. She snatched it back. "We need to find two men," she said.

The man smiled, revealing toothless gums.

"We need to talk to them." The man shuffled away. Lindy ran after him, trying not to get too close to the smell. "Wait. We're not with the police. We just want to ask them about the Gull Lady. Give a donation to her memory."

The man stopped and eyed her suspiciously.

Despising herself, Lindy pulled out another bill. "Take the dollar. If you know where the Gull Lady's friends are and can get them to come back with you, I'll give you the ten."

The man snatched the dollar and lumbered around the corner and out of sight.

"I think you just saw the last of that dollar."

Lindy sighed. "Probably. And I felt so despicable, demeaning another human being by bribing him like that. But it wasn't like I had any other leads."

"Yeah, he might hate you for it, but it didn't keep him from taking your dollar."

"I guess we might as well go back. I doubt if we'll see him again."

They walked back down the street in the direction they had come. They stopped at the corner where several people waited silently for a bus. They eyed Lindy and Rose contemptuously as they passed.

"Not a very friendly town," said Rose.

"Can you blame them? The casinos make huge amounts of money, while their homes are sold off, their schools are disintegrating, their businesses are barely making it. Some quality of life. Yuck, I wish I had my dollar back."

They stepped off the curb. Lindy looked to the left for oncoming traffic and saw the man who had just left them, hobbling up the street. "Then again, maybe not."

They watched him approach. He stopped several feet from them and motioned for them to follow. They did.

"I hope your martial arts skills are in working order," whispered Lindy.

"No problem," said Rose.

They followed the man to the end of the block. There he crossed the street and squeezed between two iron gates that enclosed a playground area.

"This is really stupid," said Lindy.

"Probably," said Rose. "Won't be the first time we did something stupid. Just keep them in front of you and run like hell if they start getting violent."

Ahead of them, two men were stretched out on steps that led up the side of a church building. The man who had brought them waited long enough for Lindy to give him the extra ten, then he scuttled away around the back of the building.

Lindy felt Rose poised beside her. She took a deep breath. Cleared her throat. "I'm sorry about the Gull Lady."

Neither of the men replied. The smaller of the two was slouched across the steps, clearly in a drunken stupor. But the big one, who had frightened her the day before, sat upright, smoking a cigarette and watching her through a curtain of haze.

"What da ya want?" He dragged on the cigarette and flicked it onto the pavement. Smoke seeped between his teeth, while he waited for an answer.

"We know the Gull Lady was killed by flying debris," said Lindy. "We know the police found some earrings in her bag."

The sleeping man raised himself onto his elbow, making slurring sounds, but no discernible words.

"You got money?" the big man growled.

Lindy flicked a look at Rose. Rose didn't look back. She was concentrating on the two figures on the steps. "A little," she said.

He coughed out a laugh. "Bring your bodyguard wit'cha today?"

"Don't underestimate her," said Lindy, hoping they wouldn't have to prove Rose's prowess. "I just want to know about the earrings. I'll be happy to pay for the information."

"Happy to pay," whined the drunk man. "Get her. Happy to pay."

"Shaddup." The big man shoved him.

He slid down a step and sat up. "What's wit'chu, man?"

"Nothin'." He darted disjointed looks around the playground, then zeroed in on Lindy. "Show me da money." Lindy pulled out a twenty. He slid his tongue along crusty lips. "Nothin' to keep me just takin' it."

"My bodyguard."

He coughed out another laugh.

"Don't doubt it for a minute," said Rose in a low voice that almost brought a laugh from Lindy. It didn't have the same effect on the man. He squinted his eyes at her.

Lindy didn't like the look. This was the dumbest thing she had ever done. How could she have put them in such jeopardy? "Look," she said quickly. "We don't mean anyone harm. We're just trying to find out if one of you saw who killed the man on the beach, and how the Gull Lady got the earrings." She rushed on when she saw movement from the big man. "We know she didn't steal them. Just found them."

"Shoulda split 'em up, like we ahways do," whined the drunk.

"Shaddup."

"But no-o-o. She had ta haff both of 'em. All I got was a dirty old coat. And I left it somewheres."

Dawn's coat, thought Lindy. And now the police have it.

"I said shaddup." The big man grabbed him by his shirtfront and lifted him up until they were nose to nose. The smaller man cringed back and whined, "I coulda used the money and now nobody but the p'lice'll get 'em."

"Did you see anybody on the beach before you found the body?"

"She should've shared."

"But did you see anyone?"

"Shee-ut." The big man jumped up and grabbed the other man. They started running and scrambled around the side of the building just as Lindy heard footsteps running across the pavement. She turned. Two policeman were running their way. One stopped beside them while his partner ran after the two men.

"Are you two okay? We were cruising by when we saw them accost you. We got here as soon as we could. You shouldn't be in this area. It isn't safe."

"We figured that out," said Rose.

His partner returned. "Lost 'em. What were you two doing out here?"

"I'm interested in architecture," said Rose. "I was just about to point out that arch above the door there. Did you know this is an excellent example of Late Victorian Neo Gothic?"

The patrolmen exchanged glances. "Are you staying at one of the casino hotels? We'll give you a ride back."

Lindy and Rose followed them back to the squad car and got in the backseat. A block from the hotel, Rose said, "If you don't mind, could we get off here?"

The car slowed down and the officer who was driving smiled over the back of the seat. "Don't want to cause any gossip? I understand. But go straight to your hotel and please don't do any more sight-seeing on your own."

"We won't," Lindy assured him. They scrambled out of the backseat and walked toward the hotel. The officers waved as they drove away.

Three minutes later, Lindy and Rose were back in the lobby of the Grand Pavilion.

"Well, that was a bust," said Lindy. "At least I still have my twenty dollars. I'm sorry I got you into that. It was a really stupid thing to do."

"You didn't. I wanted to go; it was worth a try. I'm going to shower and order room service. All that excitement whetted my appetite."

"I can't believe you just lied to the police," said Lindy.

"I didn't," said Rose. "I *am* interested in architecture."

Chapter
Twenty-one

Biddy and Jeremy were waiting for her when Lindy arrived at the theatre for the two o'clock rehearsal.

"Oh, good," said Biddy. "When you didn't come back last night, I figured you must be with Bill. But when I didn't see you all day, I didn't know whether I should worry about you or not. I called the room twice and left kinda nervous Nellie messages."

"Not to worry. I didn't even notice the blinking lights."

"So?"

Behind her, Jeremy was giving them his full attention.

"I was with Bill."

Biddy and Jeremy smiled goofily.

"And Rose." The expressions shifted to confusion. "And Dawn and Katja." She sat down and told them about the last twenty-four hours.

"So, they've arrested Dawn?" asked Jeremy when Lindy had finished.

"More or less, though I think Detective Dean isn't convinced that she did it. I guess there's a lot of evidence against her."

"How's Rose taking it?" he asked.

"She doesn't believe it. She's determined to find out who really did kill Shane."

Jeremy knit his eyebrows. "I was afraid of this. And it looks like the movie people are going to offer a deal to Andrea and Paul."

"We'll have to let them go."

"I know. I'm happy for them. Sort of. We can make do. Shuffle around some parts. Give Eric some more leads. Mieko and Kate can share Andrea's roles and I can move up Laura H. She's been working out well." He slapped his palms on his thighs. "So. It calls for a celebration. Company dinner tonight. Eight o'clock. Someplace in the hotel."

"Emperor's Garden on the twentieth floor?" suggested Biddy. "Four-star classic Szechwan cuisine. Or the Forbidden City? I think *it* has a floor show."

"No floor shows. Make it the Emperor's Garden. Tell the kids, will you, Lindy?"

Kids. Lindy smiled. They sounded like one big happy family. She felt a niggle of unhappiness, pushed it away. They *were* a happy family. Even if these kids were in their twenties and early thirties, and two of them might be moving on.

Peter called places and Kate, Mieko and Andrea took their places onstage for the *Gershwin Preludes*. Lindy pulled out her notebook and sat down. The lights faded to black, then rose again, light catching the fabric of their 1930s-style dresses as they moved through a brief trio to the tape accompaniment. They were joined by Paul, Rebo, Eric and Juan. As the melodic line and harmonies wove together and separated, so did the dancers, pairing off and coming together. Duets, trios, solos, and at the end, duets again, everyone having found their counterpart in the music and in life, except the lone male dancer who closed the piece alone onstage.

Lindy had often thought that this was an autobiographical piece, with Jeremy being the odd man out. He had been to hell and back. But now he had Biddy, and Lindy guessed that the Gershwin would be leaving the repertory in the near future.

She leaned back in her seat, the notebook on her lap, her pen held loosely in her fingers. The piece was well rehearsed and her mind wandered from dancing to partners to murder. Unlike concert dance, you needed a consistent partner in ballroom dancing. Was Shane's death about partners? Because he wanted to leave the one he had for a new one? And what about Timothy? He would have been left partnerless if Shane had taken Felicia. Now Felicia would have to stay with Timothy and Timothy couldn't afford to compete. Vincent couldn't even get a partner and his career was kaput. Still he hung around, waiting for what? Another chance? Retribution? Or was he just torturing himself?

And why was she torturing herself? Going round and round in a quagmire of relationships with no real leads, except Dawn's gun, Dawn's coat, and Dawn's confession.

She brought her thoughts back to the Gershwin as the lights faded on Eric turning slowly, but not unhappily, on the stage. An upbeat, not depressing ending. A salute to self-sufficiency. Something the ballroom world could learn from. Something she could learn from, too.

The lights came on and the dancers went through the bows. The lights faded and the houselights popped on. Lindy walked down to the stage and gave a few notes. Nothing major. They were ready.

"This is getting boring, boss," Rebo yelled out to Jeremy. "You want us to try it all to the left, or maybe retrograde it? We could start at the end and do all the steps backward to the beginning."

"He just wants to rehearse more, 'cause he lost his per diem at the slots," said Juan.

"Lucky for you," said Lindy. "Jeremy has invited you all to dinner tonight."

"A company dinner," crooned Juan. He fell to his knees and kowtowed toward Jeremy. "Thank you. Thank you."

"You just made some dancers very happy," Lindy told Jeremy as she returned to her seat.

"I thought they might be running low on funds. See you at eight. Bring Bill."

Rose yelled from the stage, "Hey, wait a minute." She jumped to the floor and loped across it, pumping her arm in the air as if she were hailing a cab. "Junie and Rusty are on their way over. They want to talk to us." She turned to Jeremy. "You and Biddy should stay, if you have a minute. I don't know what they have in mind."

"But think you might need witnesses?" asked Jeremy.

"Or moral support," said Biddy and opened her notebook.

Junie and Rusty came through the door a few minutes later. They crossed directly to where the others were seated and pulled up two empty chairs.

"Thanks for seeing us," said Rusty. "I know you must be busy." No one denied it.

"Listen, Dawn has gotten herself in a mess. We need help. She didn't kill Shane. She just wouldn't. The whole situation is preposterous."

"Then why did she admit to killing him?" asked Lindy.

"Hell, isn't it obvious? She thinks she's protecting Katja," said Junie. "It's this children thing she has. Any normal person would have gone out and gotten a husband and had a family when we broke up, but Dawn just couldn't let go. It's pitiful. Her life has been a series of young girls that she tries to mother. They always end up dumping her and moving on to something bigger and better. But she just won't learn."

Rusty nodded his head in agreement. "Katja's the worst case yet. I mean, the girl's all right. Nothing to write home about if you ask me. But Dawn has been preening her for championship since the day she walked into the studio. I just don't get it. We have other female teachers who dance as well. I don't know what she sees in her."

"But we think she's covering for her," Junie continued. "We've got to figure out a way to make her tell what she really knows."

"You know her better than anyone else," said Rose. "Have any ideas?"

Junie slumped back in his chair. "No. God, what are we going to do?"

Everyone fell into silence. Lindy certainly didn't have any ideas and it seemed that no one else did either.

"We've had such a long-standing feud, I've gotten dependent on it. And it keeps her going. Some people just need adversity. Dawn's one of them. She thrives on it. Maybe I'm one of them too. What am I going to do without her?"

An interesting question, thought Lindy. Especially since Dawn thought that he and Rusty were trying to get rid of her. She had a question of her own.

"I saw the two of you leaving a restaurant the other night, the night Dawn made you promise not to sell the studio to Junie." She paused and watched Rusty cast a chagrined look toward Junie. "Are you planning on selling? Ousting Dawn out of the partnership?"

"No, it isn't like that at all," protested Rusty. "But I'm not going to sue Junie. Dawn and her four point eight miles. Totally absurd. It would cost us more to sue than it would be worth. And besides, there's enough business for both studios. That's why we were having dinner. We're thinking of incorporating, possibly opening up three or four more studios on the East Coast. Dawn would have a share in the franchise and she would run Stepping Out."

"Obviously we had to work out the details without her knowing about it," said Junie. "She'd fight the idea just for the hell of it, even though it's to everyone's advantage."

"But the whole idea will be shot to shit if we have to spend everything on lawyers," added Rusty.

So this visit isn't completely over concern for Dawn, thought Lindy. Why did that not surprise her?

The door to the theatre swung open. Bill stepped inside, frowned at the group sitting at the banquette, and strode toward them.

"Uh-oh," said Rose under her breath.

He stopped at Lindy's chair. "I need to talk to you." There was a pulse beating in his temple. She had only seen that once before and the memory still sent shivers of dread down her spine. "Now." He wrapped his fingers around her arm and pulled her out of her chair. She stared at him, speechless. He was hurting her arm.

Jeremy stood up.

"Stay out of this, Jeremy." Bill pulled her toward the door.

She broke away. "What the hell—"

He grabbed her again and pushed her into the hallway, where he pinned her up against the wall.

"What is the matter with you?" she demanded, though she could hear her voice quavering with shock.

Bill's fingers dug into her shoulders. "I just got a call from Andrew. Seems his patrolmen picked up two women in town today. Talking to a couple of derelicts. Figured from the description that they might be you and Rose."

"So?"

He shook her. "What the hell were you trying to prove? That was the most irresponsible thing you have ever done. Didn't you stop to think of the potential danger? You both could have been hurt or killed. How could you do something so insane, and drag Rose into it with you?"

He was right. She had already come to the same conclusion and knew she had been thoughtless and stupid. But she didn't need for him to tell her so, at the top of his lungs, as if she were a naughty child, humiliating her in front of everyone.

Off to the side, Lindy could see Rose, Biddy and Jeremy standing in the doorway. She could feel her eyes tearing up. "Leave me alone," she cried. "If I'm so stupid, why don't you just go out and find someone more up to your caliber?"

"Goddammit, Lindy."

She struggled ineffectually against him. "Get away from me. Just get the hell out."

He stopped shouting. Stopped moving.

"Go away!" she cried.

He dropped his hands and took a step backward. Then he turned and walked away, down the stairs, past the elevators and the Pagoda Bar.

She watched his back, each measured stride, knowing she had gone too far. And hating herself because she didn't mean any of it. She pressed against the wall, shaking, her knees so weak that she knew if she tried to move she would fall. What had she done?

Jeremy moved away from the others, came to her, pulled her into a hug. "This is not what you want." He spoke quietly, like he could do and still command your attention. She shook her head. Felt hot tears running down her cheek. She closed her eyes.

"All this stuff between the two of you," he said, "isn't about the two of you. You know what I mean?"

She nodded. She did know what he meant. And he was right. "What am I going to do?"

"Grovel." Jeremy pushed her away so he could look at her. "When in doubt, grovel."

She gave him a half smile, all that she could muster. "All right."

She would grovel. She deserved to grovel. She had been incredibly mean to Bill, the whole time he had been there. He had come expecting a vacation and instead he had gone without sleep, tramped through freezing marshes, been accosted by gun-toting ballroom dancers, and she hadn't even been nice to him. All because her life was a mess and she didn't know what to do. And she was hurting the one person who still loved her. Or at least had loved her until now. That thought almost set her off again, so she stopped thinking. Someone handed her her dance bag, and she was walking down the hall on rubbery legs.

She stopped in the ladies' lounge and washed her face. Then she repaired her makeup. If you had to grovel, better to do it looking your best. She took the elevator upward.

She stood in front of Bill's door, taking even breaths, trying to calm the butterflies in her stomach. She raised her hand to knock but couldn't make herself go through the action. She hadn't thought of one thing to say when—if—he answered the door. If he was even here. Maybe he was slugging back a drink or two in the Lotus Lounge and she didn't need to come at all. She began to feel foolish. Maybe she was overreacting. She almost turned away.

She knew the hardest part was taking that first step onstage. It would be okay after that. She knocked. Waited. Jumped when the door opened a crack. Bill looked at her from the other side.

"Hi," she said.

He opened the door wider, but he didn't step back to let her in.

He had taken off his sweater and was wearing a navy blue T-shirt. He had a glass of something that looked like scotch in his hand. Scotch, the "when you can't take any more" drink, he had once told her.

"Has something happened?" His voice was so subdued that it frightened her.

She shook her head.

"Just drop by for a chat?"

"If that's okay." For a minute she was afraid he might say no. Then slowly he opened the door wider and stepped aside, leaving only a narrow path for her to pass through. She was careful not to look at him, afraid of what she might see. There was an open suitcase on the bed and an open drawer in the dresser.

"You're leaving," she said, stricken.

"It seemed the obvious thing to do." He crossed behind her to the table. Opened another minibottle of scotch and poured it into his glass.

She felt her mouth twist, tried to relax it. He turned his back to her and looked out the window. She felt rooted to the carpet. "Bill, I know I've been awful to you since you've been here. But it isn't you. It's me."

"Lindy, don't say any more, okay?"

She was shocked that his voice was no more under control than hers was.

"It doesn't matter. I'm leaving. I won't bother you again."

"What? . . . Bill?"

He leaned his forehead against the window. "I know I'm a thick-skulled barbarian but even I"—his voice cracked—"know when I'm not wanted."

"You're not a barbarian. You're the most cultured, intelligent man I know." Why were they talking about barbarians? It was absurd. She wanted to laugh or cry or shake him until his teeth rattled. Then in a hot searing flash, she realized that he thought she really wanted him out of her life, and that he had played this scene before, long ago. She wanted to scream, "I'm not Claire," but she said, "I want you."

Bill didn't react, just continued to look out the window.

"Do you hear me, I want you."

He turned slowly, his face a mixture of distrust, hurt and hope.

"I—want—you."

He put down his glass and opened his hands. More a gesture of defeat than an invitation for an embrace. She opted for the invitation, and his arms closed tightly around her.

They stood without moving, without talking. They had hugged plenty of times before, friendly hugs, sympathetic hugs, hugs that were never allowed to be more than just that. This could have been one of those, at first. But then Bill's hands began to move over her back, along her spine. She knew she was about to make a choice, a choice that she now knew she had wanted to make for a long time.

"Is that you trembling, or me?" he asked.

"Both, I think."

Bill moved. She heard the suitcase hit the floor, and she fell with Bill onto the bed. She had made her choice, and for the next few hours, she had no doubts at all.

Chapter
Twenty-two

The bedside clock said it was seven-twenty. Bill's arm lay heavily across her.

"Well," he said.

"Well, what?" Lindy nestled closer. "You want a review?"

He pulled away and looked at her. "I want to know if you're sorry we did that."

"Bill . . ." she began, then stopped. She didn't want to think about the ramifications of what had happened, or deal with all the baggage she had been carrying around for months. She just wanted to enjoy the moment, but she could feel Bill's body tensing. She smiled. "Are you kidding? If I weren't such a numbskull, it would have happened much sooner."

Bill let out his breath. "It was worth the wait. Though not exactly what I intended."

She sat up. "Are you telling me—"

"I just meant that I wanted it to be the quintessential romantic experience, candlelight and champagne, take it slow and skillfully, not act like a hormone-ravaged teenager."

"Skillful was good. We can go for slow and skillful later."

He smiled and his hand drifted back to her stomach. "How about now?"

"Later," she said, removing his hand. "We've got a company dinner to go to."

Bill groaned and fell back against the pillow. "I suppose we have to."

"Yes, we do. Everyone will be wondering if we killed each other." She rolled into him and he wrapped an arm around her. "But don't say anything."

"Not to worry. That kind of razzing, I don't need."

The Company was sitting at a back table in the Emperor's Garden. She and Bill had agreed that Lindy would arrive first to dispel any concern about their recent argument. She felt absurdly happy, something she hadn't felt in a long time. She carefully arranged her face into an expression of nonchalance and made her entrance. Biddy jumped up and ran to meet her. She was frowning with concern.

"Are you okay? We—" She stopped and slowly her mouth lifted into a smile. "Ohmigod, you did it!" she said. "I can't believe it, you finally—"

"Biddy, shush. How can you tell?" Biddy's smiled broadened into a grin. Lindy grasped her elbow. "For crying out loud, don't say anything."

Biddy shook her head and tried to wipe off her smile. It was a losing battle.

"Biddy," Lindy pleaded.

Biddy took a deep breath and relaxed her face. "Not a word." She led Lindy to the table and sat down, carefully avoiding looking at anyone. Lindy sat down next to her and picked up her menu.

"Damn," said Rebo from his place across the table.

Lindy looked up. "What?"

"Two hours ago we thought there was going to be a fight to the finish. Wow."

"What?"

He frowned, then broke into a toothy grin. "What are we gonna call the wannabe now that he is?"

Lindy's mouth opened, then closed. "God, how can you tell?"

"Do I have to start singing about little glow worms? How was it? Was he the best? We want the whole blow by blow."

"No!" she squawked. She leaned forward and lowered her voice. "Don't say—"

Juan started humming "Here Comes the Bride." Lindy darted a frantic look toward the door. Bill was headed toward them, wearing his cop face. *Good try, but too late,* thought Lindy. "Don't say anything," she pleaded.

Everyone picked up menus and stared at them.

Bill reached the table. "Evening," he said.

There was a sputter behind Juan's menu. Rebo looked over the edge of his menu, eyes round. "Hi," he said in a strangled voice.

Bill's eyes narrowed. They moved from Rebo, to Juan, to Rose, who was sitting next to him. Rebo and Juan lowered their menus and grinned at him. Rose gave him a thumbs-up. Next to Lindy, Biddy and Jeremy were beaming like proud parents. Beyond them, Peter and Mieko looked on expressionless. Their sign of approval.

"Christ," Bill muttered and sat down.

"I didn't say a thing," Lindy whispered.

"Well, this calls for champagne," said Jeremy, motioning for the waiter. He turned to Bill. "Paul and Andrea have a movie offer," he explained, eyes twinkling.

"Congratulations," Bill said to the other end of the table. Paul and Andrea smiled back. Jeremy coughed and brought his hand to his mouth. It didn't quite conceal his grin. There was a faint flush of color across the ledge of Bill's cheekbones. It was something Lindy had never once seen in the two years she had known him. If he ordered scotch, she was in big trouble. Then she felt his fingers brush her thigh, and she sat back to enjoy the rest of the evening.

As soon as dessert was over, Rebo and the boys beat a hasty retreat, making goofy faces from behind Bill as they left the restaurant. The others left a few minutes later. Rose moved into Rebo's chair, and motioned Jeremy and Biddy to pull their chairs closer. The conversation turned to the subject of Dawn's confession.

"If ballistics pans out," said Bill, "they'll arrest her. If not. I daresay she'll be back at the hotel in full neurosis tomorrow morning."

"I hope so," said Rose, choosing to ignore his sarcasm. "Then what do we do? And don't bother telling me to stay out of it."

Bill gave her a long look before answering. "You and Lindy will have to find out a way to finagle the truth out of her. She knows something. Maybe she isn't sure of what she knows, but she knows something. My money is on Katja. If Dawn has a .38, there's a good chance Katja does, too. Dean will run a registration check, but they might not be registered."

"And Katja had access to Dawn's coat and the earrings and the dress," added Lindy.

"Yes, but don't go in with preconceptions. It could be anybody."

"But Katja had the biggest motive," said Rose.

"That we know of," said Bill. "But motive isn't that important. A guy can destroy the lives of countless people, all of whom would love to see him dead, but get shot in the head by a stranger he cut off on the turnpike."

Rose frowned. "Means and opportunity, then."

Bill smiled. Lindy knew he was trying not to appear condescending. "You two stick with questioning Dawn. Let the professionals find out who *could* have killed Shane. These ballroom people live in an alternate reality. They've created their own little world with its own rules and power structures. They thrive on the intrigue. It's taken over their sense of what is really important, or what is right or wrong. I don't want any more victims of their delusions."

It was the same explanation Bill had given her when they first met. Only then he had been talking about the dance company.

Rose nodded. "Pretty good insight for an outsider."

"I learned it from some pros," he said, looking around the table. He smiled. "From some pros who still have a pretty good grip on the real world."

Lindy let out a breath that she didn't know she had been holding.

"So speaking as someone whose grip is pretty good," said Lindy,

She faltered when she saw Rose's eyebrows lift, then hurried on. "I still have a hard time with the idea that Shane was killed because he was leaving Dawn and Katja to dance with Felicia. It has to be something else. Right?"

"It's hard to say," said Bill.

Rose sputtered.

"Rose, give me a break."

Rose nodded and clamped her hand over her mouth.

"As I was saying. There are untold persons who might have an ax to grind."

"Shane stole Enrico's dress design and the reproduction was a travesty," said Rose.

"And Timothy would have lost Felicia as a partner," added Lindy.

"So we add Enrico, Luis, and Timothy to the suspect list," said Rose.

"You don't have a suspect list," Bill reminded her. "You have one job and that is to talk to Dawn."

"I see what you mean," said Lindy. "Once you start thinking about who might want to kill Shane you get distracted from what actually happened."

Bill gave her an approving look. If he patted her head, she might forget that they had made earth-stopping love just a few hours ago.

"What happened to his clothes?" asked Lindy.

"Yeah," said Rose. "What *did* happen to his clothes?"

"Haven't found them yet. Probably got scavenged like the coat. Or washed out to sea, though that's unlikely. It would be a hike across the beach to throw them in the ocean with a body between you and escape, and the potential even greater for being seen."

"That's right," said Biddy. "The pier is the only structure that actually goes out over the water, and that's at high tide."

Bill raised his eyebrows at her.

"You're not the only ones who go for walks on the beach."

"Okay, so tomorrow, you go to Dawn. Bring whatever she says to Andrew. Don't act on it."

Rose saluted. "You're the boss."

Bill pulled Lindy aside as they were leaving the restaurant. "You are going to spend the night with me, right?"

"If I'm invited."

"You're invited."

"Just let me deep-six these shoes and dress and get my toothbrush."

"You're not going to stand me up?"

"Of course not, it'll only take a minute."

"Afraid you'll be caught sneaking out in the morning wearing evening clothes?"

Lindy smiled. "Got it in one."

But it took more than a minute. It took over an hour. Biddy and Jeremy had come to the room while Biddy checked for phone messages. Lindy slipped out of her dress and put on black slacks and a soft raw silk blouse. She was deciding between loafers and her mules when she heard Biddy's intake of breath.

Lindy turned toward the phone. Biddy's face was blanched and she was looking unhappily at Lindy.

"What?" asked Lindy, suddenly alarmed. "Has something else happened?"

Biddy chewed on her lip.

"What?"

"One of those messages was for you, Lindy."

"God. Annie? Cliff?"

"No, nothing like that. It was Glen. He said that—" Biddy stopped and pushed some buttons on the phone. "You'd better hear it for yourself."

Lindy took the receiver. Listened to the blips, then. "Lindy, it's Glen. We need to talk. I'll be home on the twenty-fourth. Early afternoon. See you then."

She sank down on the bed, the receiver still in her hand. "Oh, God. What have I done?"

Biddy took the phone and hung it up. "You did what any self-respecting woman would have done months before you did it. Hell, Jeremy, help me out here." She sat down beside Lindy.

"I think what Biddy's trying to say is—oh, shit. Glen has left you dangling for months. He said he didn't want to be married anymore. He can't just waltz back in when he feels like it, then waltz out again."

"But he's my husband."

"Is he?" asked Biddy. "Come on, Lindy. Glen only cares about himself. He's made that clear in the last few months. How long are you going to cling to an empty marriage?"

She knew Biddy was right. Glen had deserted her a long time ago, emotionally as well as physically. It was time to get things settled. It was eleven-thirty here, five-thirty in Paris. Knowing Glen, he would already be at work. She reached for the phone and punched in the numbers to his Paris office.

"Bill," she said, while she listened to the sounds of the overseas exchange. "He's expecting me."

"Jeremy will keep him occupied." Biddy motioned him toward the door.

"Right," said Jeremy. And after a frown at Biddy, he left the room.

The secretary gave her usual answer. "Mr. Haggerty can't be reached at the moment."

Lindy had heard that answer one too many times. Something inside her snapped. "This is his wife. Remember me? You reach him, and do it within the next half hour. I will be at this number until then." She left the number to her hotel room. "Tell Mr. Haggerty if he doesn't call by then, he needn't ever call again."

"*Mais vraiment*, Madame Haggerty," the secretary sputtered, and Lindy felt vindicated at last. She had taken more haughty attitude from that woman than anyone deserved.

"Tell him." She hung up. Hands shaking. Body shaking. She leaned forward and put her head between her knees.

"Bravo, girl," said Biddy, putting her arm around Lindy's shoulders. "That's telling them."

The phone rang ten minutes later.

"What the hell is wrong with you?" asked Glen.

"Hello, Glen. How nice of you to call," said Lindy. She heard a door slam in the background. Glen must have closed his office door.

"Pauline was very upset by the way you spoke to her," he said.

Lindy bit her lip. Pauline deserved that and worse for all the times she had been rude to Lindy. But she didn't say so. She got down to business. "Glen, I needed to talk to you and that was the only way that I was certain you'd get the message."

"I left a message that I would be there on the twenty-fourth. Can't this wait?"

"No, Glen. It can't. I need to know now what you're planning." She heard him sigh. She had to stop herself from apologizing for bothering him. Soon, she would never be bothering him again. And for the first time, that thought didn't send her into tears. Maybe she was getting used to the idea that Glen no longer loved her. Or maybe it was because she had finally stopped fighting the inevitable.

There was silence on the other end of the line.

"Just a simple answer. Are you coming home for good or do you want a divorce?"

"Lindy, calm down."

"I'm calm. I've been calm since I accepted the fact that you don't want to be married anymore."

"That doesn't mean I want a divorce."

"You have to choose. Marriage or a divorce."

"Look, Lindy. My work is exciting. Paris is incredible. We've had a good marriage, but you and I both have our own interests. The kids are practically grown. They don't need us anymore. There are a lot of opportunities out there for me. And for you, too. I want to expand my horizons. I think you should do the same. No hard feelings, all right?" he said.

No hard feelings? She had invested the last twenty years of her life in her family and no hard feelings? "You mean, it's been a great run, but it's time to close the show?"

"Well, yeah. Since you put it like that. I knew you'd understand."

Lindy took the receiver from her ear and stared at it as if she could see him in it. This was her staid, conservative husband who made a five-year plan for every decision? Had he been planning this for five years? How long had this been going on? The Gershwin melody made a brief, frantic course through her mind.

"Fine," she heard herself saying. "Start divorce proceedings."

"You can do that. It will look better if you divorce me." How very gentlemanly, thought Lindy, then pulled her attention back to what he was saying. "I talked with Howard Porter a couple of weeks ago. Not about a divorce. I was just trying to arrange a financial plan that would be fair to all parties. But you can have him draw up a settlement based on the same figures. You and he can work out the details."

Lindy was struggling to keep up. Beside her, Biddy's eyes were glued to the phone as if she could see Glen's side of the conversation.

He didn't want to be the one to initiate the divorce, even though he had set up the guidelines for the settlement. It was just getting stranger and stranger. And the odd thing was, she was accepting it. Not in defeat, but in agreement. He was right. They had been living separate lives for a long time. She just hadn't noticed it. And even odder was that instead of feeling rejected and heartbroken, she felt relief that it had finally been exposed.

". . . and their education funds will see them through school, plus allowance . . ." She drifted in and out of his explanations. He was on firm ground now, talking about investments and collateral loans. ". . . the house. It's worth close to a million with real estate being the way it is. If you want to sell . . ." So this was it. Of course, she would be left to explain things to Annie and Cliff. She hoped they wouldn't blame her, like kids often blamed their mothers in cases like this. Cases like this; she was about to become a statistic. No. She was a person who had a life ahead of her as well as a good life behind her. She wouldn't throw blame anywhere. It was no one's fault. Not even hers. Glen was right. She would have no hard feelings. Not if she could help it.

"But there are a few things I'd like out of the house—" *Like the Surround Sound,* she thought. She couldn't remember him talking this much at one time in years. Maybe they hadn't had that much to say to each other. ". . . the twenty-fourth, if that's convenient. I'll have to leave right away . . ." She could go somewhere for Christmas. Not Club Med. The thought made her smile. She'd never have to take a Club Med vacation again. "Two weeks at Club Med in Tortuga."

"Fine," she finally broke in, dazed by the whirlwind of mono-logue. "The twenty-fourth's fine. Unfortunately, I'll be out of town. Can you manage by yourself? I can ask Haddie to come in for the day."

"That would be great, could you call her? Probably four or five hours will do it. Don't worry about paying her. I'll take care of it."

God, it was just like a normal conversation. Life was bizarre. Biddy was frowning at her. Lindy crossed her eyes at her, but Biddy didn't smile. She looked like she might cry.

". . . so if that's it . . ."

Lindy realized he was about to hang up. "Wait," she said. "Wait." Silence.

"There's just one thing I need to ask. And be totally honest. Don't worry about what I might think or feel. Have you—been with anyone?" He was going to deny it. She cut him off. "I don't want any details. I just need to know if I should get an AIDS test."

Silence. Then, "How can you even ask something like that?"

Because it's a matter of life and death, she thought, feeling sick for the first time since the conversation began.

"I'm a totally responsible person."

"Yes, Glen. I know. Just tell me. Have you had unprotected sex with anyone? I need to know."

"God, Lindy. You know me. I would never risk getting a disease."

"Please, just say the words. Yes, I have had unprotected sex, or no, I haven't had unprotected sex."

"No, I haven't had unprotected sex." The words were mechanical. She was glad he had difficulty saying them, but she knew they were true.

"Good. Well, if that's all, I guess you'll be hearing from Howard in a few weeks."

"Are you okay?"

"Yes. Good-bye." She put down the receiver. Gently. Just to let everyone know she was okay. That she had no hard feelings. Then she put her head on Biddy's shoulder and cried the last of the tears she would shed over the past.

After a few minutes she sat up. "Come in the bathroom while I try to make myself look normal again, and I'll give you the *Readers' Digest* version." She took a deep, shaky breath. "Then I have an affair to jump-start and a murder to solve."

Ten minutes later, she was walking along the corridor toward Bill's room. Jeremy answered the door with a worried look.

"*C'est fini,*" she said and gave him a hard-fought-for smile. He gave her a quick kiss and stepped into the hall. She closed the door behind him.

Bill was standing by the window with a glass of scotch.

"I hope you're not getting drunk," she said.

He shook his head. Kept looking out the window. Waiting to be told he was history. She could see it in the set of his shoulders. She crossed the room, took the glass, and put it on the table.

"Good," she said. "Because it's time to slip into something slow and skillful."

Chapter
Twenty-three

The phone rang at eight o'clock the next morning. Bill answered it before the first ring ended.

"Brandecker," he barked. After a few minutes of listening in silence, he hung up. "That was Andrew. He's downstairs. Dawn is back at the hotel."

"In spite of all the evidence against her?" asked Lindy.

"He wants us to meet him. Twenty minutes. Call Rose." He jumped out of bed and headed to the bathroom. Halfway across the floor, he stopped and turned back to her. "I—I'm not a cop anymore. I don't usually just jump out of bed and leave, I mean—"

He looked so guilty that Lindy had to fight the urge to laugh out loud. "Bill," she said, "chill."

"Right." He came back long enough for a prolonged kiss and was gone again. She pulled on her clothes, just as the sound of the shower burst into the room.

Twenty minutes later, Lindy, Rose, and Bill were sitting in front of Andrew Dean, cups of coffee in hand. A metal desk separated them. Two Atlantic City detectives stood against the wall behind them and a CSI detective, whose office had been commandeered for the meeting and whom Dean introduced as Detective Morrow, sat on the windowsill behind Dean.

"I don't like to use civilians," Dean said. "But I need someone Ms. Gilpatrick trusts."

"To what?" asked Rose. "Entrap her?"

Dean smiled. "Not at all. She didn't do it, or if she did, she's wilier than I give her credit for. Which could be the case. Her .38 didn't match the ballistics off the bullet from Corbett's body. She had no idea of how he was shot, even though she gave it her best shot, so to speak. I think she's covering for someone. And I think that someone is Katja Andreyevsky aka Karen Anderson. But that isn't your concern; stay away from Anderson."

"You mean Katja's back, too?" asked Lindy. She couldn't bring herself to call her Karen.

"I'm afraid so. We couldn't really keep her. She's tough as nails and we have no physical evidence that leads directly to her. The lab should be able to lift DNA from the body, but the results won't be in for a while, and I'd like to tie this up before the competition is over."

He glanced at Bill, then leaned forward and pointed a long finger at Rose, then at Lindy. "You just talk to her. Commiserate like friends would do. She's in her room now. There will be someone covering your back."

Rose and Lindy exchanged looks.

"Tell me now if you're having second thoughts. You should be entirely safe if you limit yourselves to talking with Ms. Gilpatrick. But if you want out, I'll understand completely."

Bill made a derisive snort. Lindy shook her head. "We know what to do. We're theatre people."

"Yeah," said Rose. "Beneath the makeup and chiffon are women of steel."

Bill leaned across Lindy and pointed *his* finger at Rose. "You," he said, "don't get too cocky with that martial arts stuff. There's a rogue pistol out there somewhere. You're only good at arm's length."

"Gentlemen," Rose said, unperturbed, "holster those fingers. We'll do what we have to do." She stood up.

"Not so fast," said Dean. "I said that Mr. Corbett wasn't killed with Gilpatrick's pistol. And it is hers. Registered, all nice and legal."

Rose sat back down.

"And the other pistol?" asked Lindy.

"There was none registered to Anderson under either of the names we know her by. But there is one registered to Carl Lonigan. It may be safely tucked away in his sock drawer in Cherry Hill. We didn't find it on the initial room search. I have somebody questioning him now. As soon as I hear from them, you can get started."

Lindy let this new information settle in before she asked, "Rusty? What if he brought it with him?"

"If we find it and it checks out, then fine. We'll keep looking. If we don't find it, then we have to assume someone out there either has it or dumped it after shooting Corbett."

"So you've given up on the idea that it was a random act, while Shane was out slumming?" asked Lindy.

"We haven't given up anything. We're still canvassing the area. Maybe this would be a good time to tell me what your two friendly winos had to say yesterday."

Had it only been yesterday? To Lindy, it seemed light-years ago. "Let's see. The one, the little one, was upset that the Gull Lady had kept both earrings and he had only gotten a dirty coat, which he had lost. I guess that was Dawn's coat and you found it on the beach or under the pier."

"Under the pier," said Dean. "And?"

"He was complaining that she wouldn't share. He wanted the money that he could have sold them for. I didn't have the heart to tell him they were only paste."

Dean smiled and nodded for her to continue.

"That's about it. The big guy kept telling him to shut up. And thanks to the timely arrival of two uniforms, that's all we got." She sighed. "I wonder what the big guy got."

"How so?"

"The smaller man said they always divided the spoils. The earrings, the coat, and the what? Shane's clothes, his shoes?"

"Or the murder weapon," said Dean. "Damn, I need a mentally disturbed drunk wandering around the city with a gun. Can you give me a description of them?"

Together, Lindy and Rose reconstructed a picture of the two men on the steps. Dean motioned to one of the detectives at the door. "Put an extra detail on the search for those two." The detective left the room.

Dean stood up, walked to the window, and conferred with Detective Morrow, who had remained aloof during the meeting. He pushed away from the sill and with a nod to Bill, but not to Rose and her, Lindy noted, he left the room. Dean stood looking out the window, hands in his pockets, jingling change. Lindy poured more coffee.

A few minutes later, Detective Morrow returned with a plain-clothesman and a nervous-looking Rusty Lonigan.

Dean pulled up another chair to the desk and motioned for Rusty to sit down. Then he took his own place behind the desk. "You're Carl Lonigan?"

Rusty practically jumped out of the chair. "Rusty. Everybody calls me Rusty." He was already dressed in a tuxedo, ready for the day's events. His face was beaded with sweat. The rim of his shirt collar was tinged orange from his pancake makeup. He swallowed, which he seemed to have difficulty accomplishing. "Yes. Carl, Carl Lonigan."

Dean looked over the notes taken by the detective who had questioned Rusty. "It says here that you brought a .38, which was registered to you, here to Atlantic City?"

Rusty nodded. "But I didn't shoot Shane, if that's what you're thinking, I had no reason to."

Except that he was leaving your studio to work for Junie, thought Lindy. First Timothy and then Shane, a big loss of students and income, and a huge amount of extra work for Rusty. She saw Bill shoot her a quizzical look.

"We're not accusing you of anything at the moment," said Dean calmly. Lindy noticed that his demeanor only made Rusty more nervous. "Could you please tell us where you kept the pistol and when you saw it last?"

Rusty pulled at his collar. Blew out air. "I kept it in my briefcase. It wasn't loaded." He blew out air again. Lindy was afraid he might start to hyperventilate. "The box of ammo, too. It's not like there're any children around."

Dean gave him a sour look. Rusty's hand reached for his collar again. His fingers were shaking.

"And why did you have the .38 with you?"

"It was Dawn's idea. She was always going on about how unsafe it was. You know, leaving the studio late. We deal mainly in checks and credit cards—you can check with my auditor, everything is aboveboard—but on guest party nights we take in a lot of cash. Dawn insisted we learn to shoot and made me buy pistols. I only carry it around to make her feel better. I've never even loaded the damn thing." Rusty shivered as if the mere idea was distasteful.

"And now it's missing?"

Rusty nodded. "And the ammo. We searched—everywhere in the room, didn't we?" He looked for confirmation from the detective who had accompanied him. The man nodded.

"This is just terrible."

"And who had access to your room?"

"Um, besides me?"

Dean nodded patiently.

"Well, Dawn and Katja could have gone in. I didn't see any reason to lock it. We're respectful of each other's privacy."

"Did anyone share the room with you?"

"Huh? Oh, no. I have a wife, but she doesn't come to the comps. Katja had the other bedroom. Dawn used the fold-out couch in the living room."

Rose made a disgusted noise, but a look from Bill stopped her from commenting. Lindy knew what she was reacting to. It wasn't about whether Rusty was lying about his bedmates, but that Katja got the second bedroom, while Dawn had to sleep on the couch.

"Anyone else? Any visitors to the suite? Someone who might have passed through your room to use the bathroom, perhaps?"

"Oh—there was a party Saturday night."

"The competition didn't begin until the next day, is that correct?"

"Yes, but Dawn is one of the sponsors so we were here a few days early setting up. We brought our Exclusive Club down the night before. You know, dinner, drinks in our suite. It's a special offer to our, uh, most valued students."

Read big money people, thought Lindy and saw that Detective Dean was thinking the same thing.

"It would be helpful if you could give us a list of those present."

"Of course, but would it be possible to do this later? I'm supposed to be on the floor at nine o'clock. You don't know what those ladies are like if you're late."

Dean pushed a yellow legal pad toward him and tapped the tip of a pen on the paper. "Now, if you would, Mr. Lonigan."

With a worried look, Rusty wiped his hands on his trousers and began to write. As soon as he finished, he jumped up.

"Just a minute," said Dean, looking over the list. "These are all students of yours?"

"Mostly. And their teachers. I put an asterisk next to the teachers' names."

Dean nodded. "And all these people are still at the hotel?"

"Yes, except for Mrs. Perkins. She had a fit when Shane didn't show up for the Monday morning session and went home in a huff. She's like that. She'll be back next week having forgotten why she was mad." He sat down again. "Damn, she probably doesn't even know about Shane."

"Anyone else?"

Rusty shook his head. "Dawn used Katja's bathroom." He hesitated. "Well, Junie came in the night we went out to dinner. He had a drink in the living room while I took a quick shower."

"Could he have gone into your room while you were in the shower?"

"I guess, but why would he? And he didn't even know I owned a .38. Hell, it was too embarrassing."

Dean grunted. "You can go for now, Mr. Lonigan, but don't leave the hotel, please."

Rusty jumped up. "Thank you. I won't. I'll be in the ballroom until noon if you want me for anything else. Then again from one to four." He crossed the room in three steps and was gone.

"Whew," said Dean. "I don't know whether he was more afraid of being questioned by the police or of being late to the dance."

"The latter," Rose assured him.

Dean pushed the legal pad toward Rose and Lindy. "Any of these names familiar?"

"Just Rusty, Junie, Katja, and Dawn," said Lindy. "Some of the other names, I recognize from the ballroom, but I've never met them."

"Same here," said Rose.

"We'll check them out. And this Mrs. Perkins who left in a huff. I'd like you to get up to Ms. Gilpatrick's room before she's off to the ballroom. Check back with me if you find out anything we don't know. I'll be around." He opened a drawer and reached inside. "Take these. But only use them if you get into something you can't handle. They're set to an emergency frequency." He placed two walkie-talkies on the desk.

"Wired," said Rose. "Cool." She picked them up and handed one to Lindy.

"For all other communications call my cell phone." Two cards followed the walkie-talkies.

Lindy slipped the card into her shirt pocket. The walkie-talkie felt heavy and intrusive in her hand. They followed Bill into the hall and stopped at the elevator.

"Criminy, they suspect everybody," said Lindy.

Bill nodded. "I told you that it was a lengthy process. It takes determination and a clear head to sort through all the possible suspects."

"But he doesn't suspect us."

"That's because I didn't arrive until Monday morning. I'm sure he cleared that before he let us in on what was happening. And he ran the two of you through the computer."

"We're in the computer?" asked Lindy, surprised.

"I don't know about Rose, but you are. Remember Connecticut? They have your fingerprints, your telephone number, even your dress size."

"You're kidding."

Bill tapped her nose. "So think about that if you ever consider stealing the Hope diamond."

"I will," she said.

Chapter
Twenty-four

Dawn opened the door. Her hair was wrapped in a purple terry cloth turban and she was wearing a paisley robe that she held together in a tight fist. "They let me go," she said in a voice tinged with bewilderment.

"Of course they let you go," said Rose, pushing her way past her. "You didn't kill Shane."

Dawn sighed and stepped back to let Lindy enter.

"Why on earth did you say you did?" asked Rose. She turned on the shorter woman so abruptly that Dawn skittered backward and banged into the open door. She pushed it shut.

"They searched the suite," continued Dawn, either oblivious of or choosing to ignore the question. "They were leaving when we got back. And they had Rusty. Where were they taking him? Do they think he killed Shane?"

Ignoring her, Lindy asked, "Where's Katja?"

Dawn glanced toward the closed door to Katja's bedroom. "She came in and locked herself in her bedroom. She won't talk to me. She thinks I murdered Shane. She's afraid of me."

Lindy doubted it, but she, for one, was afraid of Katja. She glanced at Rose. Rose merely lifted an unbelieving eyebrow, walked to the couch, and sat down—a position from which she could keep her eyes on the door to Katja's room, Lindy noted.

Dawn followed them into the living room, picking up stray pieces of clothing on her way. She shoved them into a drawer of the television hutch, then made a sweep of the room. She straightened a magazine on the coffee table, removed a glass and set it on the table.

"Have you eaten?" asked Lindy. "Why don't we order something from room service?" Dawn shook her head.

"Great idea," said Rose with a touch too much enthusiasm. She reached for a menu. "Breakfast? Coffee? Tea?"

"Just coffee, thanks," said Dawn and continued her circuit of the room. "They made a mess," she said.

The room looked fine to Lindy, but she didn't say so. Dawn obviously needed something to keep her occupied. She kept moving through the room, casting nervous glances at the closed bedroom door. Lindy sat down to wait. When Dawn had worn herself out with useless puttering, she would be more likely to confide in them.

"Why won't she talk to me? She can't really believe that I killed Shane."

"Why not?" asked Rose. "You confessed."

"I had to."

"Because you believed she had killed Shane?"

"No, of course not," said Dawn indignantly. "But I was afraid that everyone would think she had killed him. Katja is very special and people are jealous of her."

"So now you're saying you didn't kill Shane," said Lindy, as gently as her impatience would allow.

"I didn't." Dawn's face crumpled and she reached for the ever-ready tissue box. Then she dropped onto the couch and tucked her feet beneath her. "But I could have. Doesn't that count?"

Lindy was certain she couldn't have heard correctly, but Rose's expression as she hung up the phone said that she had.

"Get a grip, Dawn," said Rose. "No, it doesn't count. What counts is that someone else murdered Shane. And you're not help-

ing anyone by these flights of fancy. Not anyone. Do you
hend that?"

Dawn snatched up a throw pillow and hugged it to her c
don't want to talk about it. I'm so confused."

Rose flicked a glance at Lindy. She took the cue. "I'm sur
must be," she said gently, slipping into the role of good co
Rose's bad. She'd have to give Rose a lecture about her own flig
of fancy someday. "It's so awful, isn't it?"

Dawn nodded.

"You know, Rose and I were suspected of murder once. In
Connecticut." Rose's eyes rounded. She hadn't even worked for
Jeremy then. "Someone in our company was murdered, and the po-
lice were everywhere, asking all sorts of questions.

"I never knew what to tell them. I mean, all the people in the
company were my friends. I just couldn't believe one of them would
do something like that. My first instinct was to protect them."

No response from Dawn.

"But then I realized that I wasn't protecting them. That they
might be in mortal danger." At least she had Dawn's attention now.
"If the murderer had killed once, he might kill again."

Dawn gasped. "You mean, he might try to kill Katja?"

It was an effort not to let her exasperation to Dawn's obsession
show in her face. Rose didn't bother, but Dawn was giving Lindy
her full attention and didn't notice. Lindy shrugged. "It's always a
possibility."

"We've got to get her away from here." Dawn pushed the pillow
aside and started to get up.

"You can't. Neither of you is allowed to leave the hotel."

Dawn sat back, deflated. "What should I do?"

"I think it's time you told the truth."

Rose cleared her throat. Lindy took her eyes from Dawn long
enough to see Rose cut her eyes toward Katja's bedroom. Lindy
leaned over to straighten the already straightened magazine and saw
that the door was ajar. So, Katja was listening. What would she do if
Dawn actually incriminated her? Should they wait and see?

Rose took the question out of her hands. "We know you're listening, Katja. Why don't you come out and join us?"

The door opened all the way. Katja stepped out, fully dressed in a calf-length iridescent dress and heels. Her false eyelashes were in place and bright red lipstick accentuated the scowl on her lips. "I have students waiting for me in the ballroom. *I* have work to do." She stepped back into the bedroom and came out a moment later carrying a burgundy dance bag, which she slung over her shoulder. After an accusing look at Dawn, she marched out of the room, slamming the door behind her.

"I—I should be going down, too," said Dawn, a tremor in her voice. "They'll wonder what's happened to me."

I doubt it, thought Lindy, not after Katja spreads the news.

There was a knock on the door.

"Katja," said Dawn.

"Room service," said Rose and got up to answer it.

The waiter came in with a covered tray. Rose didn't follow him inside but stepped into the hallway. As soon as he hefted the covered tray onto the table, Lindy signed for the food and hurried him toward the door, searching her bag for the tip as they went.

Rose was waiting just outside the door. "I'll get it." She fumbled in her jeans pocket, while she danced the waiter in a half circle, all the time looking over the man's head and down the hallway. Then suddenly she stepped back into the room. "I guess you'd better get it," she said to Lindy. Lindy handed over two dollars. Rose pulled a five out of Lindy's open wallet and stuffed it into the man's hand as well. She shut the door on his "Wow, thanks."

"What was that for?" whispered Lindy.

"Katja didn't go to the ballroom. She was at the other end of the hall when I opened the door. Thank God for room service. There's no elevator at that end, only a short corridor of rooms on the street side of the hotel. And she was fumbling in her bag, maybe searching for a key card, like she was going to someone's room. Someone on a budget. Too bad I couldn't follow her. She's up to something. I'm going to call Detective Dean and have him check into it. Get Dawn started on some food."

Lindy coaxed Dawn to the table, while Rose went into Rusty's room to make the call. A minute later she was back, gave Lindy a surreptitious thumbs-up, and sat down in front of a plate of pastries.

"Great view," said Rose, looking out the window.

Dawn frowned at her.

"I've got a great view from my room, too. Does everybody at the comp have an ocean view?"

Dawn continued to stare at Rose as if she had lost her mind. Rose smiled at her, waiting for an answer. "No," Dawn finally said. "Most of the competitors, students and teachers are at the back of the hotel in the cheaper rooms."

Rose's face fell. "Almost everybody, in other words."

"Yes."

They ate in silence, while Dawn pushed flakes of pastry around her plate with the tip of her fork. Lindy reached for another piece of cantaloupe. It was amazing how hungry she was.

"So what happened that first night after you and Shane and Katja left the ballroom?" she asked. Realizing she sounded more like an interrogator than a gossip, she hurried on. "I mean, what a scene. And poor Katja—finding out that Shane was leaving, in front of everybody."

Dawn pushed her plate away, pulled her coffee cup closer, and wrapped both hands around it. "She was so upset. I followed her back to the room. I tried to reassure her that she didn't need Shane, that I'd find her a better partner. Oh, Damn. I forgot about the Hollingfords. I should call him and see if he's still available."

"Dawn," Rose urged, "what happened after you left the ball-room?"

"Shane caught up to me. At first I didn't want to let him in. Then I decided we might as well get it over with." She made a giggling sound. "Me, who never lets go of anything.

"He came inside, but Katja wasn't here. I checked her room. She hadn't been back. There was no dress or dance bag or anything. Shane was livid. He said he had found out about Katja not being Russian. He had her driver's license. She was always so careful not to let anyone see it. He must have stolen it from her wallet. Can you believe it?"

"He threatened you?" asked Lindy, trying to guide Dawn back to the pertinent facts.

"He said he'd make sure everyone knew that Katja was a fake. Her career would be finished, and I'd lose all credibility on the circuit. I couldn't let that happen to Katja. I told him fine. He could leave. I wouldn't sue him like I was planning to do to Timothy. He told me that wasn't good enough."

"What did he want?"

"Want?" Dawn shrugged. "He wanted the dress. He said he would give the license back if I would give him the dress. That we could keep up with our 'little charade'; he wouldn't tell. Such a hoo-ha over a dress. I told him he could have the damn thing. Felicia could make all the copies she wanted. But I didn't have the dress. I called around to see if any of the girls had seen Katja, but they hadn't." Dawn stopped on a shaky breath, her eyes filling with tears.

It *was* a lot of to-do over a dress, thought Lindy. But then Enrico had said his dresses always took first. "Why do you think Shane was so determined to have the dress? Enrico could have made one for them. Hell, he had a display full of them."

"Except that they had all been destroyed by the next morning," said Rose.

"Even if they hadn't been, Shane and Felicia could never have afforded one," said Dawn. "None of his gowns cost less than three thousand dollars and that was three or four years ago. The one he loaned me was just a prototype. He was going to list that design for four or more. And he would have gotten it, too."

"Do you think Felicia could have gotten back on the floor in his dress without Enrico stopping her?" asked Lindy.

"What's to stop her?" asked Dawn. "Enrico hasn't been seen since the morning of his big opening. Poor guy. I should probably send him something. Do you think flowers would be inappropriate?"

Lindy rolled her eyes. "Do you think that Shane really believed Enrico's dress would win a competition for them?"

"I don't know. He wanted it because of the movie. Harold approached me with the idea of using the comp to talent scout for this Fred Astaire movie he's producing. I invited them expense free. I meant to get the part for Shane and Katja. But Shane wanted the part for himself and Felicia. Enrico's designs are from that period, I guess, and Shane thought the dress would make them appear right for the part. He said a movie contract would bankroll their ballroom career."

More than *from* the right period, thought Lindy. They *were* the period. And at least Shane was smart enough to know that. "So then what happened?"

"He told me to go find her. He was getting kind of scary, so I left him here while I went to look for her."

"And did you find her?"

"No." Dawn seemed to withdraw inside herself. She took a sip of coffee and grimaced. "When I came back, he was gone. I hoped maybe Katja had come back and they had made up." She smiled ruefully. "Pretty silly of me, wasn't it?"

It certainly was, thought Lindy. Most likely Katja had come back, somehow lured him outside and shot him. Had she then slipped into the vendors' room and destroyed the remaining gowns? Did she think that would draw suspicion from her? It didn't make sense to Lindy. Then again, getting murdered over a dress didn't make too much sense, either. She had so many questions she didn't know what to ask first, and she was afraid if she pressed too much, Dawn would get nervous and clam up.

"So how did you find out that Katja was at the beach house?" asked Rose. She had dropped her hard edge, and her voice was soothing and honey-toned.

"She called. Not that night, but Tuesday. She said that she had returned the dress to Enrico and he was so nasty to her that she

freaked. She drove to the beach house just to get away and think."
Dawn sniffed. "See? She couldn't have killed Shane. She didn't
have the dress anymore. She didn't even know that he was dead
until I told her." She stopped and looked from Lindy to Rose. For
the first time since Lindy had met her, she seemed to be aware that
she was the only one talking. The room became quiet.

"Luis said she didn't return the dress," said Lindy.

With a flick of her nail tips, Dawn waved the remark aside. "What
does Luis know? He's just a lapdog and he does good diamantés."

"Did he or Enrico ever come here?"

"To the suite? Luis did. He brought the dress Sunday afternoon
when they first arrived and did a fitting. Enrico was hiding out in his
room the whole day, so nobody would see him." Dawn tapped her
nails against her coffee cup, then gasped: "That's it! Enrico must
have killed Shane."

Lindy blinked as she tried to catch up with Dawn's shift of ideas.

"Don't you see? Enrico is lying. Katja returned the dress. It had
to be him. He has a vicious temper. And he's big enough that he
could have put Shane in that dress even after he was dead. That
must be it." Dawn jumped up, her body humming with febrile excitement. "Do you think I should call that Detective-what's-his-
name and tell him I was mistaken? It really was Enrico that killed
Shane, not me. And I won't send him flowers."

This time both Lindy and Rose rolled their eyes.

Rose reached for the coffeepot. "Sit back down and have another
cup of coffee first. I want to know why you ran away at the beach
house. We were only trying to help. If it hadn't been for Bill, you
could have died."

Dawn picked up her cup. "Who is he? A friend of yours? When
he crashed in like that, I thought he might be the murderer."

Lindy groaned inwardly, but didn't point out that Bill had not
crashed in, only stepped quietly into the room just in time to save
them from being brained by the fireplace poker.

"And the way he badgered Katja. It wasn't fair. He frightened
her."

"He also pulled her out of the marshes, then went back to get you. At much risk to himself, I might add," said Lindy.

Rose shot her a warning look. Lindy took a deep breath.

"And now I'm car-less," said Dawn. "I'll have to get a loaner. Maybe I can get Rusty to deal with the insurance. If he hasn't been arrested."

Lindy gritted her teeth. She reached for a crescent roll and bit into it to save her enamel.

Dawn stood up. "Well, this was nice, but I really have to get dressed and make an appearance in the ballroom. Students get nervous if you're not around to stroke them every now and then. Are you going down? Maybe you could just make sure Katja's got everything she needs."

Dawn pulled the turban off her head. She used it to towel-dry her hair while she rummaged through her underwear drawer.

Rose and Lindy stood up. "We'll see you down there."

Dawn waved over her head at them and they let themselves out.

Chapter
Twenty-five

Rose and Lindy stopped on the lobby level to report what they had learned to Detective Dean. He added Luis to the list of those who had been in the suite during the week. The one depressing piece of news that Dean had to share with them was that although there were only twelve rooms along the far corridor, most housed two to four registered guests and possibly more unregistered ones.

There were only a few people in the ballroom that morning, and only one couple on the floor. Their routine ended to a smattering of applause, and Rusty Lonigan and his student replaced them on the dance floor.

"Spotlights," said Rose.

"Where?" asked Lindy, looking around for the heavy equipment.

"That's what they're doing. Individual routines. Choreography, not just school figures. We might as well sit down. This could take hours." They were making their way toward the Stepping Out tables when Rose pulled up short. "Damn. She beat us here and she's not alone."

Dawn sat at the Stepping Out table and Junie was sitting beside her. Junie jumped up when he saw Lindy and Rose approaching. He looked like he would have run for it if there had been anywhere to run, but they were between him and the door. Lindy and Rose sat down just as "Black Magic Woman" sounded through the speakers, making it impossible to talk. Rusty and his partner began their routine. As soon as it ended, he escorted his lady to the edge of the floor, gave her a quick pat on the shoulder, and hurried toward Dawn's table.

"What did they say after I left? They don't think I murdered Shane, do they?"

Lindy shrugged. "We don't know what they think. He just called *us* in to get our statements about what happened at the beach house."

Rusty dropped into the chair next to her and patted a towel across his face. "I can't wait until this is all over." He leaned across Lindy to get Dawn's attention. "How are you holding up?"

Dawn didn't hear him. She was looking in the direction of another table. "What's she doing at the Ballroom on Main table?"

They all turned to see Katja holding court at a nearby table, surrounded by a group that was listening avidly to what she was saying. Sitting next to her was Vincent Padrewsky.

"Her fifteen minutes of fame," said Rusty. He threw his towel on the table. "I'm on again." He got up and walked toward the dance floor. Lindy watched him pick up another lady. He was all business now, calm, and secure, but he had fallen apart when the police had questioned him. Of course, the police had that effect on some people, herself included.

"Some fame," said Junie. "I hope she enjoys it before they lock her up for good." He turned to Dawn, waiting for the harangue he knew he was about to receive and that he seemed to relish as much as she did.

But Dawn didn't rise to the bait. She was staring at Katja and Vincent.

Lindy watched Vincent Padrewsky with interest. She hadn't seen him on the floor all week. "Does Vincent work for Ballroom on Main?" she asked.

Junie grimaced. "When he's not too drunk. But only front end. He's not reliable enough to take on the full-program students."

Rusty's showcase came to an end and the emcee announced the lunch break. Couples from around the room started for the door. A few couples moved onto the floor, which would be available for practice. Vincent stood up and said something to Katja. She shook her head. With a shrug, Vincent rummaged through his dance bag and pulled out a pack of cigarettes. Then he left the table and meandered toward the service hall. Katja picked up her own bag and went in the opposite direction.

Lindy wondered how many people used that hallway for a quick cigarette between heats. Had one of them discovered the door to the vendors' room and taped it open, then sneaked in to destroy Enrico's dresses?

Rusty was back again. "I'm going to the teachers' room for lunch. Anybody coming?"

Junie stood up and pulled Dawn to her feet. "We'll all go." He looked at Rose and Lindy. "You'll join us, of course."

"Isn't the room only for teachers?" asked Lindy.

"With the number of students we have at this comp," said Rusty, "they wouldn't dare call us on a couple of extra ham slices." He grabbed his dance bag, which was the same color as most of the bags in the room, and motioned them toward the door.

"All those burgundy dance bags must be freebies," said Lindy as she and Rose followed Rusty across the hall. "It's amazing that anyone ends up with their own."

Several doors down from the lounges, the teachers' room was doing a lively lunchtime buffet. Tables were filling up. They joined the queue to the food table.

Lindy was just reaching for a plate when Katja passed by, blatantly ignoring them. She balanced a plate piled high with chicken fingers, French fries and mozzarella sticks in one hand and a piece of pie in the other. Not diet food. Comfort food. Lindy felt her first pang of misgiving. So the girl had lied about her nationality. So she had panicked when Dawn told her about Shane's murder. It was a natural reaction when you thought about it. Maybe she *had* gone to the beach house to think things over. Try to patch up a career that was suddenly floundering. Had they been too quick to judge her?

Katja paused at a table and glowered at the people who sat there, Felicia Falcone and Timothy Saunders. Felicia jumped up. "How can you eat when Shane is dead?" she demanded. Around them people looked on, expecting, perhaps hoping for, a fight.

Katja turned away. Felicia knocked the plate out of her hand. Food went flying. So did diners.

Katja launched herself at Felicia; they fell against the table. "He was *my* partner. *My* boyfriend," she cried in her thickest Russian accent.

"You moron. He was leaving you. In every way. I should know."

Katja reached for her throat. Rusty leapt from the food line and latched on to her wrist. Timothy jumped up and grabbed Felicia from behind.

"Oh, no," said Dawn. "There's Danny Hollingford at the door. He'll never dance with Katja if he sees this catfight." Dawn dropped her plate onto the nearest table and ran to cut off Hollingford's entrance.

Junie took two smooth steps toward the table. He jabbed a finger at Katja. "Any more trouble from you and I'll have you expelled from the competition." He looked sternly at Felicia. She brushed off her skirt and sat down. After a moment's hesitation, Timothy sat down, too.

Junie and Rusty resumed their places in the food line and within a few minutes, they all, including Dawn, were angling their way toward a back table.

"Junie, sit here, we were just leaving." A young dancer, probably no more than fourteen or fifteen, stood up. He was tall and skinny. Like the adults, his hair was sprayed in place and he was wearing makeup. The girl next to him was a head shorter than he. Another miniature adult; false eyelashes, glitter-blue eye shadow, the whole regalia. She was wearing a Latin dress with so little fabric, Lindy wondered how she had gotten past her mother. She smiled saucily at Junie before they hurried away.

"Nice boy," said Junie. "Good line, perfect rhythm. He'll have to dump her though. She isn't going to grow."

"Not up, anyway," agreed Rusty. He deposited his plate and silverware on the table and waited for the women to sit down. "A shame really. At six she was knocking out steps like a pro."

Not even arrived and a has-been already, thought Lindy with a pang of compassion. Though perhaps it was better that way. Better than having arrived and then become a has-been like Vincent Padrewsky.

Lindy and Rose spent the rest of the afternoon following Dawn in and out of the ballroom. At five o'clock, they left her at the elevator and went to the theatre. With dress rehearsal an hour away, only the professional stage dancers were warming up. At five to six the formation team and the honor dance couples came in complaining about having to rehearse during their dinner hour.

At eight o'clock, everyone was back in the ballroom. Lindy scanned the room looking for Bill. He was standing against the opposite wall, talking to Andrew Dean. He had met them briefly for dinner, but he was clearly preoccupied and Lindy didn't think it was with her. She sighed. Nothing was going to happen, and time was running out—for catching a murderer and for spending time with Bill.

"Some vacation," she said dejectedly.

"You and Bill should spend a quiet Christmas together," commiserated Rose.

"Can't. He's going home for the holidays."

Rose grinned. "Afraid to meet his mother?"

The ballroom was packed. This was the culminating evening of the weeklong competition. Latin dancing was scheduled throughout the evening. It was obviously a big draw. Probably why they had saved it for last.

The evening passed—at a snail's pace in spite of the frenetic music and movement. Rusty led women back and forth from the floor for pro am heats and general dancing.

Katja was sitting at the Ballroom on Main table and only came near the Stepping Out tables long enough to pick up one of her students for a dance and drop him off again. She didn't look at Dawn, who sat morosely watching the competition.

During one of the short breaks, Rose leaned over to Lindy. "They've opened a bar at the back of the room for the final night. We can get a drink and not miss anything."

"Works for me, get in line. I'll just say a quick hello to Bill and I'll join you." Rose went off in the direction of the bar. Lindy had almost reached Bill when Junie and Rusty crossed in front of her and left the room. Bill and Andrew Dean slipped out behind them. Lindy hurried after them.

The hallway was crowded with practicing couples and people talking or heading toward the Pagoda Bar. But she didn't see Junie and Rusty or Bill and Andrew. She was tempted to look for them, but she had left her evening bag that held the walkie-talkie on the table. Not bright, she thought. She went back to retrieve it.

She had just stepped inside when she saw Katja standing at the Stepping Out table. She leaned over and said something to Dawn. Dawn got up and the two of them walked together toward the exit.

Lindy slunk back behind a group of people as they passed. She looked for Rose but couldn't see her for the crowd. Her eyes on the departing women, she wondered if she had time to get to the table for the walkie-talkie and still catch up to them. They might be going back to their suite, but Lindy doubted it. And they might elude her if she wasted time getting to the Stepping Out table.

Lindy stepped outside. Katja and Dawn were walking quickly down the hall, not toward the elevators, but toward the escalators to the casino. Katja was wearing a thick sweater coat over her dress and had changed her dance shoes for sneakers. Her dance bag was slung over one shoulder. Not a good fashion statement, thought Lindy, but appropriate if you were planning to leave the hotel. Dawn was wearing heels and had to run to keep up.

Katja guided Dawn onto the escalator and stood behind her as they descended. Lindy waited until they reached the casino level before she started down, praying they wouldn't turn around and see her. They didn't turn. They didn't even slow down when they reached the casino but skirted around the perimeter, past the coffee bar, past the change and token office, and into the all-night souvenir shop.

Lindy hesitated. What were they up to this time? And what the hell was she going to do about it? She stood close to the wall and peeked around the glass door of the souvenir shop, while at the same time trying not to look suspicious. All she needed was to be escorted away by one of the many security guards employed by the casino and let Dawn and Katja get away. They were arm in arm on the other side of the store. Dawn was shaking her head, her lips compressed. Katja rummaged in her dance bag. Looking for money? Were they shopping? Then Lindy saw a second door that opened onto the boardwalk. Oh, shit, it *was* happening.

Lindy looked quickly over the casino. Of all nights not to find Rebo, Juan and Eric at the slot machines. But they were sick of ballroom and gambling and had taken a cab to the mall as soon as the dress rehearsal ended. Damn. She could alert one of the guards, ask them to contact Dean. But would they believe her? Or think she was drunk or crazy and detain her while Katja and Dawn got away? She couldn't take the chance.

She searched the room, praying for a familiar face, but the only person she saw was Vincent Padrewsky, sitting at his usual craps tables. Great. A lot of help he would be. She glanced back at Dawn and Katja. They were huddled together now, and pushing against the exit door.

Lindy hesitated for only a second. Vincent was her only hope. She hurried over to the craps table.

"Vincent." She shook his shoulder. The dealer looked at her and frowned. "He's had enough," she said and smiled at the man with a mouth that had to be feral. He had probably seen worse expressions on angry spouses. He nodded. Lindy scooped up the pile of chips and stuffed them into Vincent's jacket pocket. Vincent looked down at her hand, then slid off the stool.

"Vincent, this is important. You know who Rose is?"

Vincent made a silly smile and said, "Sure, the Amazon that kay-oed Enrico." He swayed slightly.

"Listen. This is really important. A matter of life and death."

Vincent kept smiling. Oh, God. She had to make him understand. She shook him hard. "Rose is in the ballroom. Find her. Tell her to come to the boardwalk. Now. Immediately." She started pushing him toward the escalator. "Vincent, do you understand? You've got to hurry."

"Sure. Tell the Amazon to come to the boardwalk."

"Yes. Tell her to bring help."

"Help? I can help."

"Just get Rose. Please."

She couldn't wait any longer. She gave him another shove and walked quickly toward the souvenir shop. A second later, she was standing outside on the boardwalk.

It was freezing and she started to shiver. At least she was wearing slacks and flat shoes tonight. She peered in both directions, hoping against hope that there was a restaurant open and Katja and Dawn had gone inside to talk. But she knew that was unlikely. And then she saw them.

They were moving along the edge of the boardwalk, passing in and out of the lamplight, heading in the direction of the pier. They were huddled so close together that they looked like one person. But Lindy knew it was them. They were having trouble walking. The wood was still slippery from rain and melting snow.

She moved after them, glancing behind her to see if help was on its way. She was cold. Alone. And frightened. What were they up to? And what could she do about it? Please, God, that Vincent was sober enough to carry out her instructions.

Ahead of her, one of the women slipped and fell. Dawn, she thought. Katja leaned over to help her up. Lindy slowed down, hugging the shadows, keeping her eyes on the two women. Katja was having trouble getting Dawn to her feet. Then with a horrifying bolt of understanding, Lindy understood why.

Chapter
Twenty-six

Dawn was struggling, her arms and legs lashing out at Katja. Katja dodged and batted her hands away as she tried to haul Dawn to her feet. Dawn wrenched to the side. Katja lost her balance, her feet slipped out from under her, and she sprawled on top of Dawn.

This was the time to stop them, when their attention was focused on each other and not on Lindy. But which one should she try to overpower? Katja? She had lured Dawn outside. She had dragged her this far down the pier. She must be the one who had murdered Shane. But if Lindy was wrong, she would put them all in jeopardy.

She hesitated only for a second, but it was time enough for Katja to regain her feet. She stepped away from Dawn, and stood looking down at her. Slowly Dawn crawled to her knees, her face lifted to the other woman.

Lindy slid to a stop but her feet kept going, and she only managed to keep herself from falling by grabbing hold of one of the lampposts. Katja turned, raised her arm toward Lindy.

She knew in that instant what Katja was going to do, but she couldn't move. She was caught in the lamplight like a startled animal. The sound of the shot and the clang of the bullet as it ricocheted off the lamppost seemed to come simultaneously. Lindy sat down hard. She was afraid to move. Afraid not to move. A sitting duck—literally.

She looked over her shoulder toward the hotel. No one was coming. They would be too late.

Katja pulled Dawn to her feet and they stumbled toward the pier. They reached the entrance, and suddenly they were gone. Lindy pulled herself up by the lamppost. Squinted down the boardwalk, but saw no movement. They had just disappeared. No. Not disappeared. They must be hiding in the shadows of the arch. There was nowhere else for them to go. There was a fence across the entrance to the pier. It was a dead end.

Lindy sprang to her feet. Adrenaline surged past her fear and propelled her forward. A dead end for Dawn if someone didn't stop them. But would Katja really kill Dawn knowing that Lindy would be a witness? That stopped her for a minute. Katja would have no qualms about killing her, too.

Grasping the rails of the boardwalk, Lindy moved as quickly as she dared toward the pier entrance. She stopped, clinging to the concrete supports of the arch, knowing that on the other side Katja held a gun on Dawn. She didn't have a plan. She just knew she had to prevent Katja from committing another murder.

She looked for something to throw into the darkness, hoping to distract Katja long enough for Dawn to escape. But in the next moment, she heard running footsteps on the pier. They had gone inside.

Lindy eased around the arch and peered into the shadows. The chain-link fence had not been repaired. The police tape had been torn from the gaping hole.

No one would know they were on the pier. And if Lindy followed them, there would be no one to tell them where to look. But if she didn't follow them, it might be too late.

She searched for a place to leave some sign of where they had gone. The thick walls of the arch blocked any ambient light from the lampposts. Even if she left something at the entrance, no one would see it.

The yellow tape skittered across the wood as the wind kicked up. She grabbed one end and stretched it toward the center of the boardwalk. But when she let go, it curled back into the archway. She needed something to anchor it with.

A piece of corrugated roof was lying next to the fence. She clutched it with numb fingers and dragged it into the middle of the walk. It made horrible rumbling noises, but it didn't matter. Katja and Dawn knew she was there. She pulled the tape back and anchored it with the roof. Then she yanked the necklace from her neck and hung it over the edge of the metal. The stones were real, but it seemed a small price to pay if it would save a life, maybe her own.

She pulled her earrings from her ears. She tried to balance them on the top, but they fell to the ground. She grappled for them, her fingers awkward with cold, every second expecting to hear another shot. She gave up and left them on the ground.

It wasn't much, but it might work. There was just enough hint of light that someone might see them. And Bill would recognize them. She looked desperately toward the hotel, then back to the hole in the fence. Katja's burgundy dance bag lay open beside it. Lindy grabbed the bag and threw it into the center of the boardwalk. The rescuers would see that, and between the bag, the jewelry, and the tape, they would know where she had gone. She climbed through the tear in the fence.

Once inside, she stopped, listening for the sound of footsteps. She heard waves breaking on the shore, the rumble of metal knocking in the wind, and at last, whimpering and scuffling feet. They were headed toward the end of the pier where the waves swelled beneath it. Katja wouldn't have to shoot Dawn. She could just push her into the ocean. She might never be found and no one could prove that she had been murdered.

Lindy knew she couldn't wait for help. Even if Vincent had found Rose, she would never make it in time to save Dawn. She thought longingly of the walkie-talkie that she had left behind. Prayed that Bill had seen her leave the ballroom. Then she took a deep breath, and hugging the frigid sides of the concession trailers, she crept forward.

She was getting closer to them; she could hear grunts as Dawn tripped and was hauled to her feet. At least she was slowing Katja down. Maybe Lindy would find a way to stop her.

At the end of the last trailer, she peered around the corner. Nothing but more darkness. She stepped quickly across the opening. Thought she heard a footstep behind her. Hope blossomed and then fear. She pressed herself into a crevice between two hand carts, but no one came.

She had to stay focused, not let her imagination run wild. That could be fatal. She inched ahead, ears alert for the slightest sound. At the far side of the pier, towers of some ride disappeared into the sky. In front of her, the ticket booth stood like a lone sentry box, to her right was the roller coaster. And in between—open, empty space. She edged along the curve of the roller coaster and slipped behind the ticket booth just as two shadows stepped onto the tracks. She pressed into the wall and held her breath.

The echoes of footsteps broke into the night. They must be climbing the tracks. Of course. There was a fence around the pier. Katja would have to lure Dawn above the height of the fence to push her into the water. Lindy leaned forward just enough to see the two women outlined against the sky. Katja was behind Dawn, pushing her upward. She was looking back over her shoulder, her eyes scanning the pier below her, looking for Lindy. The moon cast just enough light to silhouette the pistol Katja was pointing in her direction.

She dared not move. If only Dawn could upset Katja's balance, it might give Lindy time to overpower her. But Dawn was going meekly to the slaughter. Did she have any idea of what was going to happen to her? What was wrong with the woman?

And then gloriously there was the sound of running footsteps. Reprieved, Lindy turned to warn them about the gun and her words died in her throat. Vincent Padrewsky was loping toward her and he was alone. Lindy wanted to cry for the absurdity of it all. Dawn was going to die because of her stupidity. And possibly Vincent, because of his own stupidity.

"Vincent," she hissed. "Over here." She waved him toward her. But Vincent stopped and smiled stupidly at her, oblivious to the danger. He was standing out in the open, a burgundy dance bag hanging from his shoulder, and Lindy's heart sank.

The sounds of climbing had stopped. "Vincent, get down."

Vincent's face took on a look of surprise. He must have seen Katja and Dawn on the roller coaster. He clambered toward Lindy.

"Did you find Rose?" she whispered, already knowing the answer. Vincent shrugged. "Found this," he whispered back, lifting the dance bag up for her to see. Lindy closed her eyes in exasperation—and felt fingers tighten around her arm. Her eyes flew open. "What are you doing?"

Vincent pulled her from the shadows and shoved her out into the center of the pier. She fell to the ground and the cold, wet wood sent a paralyzing jolt through her. Vincent stood over her, his hands thrust casually in his pockets. She grabbed for his ankle, but he stepped out of reach, shaking his head.

"Uh-uh-uh," he taunted.

"Vincent, she has a gun."

Vincent rocked back on his heels and lifted his head toward the roller coaster. Lindy looked up. The .38 was trained on Vincent and her.

"Get up," ordered Katja.

It was amazing how she could keep that Russian accent together, thought Lindy, as she pushed slowly to her knees. She reined in her thoughts; she needed to concentrate. She had no intention of dying tonight. She had an affair to jump-start. The thought almost made her laugh. She took a controlled breath, her lungs rebelling against the cold. She needed a plan, but her mind seemed stuck on renegade thoughts. Like where Katja had hidden the gun all this time. And what part Vincent played in all of this.

Suddenly her curiosity was more demanding than her fear of dying.

"I don't get it," she said. Realized they probably couldn't hear her through her numbed lips and chattering teeth. "I don't get it," she said louder.

"Shut up," said Katja. "Bring her over here."

Vincent reached over and pulled Lindy to her feet. She could hear his teeth chattering. Her own shoulders were jerking with uncontrollable shivers. Even the pistol that Katja held was vibrating in the air.

"It's freezing out here," said Vincent.

Katja jerked the gun toward him. "Hurry."

Holding Lindy tight against his side, he dragged her toward Katja. "I see you helped yourself to my dance bag. Put the gun away. You can't kill everybody."

"What else can I do?"

Lindy felt Vincent shrug. "I don't know. Deny it. It's her word against yours. I won't tell. And Dawn will back you up. Won't you, Dawn?"

Dawn seemed comatose. She hadn't moved, nor spoken. She just stared back at Vincent.

"Won't you?" he coaxed.

Dawn's head turned slowly to Katja. Their faces were inches apart. "You really killed Shane? Why?"

Yes, tell Dawn why, thought Lindy. *Give me time to think.* She shifted against Vincent's chest. His grip tightened.

"Why don't you tell her?" asked Vincent. "I'm sure she'd love to hear this one."

The vibration of running footsteps sounded without warning. Vincent whirled around. Lindy jabbed him in the ribs and his arms flew open. She had an image of Bill racing down the pier as she threw herself beneath the roller coaster tracks.

"Help! Help!" cried Katja. "He is trying to kill us. Help!"

Lindy couldn't see Bill. He didn't know that Katja was armed. "She has a gun!" she screamed just as the shot exploded in the air. A cry of pain. Please, God, not Bill. Dawn screamed. Vincent staggered back, then began to run. Not Bill, please.

She had to do something. Had to get to him. She crawled from under the substructure just as another shot split the air. She ducked back under the gridwork. There was movement in the shadows behind her. "Bill?" she whispered. No answer. "Rose?" The shadow moved away. God, now what? Was Vincent underneath here with her? Looking for her?

There were other sounds on the pier, but Lindy couldn't seem to move. She was holding her breath, her mouth open so her chattering teeth wouldn't give her away. Someone was stalking her. He was coming closer. She shrank back; a shadow passed by a few feet away.

She heard her name being called. Bill's voice. But it was coming from a distance. Out there on the pier. She wanted to run to him, but she was afraid she wouldn't make it, even more than she was afraid of who was under the roller coaster with her. She could feel him moving in the darkness. So close. But not coming toward her; he was moving away. He hadn't found her.

She backed up on the balls of her feet, slowly, carefully, knowing the least bit of sound would give her away. She heard Bill call her name again. She turned toward his voice. Across the pier, Bill was wedged between two freight boxes. And Vincent was slumped at his feet. Then who was beneath the roller coaster with her? For a wild moment she thought that it might be Rose, but Rose would have given her a signal.

"Lindy?" Bill's voice was low, but demanding, and, Lindy realized, fearful.

She started to step toward him. Get to him somehow.

Bill leapt from behind the boxes and raced across the pier, but not toward Lindy. There was another shot. A scream. Above Lindy's head the clank of metal hitting metal; a thud as something fell to the ground. Terrible scenes flashed in her mind. Bill bleeding on the pier. Dawn fallen to her death.

Lindy stepped into the open. She couldn't help herself. She had to see.

At first she only saw Dawn balanced on the rails, bending over, but she heard Katja moaning. Abruptly Dawn sat down and cried, "She's fallen through the slats. Someone help her."

The pier suddenly resounded with echoing footsteps. *Must be a whole cavalry*, thought Lindy, dazed that she was still alive. But where was Bill? Panic seized her. The air behind her moved. And then she remembered. Someone was still hiding in the framework. She whirled around. A shadow separated from the underbelly of the roller coaster and moved slowly toward her. She could hear his breathing, harsh and raspy. And the smell—good God. It couldn't be.

"You owe me twenty dollars," he said. And with a rusty laugh, he melted back into the shadows. Lindy stared into the darkness where he had disappeared. She was still staring when she heard Andrew Dean barking orders to his men. There was activity everywhere, and it passed like a kaleidoscope of sound around her. But she didn't hear Bill's voice. She moved blindly into the open. A siren screamed down the boardwalk. She started to run.

Chapter
Twenty-seven

Bill was standing next to Andrew Dean. He looked up in time to catch Lindy as she launched herself toward him. "You idiot," she cried. "You could have been killed."

Bill grinned. "See, a term of endearment." He wrapped his arms around her. Warm arms. Really warm arms.

"Well, damn," said Dean.

Lindy and Bill looked up. Two officers were walking Katja in their direction. She was handcuffed and limping. Behind them Dawn was being escorted by two other officers.

Dean turned to Bill. "Hell, I thought you drilled her. She's not even hurt."

"Me?" said Bill. "I'm a college teacher. I don't carry."

"You don't?" Dean's voice was strident, and Lindy was glad it was directed at Bill and not her. "Jesus Christ on a friggin' cross," said Dean, running his hand across his face. "Why didn't you tell me you weren't carrying? If I had known that, I wouldn't have waited for backup."

"It didn't occur to me," said Bill. "It worked out okay."

Lindy narrowed her eyes at him. He sounded a lot like she did when he was yelling at her. He raised his eyebrows at her and held her closer.

"So what the hell did happen?" asked Dean.

"She just fell over," said Bill. "One minute she's standing up, aiming that .38, and the next she's on her back, stuck between the tracks. The .38 goes flying and discharged when it hit the pier." Bill shrugged. "A lucky break."

Right, thought Lindy. *Lucky for you.* She'd tell Bill about the man who had pulled Katja's feet out from under her and saved them all. But later.

"She's been Mirandaed," said one of the officers as they stopped in front of Dean.

"Get her into a car," said Dean.

"Wait," cried Dawn, breaking free of her guard and running toward them. "You can't take her. She's pregnant."

"Is she?" Dean asked dryly. He motioned to the guards to take her away.

"Yes, I am," said Katja defiantly. She flicked an angry look toward Dawn. "Something you wouldn't understand." Her tone was venomous, and Dawn shrank back. Then for the first time, Katja's iron will seemed to crack. "I thought he would change his mind if he knew. But he told me to get rid of it."

Lindy saw Dean raise his eyebrows toward Bill. He wasn't about to stand in the way of a confession with this many witnesses.

Katja sniffed. "So I—" She stopped to take a breath. "So I told Vincent. He was very sympathetic. But I didn't realize he was going to kill Shane. I thought he would just talk to him." She started to cry.

Dean made a disgusted sound and motioned the policemen to take her way. "She just doesn't give up, does she?" he said.

"Vincent killed Shane?" asked Dawn.

Lindy could feel Bill's silent laughter. She snuggled against him and felt him kiss the top of her head. "Some vacation," he said.

They walked back toward the boardwalk while a crime scene squad secured the area. Lindy hoped their rescuer had made his escape. He wouldn't like to have to face the police even as a hero.

A huge, shivering crowd was waiting at the entrance of the pier, held back by a line of policemen. Half of the ballroom must be there. Lindy spotted Junie and several other judges at the front of the crowd. Off to one side, the movie people were talking animatedly among themselves, their breath clouding the surrounding air, while the PA took notes in the dark. Even Enrico and Luis had made an appearance, scowling at the gurney that was carrying Vincent toward a waiting ambulance.

"Enrico," Vincent called. He tried to rise, straining against the straps that held him to the gurney.

The paramedics slowed down, and Enrico stepped forward.

"What is it?" asked Enrico in his most ominous tone.

"I just want to see your face when I tell you."

"Tell me what?"

"It was so simple. The service hall. The unlocked door Luis had so conveniently hidden behind the drapery."

"What are you saying? Luis did something to my dresses?"

Vincent sputtered, then winced. The medics started to move him away. "No, just a minute," he said. "If Luis had any balls or a tad of imagination, he would have. No, I did it all by myself. Just sneaked in, sneaked out. Pulled off the tape when I left and no one suspected a thing." He smiled, satisfied and malicious.

"You? My dresses?"

"Yes, me. I slashed each one, bit by bit, and dropped the pieces to the floor. Then I stomped on them. It was wonderful. I loved every minute." He laughed in a weird lighthearted way that infuriated Enrico.

He lunged at Vincent, but Junie and two other judges pulled him back.

"Now you know how it feels to have the thing you love most destroyed."

Enrico growled in fury. "You didn't love Junie. You were using him. Just like all the others."

"Junie?" Vincent frowned up at him. "You think I'm talking about Junie?" He slid his eyes from Enrico to Junie. He started to laugh; it turned quickly to tears. "Not Junie, you old queen. I'm talking about dancing, my career, the chance of a championship. Down the toilet because of your jealousy. You destroyed me, and I hate you." The stretcher moved away.

Enrico stared after him. "And you, my friend, are a nutcase." He turned on his heel and strode through the crowd, Luis hurrying close behind.

"If looks could kill," said Lindy.

"Fortunately, they don't," said Bill. "Let's get inside before we both get pneumonia for Christmas."

"Where is Rose?"

"Over there with Dawn. She was right behind me. But I made her stay back to wait for Andrew. I was afraid they might not figure out where we were. I've got your jewelry in my pocket." He gave her a squeeze. "Pretty clever."

"Thanks," she said. "Compliments will get you everything."

He grinned. "That's what I'm counting on."

It was probably the most unorthodox system of taking statements that Lindy could imagine. She was allowed to change out of her mangled outfit and met the others in a suite donated by the hotel.

Statements were being taken in the two bedrooms. They each waited their turn, lounging on the couch and drinking coffee and eating sandwiches, also donated by the hotel. A show of their gratitude, Andrew told them.

As soon as the questioning was concluded, Andrew thanked them and followed his men out the door. Junie, Rusty, Dawn, Rose, Bill and Lindy sat silently around the room. It seemed that no one had much to say. A minute later, glasses and several bottles of wine were delivered to the suite. Rusty uncorked the wine and passed glasses around.

"I suppose it would be rude to leave," said Bill, eyeing Lindy's crew socks and sneakers.

"Got a thing for gym shoes?" she asked.

"I've got a thing for you."

She glanced quickly around the room while heat shot right down to her toes.

Rose handed them each a glass. "Just one big happy family," she said out of the side of her mouth and reached over the coffee table to hand a glass to Junie. Then she took two more glasses and went to sit on the arm of Dawn's chair.

"She's pregnant," said Dawn. "She told me tonight."

Junie opened his mouth, then shut it.

Rusty answered, "*Maybe* she's pregnant. She's lied about everything else. Wouldn't surprise me if she was lying about that, too."

Dawn sighed deeply. "Junie, I owe you an apology."

Everyone in the room stared at her.

"What?" said Junie. "Don't even start with me, Dawn. I'm not in the mood."

"No. I mean really. I do. I always thought you ruined my life by not letting me get pregnant. But Shane ruined Katja's by getting her pregnant."

Junie threw up his hands. "Oh, jeez, Louise. Your life isn't ruined. You're sitting at the top of the ballroom industry. Katja ruined her own life by being stupid and untalented—just like Vincent."

"She isn't untalented," said Dawn.

"Untalented and fat."

"Well, she *is* pregnant."

"Eating for two? Hell, she was eating for a whole team of sumo wrestlers."

"That is the most—"

Lindy and Bill exchanged looks and put their wineglasses on the table. Rose slipped off the armchair and picked up her bag.

"Would you get a grip?" yelled Junie.

Bill and Lindy got up from the couch, nodded good night to Rusty, who nodded back.

"And if you try to steal the Hollingfords from me—"

Lindy and Bill headed for the door.

"They're getting a divorce," bellowed Junie.

"Ha. You wish. They've reconciled and they're both coming to work for—"

Rose had the door open. Bill and Lindy stepped into the hall, and the door mercifully closed behind them.

Rose shook her head. "Some things never change." She smiled at Bill, then at Lindy. "And some things do. Good night."

Chapter
Twenty-eight

Lindy felt warm and toasty, and she didn't really want to leave the comfort of Bill or his bed. It was six o'clock. It had been late when they had gotten in last night, and they hadn't spent very much of the night sleeping. She was tempted to curl up next to him and go back to sleep.

But she had an obligation. A question of a debt and she knew she wouldn't feel right until it had been paid. She slipped quietly out of bed and gathered her clothes from the floor. Then she tiptoed into the bathroom to change. Before she left, she took time to scribble a hasty note. "Don't go anywhere. Back soon. L." Then she took Bill's leather jacket and key card, and her wallet and let herself out of the room.

Once in the casino, she put on the jacket and pulled the collar up. Then she pushed the exit door open. The first thing she looked for were police cars, but the boardwalk was deserted. There couldn't have been that much evidence at the pier. They had probably collected any stray shells or casings, or whatever, the night before.

She started toward the pier, the treads of her sneakers gripping the wood. The sun was coming up on the horizon, and gulls perched across the sand. Lindy wondered who would feed them now that the Gull Lady was dead. She wondered if the gulls would miss her.

She climbed down the steps and onto the sand. Ahead of her, the underbelly of the pier loomed shadowy and no more inviting than before. She paused long enough to pull a twenty from her wallet. She owed the big man, and she intended to make good on her debt. But that didn't mean she relished going back beneath the pier.

She moved slowly, singing "We Wish You a Merry Christmas," of all things. Just so she wouldn't take them by surprise. She didn't go beneath the pier. She stopped with her hand on the foundation and called, "Hello, is anyone there?" There was a rustle of shifting cardboard. She hoped she wouldn't find a stranger sleeping there. If she didn't recognize them, she'd run like hell back to the hotel and bring Rose with her the next time she went looking.

Because she would look. She owed the man for her life as well as for Dawn's and Bill's. And even if he was a homeless drunk, he deserved to be thanked. The shadow loomed without warning and she stepped back involuntarily.

A raspy laugh came from the shadows. Lindy waited. Finally, he took one step forward and was captured by the morning sun. The light wasn't kind. His face was shrouded by a mass of matted hair and beard. The front of his coat was smeared with something that Lindy didn't want to think about.

He was wearing so many layers of clothes that he looked incapable of moving. But Lindy knew better. He had skulked through the darkness the night before like a phantom.

"I owe you twenty dollars," she said and was appalled to hear that her voice was shaking.

The man rumbled a laugh that quickly changed into a racking cough.

She was tempted to throw all her money at him and run. Not have to deal with this blighted human, face-to-face. But that wasn't the answer and she knew it. She didn't know what the answer was, or if there even was one.

"Here." She thrust the twenty dollars forward.

It was snatched out of her hand. And the man stepped back into the shadow of the pier.

"Thank you," she said.

"Git," came the answer. And she did.

Bill was sitting up in bed, reading the note she had left on her pillow, when she let herself back into his room.

"Where the hell have you been?"

"In a minute," she said. She hung his jacket in the closet, pulled off her clothes, and jumped under the covers. "Brr."

"Goddammit, Lindy."

"Umm, this is nice."

Bill jumped. "Stop that. Your hands are freezing. Why were you outside? You're going to drive me nuts."

"That sounds challenging." She took a look at his expression. "Oh, all right." She plumped up the pillow and pulled the blanket to her chin. She told him about the man—she didn't even know his name—beneath the pier. How he was a friend of the Gull Lady. How he had pulled Katja off balance by reaching up through the slats of the roller coaster track. "She didn't slip. She was yanked off her feet. He saved our lives. And I owed him twenty dollars."

Bill looked a little dazed. She took pity on him. "The day Rose and I went looking for them in town, I said I would pay twenty dollars for information. But the police came and he ran away before I had a chance to give him the money. He reminded me, last night. I just wanted to make things even, so maybe you and I could finally have a little time together not clouded by a murder investigation."

"Well, don't get too optimistic. Andrew called and I said we'd meet him for breakfast at nine."

"That's two hours away."

"So it is."

They met Andrew Dean in the Rickshaw Café. He was sitting at a booth against the back wall, far from the panoramic window. Lindy scooted in across from him, and Bill slid in beside her.

"I hope you've got good news," said Bill. "A double confession, maybe."

"No confessions, yet. They're too busy accusing each other. But forensics is coming in, and it won't be long. Unless someone screws up along the way, it'll go to trial, murder and accessory to. My bet is she pulled the trigger and suckered him into helping her."

"Vincent's out of the hospital?" asked Lindy, though she didn't really care.

"Yeah. They kept him overnight, but she just got a chunk of flesh. No big deal."

A waiter stopped to pour coffee. Lindy tried to concentrate on the breakfast menu. "I hope you guys aren't going to talk about gore and guts while we eat," she said.

Bill and Andrew both grinned at her.

"Please."

"Okay, no more gore and guts," said Dean. "We did find out how Vincent got into the vendors' room. One of the vendors confessed to taping the door so they could smoke without having to go all the way around the ballroom and into the hall. Hell, an AC casino is the only place you can smoke anywhere in peace. It was the Ballroom people who nixed it in the hallway. Anyway, when this Luis character put up the curtain, everyone just forgot about it. Like Padrewsky said, it was simple. He waited until the room was locked for the night, walked right in, wreaked a little havoc with the ball gowns, then removed the tape when he left. By the time the guards made their rounds, everything was locked up safe and sound."

"Just one question before breakfast comes," said Bill, shooting an amused look at Lindy. "How did she get Shane's feet in her shoes?"

"According to Vincent, Katja was wearing the shoes. She crushed Corbett's feet with the heels. Then she put them on his feet. Gruesome little bitch. The heels of those shoes are reinforced steel. The bruise marks match the shape of the heel, and they were . . . Let's just say there was evidence on the heels themselves."

"Thanks a lot," said Lindy, watching a waiter bringing a tray of plates toward them.

"Well, that's it," said Dean as an omelet was placed in front of him. "Dig in."

"Did you find out if Katja's really pregnant?"

"As a matter of fact we did, and she is. Probably the only truthful thing she's said since we started questioning her."

"How too bad," said Lindy, dropping her fork onto her plate. "What will happen to the baby?"

"These days, there's a good maternity ward in every major women's prison. Then they'll give custody to a relative or send it to social services, and they'll foster it out. I wouldn't worry about the baby. It'll be better off without a murderer for a mother."

The conversation changed to other topics and Lindy began to relax. As long as she didn't look too closely at the two fried eggs on her plate, she could get them to her mouth.

"You guys staying around for a while?" asked Dean as they were leaving the restaurant.

Bill groaned. "You don't need more statements, do you? We won't have to testify?"

"Nah. We have your statements. That should do it. Just thought you might want to play the slots for a few days."

"I don't know what we're doing," said Bill. "We haven't gotten that far."

"Well, whatever it is, have a good time. And thanks for the help. Next time you're in town give me a buzz."

At hour call, Rebo, Juan and Eric bustled into the theatre, carrying shopping bags. They were all wearing tiaras over their winter hats. They made a beeline for the banquette where Lindy, Bill, Biddy and Jeremy were sitting.

As soon they reached the table, they twirled and struck pinup girl poses. Their audience of four broke into laughter.

"Where on earth did you find those?" asked Lindy. "The vendors' room?"

"Nope," said Rebo. "We were over at the Miss America Pageant exhibit. We got these at the gift shop. Actually, we did *all* our Christmas shopping there. You like?" He batted his eyelashes at Bill.

"It does have a certain *je ne sais quoi,*" said Bill.

"Say what?" said Rebo. "Rose is gonna love this. I think I'll give her her present early." The three of them hurried backstage.

"I'm glad this is almost over," said Jeremy. "Sometimes I wonder if we shouldn't just stick to touring."

Bill glanced at Lindy.

"We'd be belly-up in a month," said Biddy. "Most companies lose money on tour. And in New York when you think about it. These gigs might be a pain in the butt, but they pay extremely well. We're one of the few companies running in the black."

"Thanks to a brilliant business manager I know." Jeremy smiled at her.

Jeez, thought Lindy. *The next thing you know he'll be kissing her in public.*

The performance was well attended. The applause was appreciative, but the theatre cleared more quickly than usual.

"They gotta get back and do some more slows and quicks," said Rose as she folded and packed the costumes in a theatre trunk. She was wearing a tiara.

Kate stuck her head in the doorway of the costume room. "Hey, Rose. Are we waiting for you?"

"No," said Rose. "I'm staying over tonight. I'll help Rusty and Dawn get squared away, get in a couple of pulls at the slots, and take the bus back to the city tomorrow night."

"Okay, see you. Merry Christmas."

"Merry Christmas."

"And what are you doing for Christmas?" asked Rose. "Has Bill talked you into meeting his mother?"

"No way," said Lindy. "Glen's coming to move his things out on the twenty-fourth. I'll make myself scarce until he's gone. Then I'll spend Christmas rearranging the furniture." She was embarrassed that her voice wavered. "Don't want to be living in the past when the new year arrives." She smiled. It was an effort. She wasn't even sad anymore. Not really. And she was having a wonderful time, murder aside, with Bill. But she wasn't sure how seriously involved she should allow herself to become. She knew the hazards of a rebound relationship. Everyone said they never lasted.

"Nervous?" asked Rose.

"A little. Mostly about having to tell Cliff and Annie. They'll be devastated. I guess we'll just have to rub along the best we can."

Rose closed the lid on the trunk and ran packing straps around the outside.

"What are you going to do for Christmas, Rose?"

"Me? Meet some people, have some fun. Then I'm going skiing in Vermont. Guy I know has a great set of . . . snowmobiles." She hoisted the trunk onto its side and slid it out the door. "Let it snow, doodeedoo, doodeedoo."

They passed Peter in the hallway. "This is the easiest load out I've had in years. Mieko and I are driving back tonight. You want a ride, Rose?"

"No, thanks. Have a good one."

"You too."

"Everyone is awfully festive," said Lindy.

"I think all this glitz has made them long for the discomforts of home. Are you and Bill leaving tonight?"

"No. We'll stay until tomorrow, maybe drive down to Cape May for a day or two."

"Sounds like fun. Almost as fun as meeting his mother."

They made their way to where Jeremy, Biddy and Bill were waiting.

Andrea and Paul called out a good night and the two of them left the theatre.

"And what's going to happen with them?" asked Lindy.

Jeremy shrugged. "The producer took their specs. Seems the movie's on hold." He bit his lip, then broke into a grin. "They're thinking about changing it to a murder mystery." Everyone looked shocked. Biddy broke first. A giggle erupted from her throat. She wrestled her mouth into a frown but by then Jeremy was laughing. Rose and Lindy joined in. The only one not laughing was Bill.

Rose, Jeremy and Biddy returned to the ballroom, Rose to shore up Dawn, and Jeremy and Biddy to work the crowd. There were a lot of rich dance lovers out there and after seeing the performance, they might be inspired to contribute to the Ash Company.

Lindy and Bill stood waiting for the elevator.

"Do you want to go in for a drink?" asked Bill.

"What's the matter?"

Bill shrugged off the question.

The elevator came. Bill ignored it. Lindy waited.

"Are you sure you don't want to come to Connecticut?"

"I can't. I explained why."

"I know. I'm just afraid you won't be there when I come back."

She touched his arm. "I won't be. We'll be on tour. Remember?"

Bill rubbed his forehead. Viennese waltz music blared into the hall and died away.

"But we have a few more days that we can spend together," said Lindy. "Right?"

From the Pagoda Bar, the cabaret singer broke into "Have Yourself a Merry Little Christmas."

"Right," said Bill. "What do you want to do?"

Lindy looked up at him and frowned. "Do you know how to dance?"

"What? No. Well, I can sway back and forth to the music."

"Show me."

"Here? Now?"

"Sure," she said. "Everybody is in the ballroom or the bar. We're all alone and I love this song." She held up her hands.

Bill narrowed his eyes, but finally stepped forward and took her hand in his. His other hand went to her waist. Then he pulled her close.

He was right. He could sway to the music. And he could stay on time, too. It was a good sign, she thought. They were comfortable together. Another elevator came and went. The singer sang only for them. "So have yourself . . ."

"Merry Christmas, Bill."

"Merry Christmas."

This time when the elevator came, they danced inside, and the doors closed behind them.